Backwaters

1979
Chapter 1 – Whitehall Court SW1
Chapter 2 – Gretchen
Chapter 3 – Thomas
Chapter 4 – Lulworth
Chapter 5 – Bentley and Hacket
Chapter 6 – The Army Truck
Chapter 7 – Soppy Joe's
Chapter 8 – Birthdays
Chapter 9 – John Muir
Chapter 10 – Tall Black Russian
Chapter 11 – Ground Rules
Chapter 12 – Hors d'oeuvres
Chapter 13 – Just Desserts
Chapter 14 – Primrose Hill
Chapter 15 – John
Chapter 16 – Spin
Chapter 17 – Grey Notebook
Chapter 18 – Malvern
Chapter 19 – Homo Erectus
Chapter 20 – Backwaters
Chapter 21 – Lady Di
Chapter 22 – The Abbey
Chapter 23 – The Baker
Chapter 24 – The Gospel according to Versace
Chapter 25 – Numbers
Chapter 26 – The Stowaway
Chapter 27 – Jem
Chapter 28 – Train North
Chapter 29 – Port
Chapter 30 – The Facts
Chapter 31 – Sandy
Chapter 32 – A Long Hot Bath
Chapter 33 – Lochbay
Chapter 34 – Pin Mill
Chapter 35 – The Neist Inn
Chapter 36 – Coire Ghrunnda
Chapter 37 – Doubting Thomas
Chapter 38 – The Cider Salesman
Chapter 39 – Pallbearers

Chapter 40 – INTJ
Chapter 41 – Mollie's Ribbons
Chapter 42 – Inn Pin
Chapter 43 – Hot Pig
Chapter 44 – State
Chapter 45 – In Deed
Chapter 46 – Crux
Chapter 47 – Time
Chapter 48 – Ambulance
Chapter 49 – Magical Artefacts
Chapter 50 – Jock
Chapter 51 – 4Cs
Chapter 52 – The Misty Isle
Chapter 53 – SW1 2006

Backwaters

"Action and adventure, alcohol and misadventure"

BACKWATERS

by

Matt Swain

Copyright © 2011 Matt Swain

All rights reserved. No part of this publication may be reproduced, stored in a retrieval system or transmitted in any form or by any means electronic, mechanical, audio, visual or otherwise, without prior permission of the copyright owner. Nor can it be circulated in any form of binding or cover other than that in which it is published and without similar conditions including this condition being imposed on the subsequent purchaser.

All characters appearing in this work are fictitious and any resemblance to real persons, living or dead, is purely coincidental.

ISBN: 978-0-9570708-0-6

Published by Cuillin Books in conjunction with Writersworld Limited and is available to order from most bookshops and Internet book retailers throughout the United Kingdom.

Printed and bound by www.printondemand-worldwide.com

www.writersworld.co.uk

WRITERSWORLD
2 Bear Close
Woodstock
Oxfordshire
OX20 1JX
England

The text pages of this book are produced via an independent certification process that ensures the trees from which the paper is produced come from well managed sources that exclude the risk of using illegally logged timber while leaving options to use post-consumer recycled paper as well.

Thanks Bro

Locations

Montenvers	45°55'54.22"	N	6°55'03.27"	E
Sax	38°32'15.36"	N	0°51'39.61"	W
Lulworth	50°38'04.94"	N	2°09'16.03"	W
Olduvai Gorge	2°59'46.47"	S	35°21'08.47"	E
Primrose Hill	51°32'23.18"	N	0°09'38.84"	W
King's Canyon	36°44'48.84"	N	118°58'18.82"	W
Crystal Cascades	16°57'50.59"	S	145°40'31.82"	E
Annie's Grave	52°06'39.58"	N	2°19'41.76"	W
Backwaters	51°52'47.80"	N	1°12'55.44"	E
Burgess Shale	51°25'18.52"	N	116°30'22.17"	W
Beedjen Drim nan Rarve	57°14'07.99"	N	6°13'00.70"	W
The Table	57°38'31.08"	N	6°16'28.18"	W

1979

  Pure light bounces off the granite and breaks on the glacier. Cameras click in vain attempts to capture the image. A nine year old girl stands at the railings and scans the glacier below. She is hardly aware of the snow-capped walls and jagged peaks of the Aiguilles. People come and go, admiring the scenery of the Vallee Blanche; 'awesome' being a much used word by the English. The clean air is also noted and consumed in great lungfuls. None of this permeates the girl's consciousness as she maintains her watch.

  Starting first as streams of coloured dots high up in the valley, groups of skiers sweep below. Her look-out point is now in shadow, the temperature drops, but still she does not move.

  Occasionally her brother joins her vigil. He drums his fingers on the cold metal railing and stays long enough to crack a joke. Then he retreats to the shelter of the cafeteria where their mother watches events from behind her book. Snow begins to fall and the girl pulls up her hood, but otherwise remains at her post.

  A man in a red jacket leans against the railings next to her, staring in the same direction.

  "A watched glacier never moves," he says.

  "Daddy!" the girl cries, her face lighting up as she presses against the coarse fabric of the man's jacket.

  "Sorry I'm late," he says, hugging the girl to his chest. "We had a bit of a detour - new crevasse."

  "It's okay - we haven't been here long," she says, not letting go as her mum collects their things.

  "Liar," says the boy behind them. "We've been here since the beginning of the bloody Ice Age."

  The four of them laugh and make their way to the train, the girl proudly carrying her father's rucksack, not leaving his side.

Chapter 1 – Whitehall Court SW1

Thomas leant forward on the counter to read the label of what looked like a very old bottle of wine. It was hiding above the optics and Thomas had to stand on the spindle of his stool to get a better view. As the faded script came into focus his hands slipped on a bar towel and Thomas toppled over the bar. "Bollocks," he muttered, his legs dangling in the air. "Roddy, can you…"

With some effort the barman re-seated his favourite customer who, after checking himself for injury, reached for his cigarettes.

Tapps, in common with many London clubs, had seen better days. It had moved to its SW1 address in 1913 and in the ninety years since, whilst aspiring to high ideals, had in essence become a discreet drinking club. Its most cherished asset was the many possible escape routes through Whitehall Court which had helped to keep the club under the tabloid radar. Only once, when London clubs were under scrutiny for sexism, did *Tapps* become momentarily visible. When interviewed on the subject, the president had vehemently denied any bias but had then been widely quoted as saying, "No right-minded woman would want to join and, while we don't have a policy on gender, we do have one for sanity."

And thereafter, male members had been once again left alone to their serious drinking, subscriptions had risen substantially and no one ever suspected that the quote had actually come from the ad agency Bentley and Hacket.

Thomas drained his cocktail.

"Another? Mr Thorpe?"

Stifling a yawn, Thomas looked around the bar to see he was the only one left. "Thank you, Roddy, but it's time to wend my way."

"Would you like me to ring for a taxi?" asked the barman.

"No no. I'll hail a cab from the roadside. One gets a thrill, as one teeters between kerb and gutter, in wondering whether the cabby will resemble Beau Brummell or... Bob Hoskins."

The barman began filling the glass-washer but remained politely attentive.

"You know, Roddy, he took so long with his ablutions that George the Fourth and assorted cronies would gather to watch him dress." Thomas raised an eyebrow.

"Who? Bob Hoskins?"

Thomas considered his answer but, through the mist of alcohol, soon lost track of the question. "Apparently," he replied mechanically. "Better retrieve my coat."

He made his way past old leather sofas and into a larger room still half full of men, some of whom called to him. Lifting his arm in acknowledgment, he swayed across the room and pushed through a light-oak door whose gold-embossed label announced 'Gentlemen's Cloakroom'. Thomas trailed his hand along the wall until it touched tile where he stopped in front of a urinal and leant his head against the cool surface. He closed his eyes and rested.

Something was different about the cloakrooms and he tried to re-run his last few steps. Rolling his forehead from side to side on the tiles he caught sight of a large metal box on the wall. As he pondered this new addition to the familiar room a toilet flushed and a man emerged from a cubicle. The man washed his hands, only noticing Thomas when he reached for a paper towel.

"Tom, hi!" he said, appraising Thomas's position. "Good to see you looking so fit."

Thomas raised his free hand and gave a slight wave. The man withdrew some change from his pocket and, inserting it into the metal box, pulled the silver handle to retrieve a small matchbox size container. He held it up to Thomas with a grin.

"Monogamy – not natural is it."

"Quite," replied Thomas.

"Roddy. Am I going mad or do we now have a Johnny machine?"

"I believe the club has yielded to members and we now have a contraceptive machine."

"Contraception? I thought we were all queer."

"No, sir."

"Really?" said Thomas. "This place is going to the dogs."

"Did you find your coat, sir?"

"Was I looking for it?"

"I believe you were going home."

"I was? I was... that's right."

Thomas sat down on the bar stool.

"How long have you worked here, Roddy?"

"Since I left school, sir. Twenty years ago."

"Ah, that would make you about my age. Are you queer?"

"No, sir."

"Ah, I suppose not... you stand on the other side of the bar. Did your father warn you about people like me?"

"Only *not* to go south and *not* to work in a Gentleman's Club."

"So you did exactly the opposite."

The barman smiled.

"Good man. Did you want to spend your life serving hopeless cases?"

"It's a fair job, Mr Thorpe."

"Ah ha. An evasive answer. Come come, Roddy – you can tell your Auntie Thomas. I promise I won't remember a thing in the morning."

"Well, sir, I wanted to be a blacksmith like my father but he was so... well..." The barman's voice tailed off.

"And is you father still a 'smith of the black?'" asked Thomas.

The barman nodded and opened the glass-washer. Thomas watched the steam slowly rise up the back of the bar, fogging the mirror. He tried to remember his own father; the fights, the prideful sulks.

"And you, sir?"

Thomas realised he was being addressed. "Me? Oh well, my father Roddy is a..." He cast his eyes around and drummed his fingers. "My father is a jigsaw piece without a shape. A jigsaw piece whose pattern has been misplaced."

"Sorry to hear that, sir."

"Hear what?"

"I heard nothing, sir."

"You know, Roddy, you could play the Admirable Crichton... admirably."

"Thank you, sir."

Thomas rubbed his chin and sighed. "Unfortunately I seem to be sober again."

"Your usual, sir?"

"Certainly, I can't go home in this state."

Chapter 2 – Gretchen

Dawn broke over Sax. The picturesque Spanish town, tumbling down a hillside, lit up as the Vinalopó Valley showed itself to the new day.

A narrow beam of sunlight made its way through the dark wooden shutters and dropped very slowly over stippled whitewash. It hesitated at a picture frame as if unwilling to reveal the subject – a donkey in a hat – before spilling across the canvass. Underneath the descending ray was a bed with white sheets covered partially by a grey fleece embossed with pink writing. Over the pillow flowed long brown hair, at the centre of which nestled a girl's face radiantly youthful. From the opposite bed, David enjoyed an all too rare moment, his job nowadays affording little spare time for his family. Carefully moving his hand free of the sheet he checked his watch. Across the room a large brown eye twinkled and half a mouth became a large grin.

"Morning, pumpkin," David said quietly, not moving.

"Hi, Daddy. Did you sleep well?"

"Fine. Happy, happy, happy birthday and many more returns."

"Thank you, I'm not sure I should be happy. What age should I start worrying about getting old?"

"Hmm – another twenty years."

"Thirty three – that's ancient!"

David smiled. "You wait until forty three." He eased the sheet back and sat up gingerly, allowing his lower back to adjust. "Birthdays always start with a cup of tea," he said, standing up and rummaging around his bag.

"I thought I would get buck spiz."

"It's 'fizz', sweetheart, and no you bloody can't."

"Harrumph!"

"Well maybe tonight."

"Thank you, Daddy."

David poured bottled water into the kettle and switched it on. He reached back into the bag and took out two gift wrapped parcels; one large and one small.

"Happy birthday, Gretchen!" he said, handing her the presents.

"Ooh thanks."

"You have some more at home but I thought you may like these now."

Gretchen opened the small one first. "Wow," she said, "what is it?"

"It's called a Leatherman. I got it in America. It's like a Swiss Army knife so you can stop borrowing mine."

"Great – are they as good?"

"I think so, it's only just been launched but if it is, you can ask mum to get me one for my birthday."

Gretchen examined the device as her dad prepared the tea.

"Now this," she said, starting to unwrap the second present, "feels like clothes. You haven't been trying to buy clothes for me have you?"

"I confess I asked your brother," said David as Gretchen held up a large-necked baggy sweatshirt. "Apparently you went to see a film called Flashdance?"

"Oh daddy it's perfect," she cried, putting it on over her pyjamas. "I do love you."

While David began getting ready for the day, Gretchen opened the climbing guide for the area.

"'The uplands,'" she read aloud, "'to the west are part of the…'" She held the page up to her father, pointing to the word.

"Baetic Cordillera," he said.

"'…a mountain system made up of multiple ranges reaching from And… alusia to Va… lencia. The local climbing is exceptional in quality if not severity though within an hour's drive are numous crag… '"

"Numerous."

"'…numerous crags to test the best. Most routes are sport routes and there are a number of scrambles for non-technical climbers.'"

"Daddy, it says they're sport routes so we don't need any protection gear, just…" she picked up a short leash with spring clips at each end, grinned and said very clearly, "…quick-draws."

"Sounds like it," he replied.

"Do you think I might be able to lead one then?"

"Well I suppose you are a teenager now."

"Oh yes, oh yes," said Gretchen as she leapt between beds.

David looked lovingly at her. "Do you know what I love most about you?"

"My big muscles?" replied Gretchen, flexing her skinny arms.

"Not even that. It's because you smile with your eyes and they light up the room."

Gretchen smiled, proving his point. "What's that on your shirt?"

David looked down at the five white objects printed onto the blue cotton. "Trilobites."

"And where do they come from?"

"All over but you would have to go back five hundred million years to find them."

"Are they fossils then?"

"Yes, I went to a place in Canada to see a very important find, which is where I got this tee-shirt."

"Will you take me one day?" asked Gretchen, her eyes sparkling.

"Darling, the list of where I'm taking you is getting a bit long. Perhaps you can visit yourself. You know it's more fun sometimes to discover things for yourself."

Gretchen went quiet. "Daddy, I just want to be with you."

"I know that, shnuggle," said David, holding out his arms.

She swung her arms back and bent her legs. Before he could say "no", she had launched herself and they were falling over together, David letting his daughter apply a judo hold.

He tapped the floor. "I submit."

She jumped into the air raising her hands, "Ippon!"

Gretchen started as the phone light flashed and, reaching across a stack of bound reports, pressed the hands-free button. "Hi, Mavis."

"Gretchen, sorry to disturb you but it's your brother on the line. He says it's urgent. Shall I put him through?"

"Urgent urgent or has he just lost his car keys urgent?"

"I'm not sure, would you like me to say you are in a meeting?"

"Thanks, Mavis, but I'd better take it."

Her speaker buzzed and clicked.

"What's up, Tom?" said Gretchen, frowning at the poor sound.

"Grae – hi – just ringing to wish you good luck with the presentation."

"Hang on, Tom, I can't hear you, I'll pick up. Are you in a phone box?"

"Yes," replied Thomas, "at the top of Wardour Street – fascinating adverts in here you know, a girl could blush!"

"What happened to your mobile?"

"Oh, good lunch with a client, drowned I'm afraid... my mobile not my client. You know how it is."

"You know I don't know how it is!"

"Well now you're just being obtuse."

"I'm being busy, Tom."

"Don't I know it, darling, Mavis sounded like Mother Superior. Anyone'd think I was a homosexual drunkard loose in Soho."

"Tom! I've got to get to my presentation..." There was no reply. "Tom! Thomas!"

"Sorry, darling, I was just reading a business card. Apparently a husband and wife do 'daily shows'. I was just wondering if I rushed, I could catch the matinee."

"Tom, this phone is going down in five seconds."

"The point is, I love you and hope the meeting goes well."

"Thank you, Tom, it's kind of you to remember – I will see you on Saturday."

"How could I forget your big day, now be a darling and put Mavis back on the line, I want to have some fun."

Gretchen replaced the phone, took a deep breath and rubbed her eyes. Through the door she could hear Mavis, professional as ever, politely resisting her brother's afternoon invitation. She checked her cup, which was empty, got up and stretched. Out of the window she could see across to HMS Belfast, its grey paint matching the ashen sky. She took in a long deep breath and slowly exhaled. Beneath her a steady stream of expensive-looking cars divulged her audience, who greeted each other with varying degrees of enthusiasm. The phone light flashed again.

"Mavis?"

"Gretchen, the boardroom is clear for you. Do you need a hand with anything?"

"Thanks, I should be able to manage."

"Oh there was another call for you, Guy? Didn't leave his second name. I told him you were busy."

"Okay thanks. Oh, and Mavis?"

"Yes."

"Sorry about my brother."

There was a giggle. "He sound's lovely."

The empty boardroom was quiet and had that eerily dead quality of meeting rooms. Gretchen clicked through her presentation slide by slide closing her eyes occasionally, attempting to recall all of the points without relying on her notes. Eleven solid months of preparation for this day had uncovered many inconsistencies between company myth and reality. She had done all that she had been asked to but it didn't mean that they were going to like it.

She looked around the room and to the stack of reports at the back. Maybe Mavis had been right to suggest someone should hand them out. Gretchen had also kept refreshments to a minimum with no alcohol, another move that Mavis had considered 'bold'.

She checked the time and dialled a number on the phone.

"Hi Grae," came a voice.

"Hey Guy, you rang."

"Yes I managed to get as far as reception."

"Sorry, lot going on today. Are we still okay for tomorrow?"

"Ah... Gretchen I'm afraid... No."

"Oh no, I was kind of relying on you. There's a lot of pretty physical stuff."

"I'm sorry – I don't really think I'm suited to this."

"Don't worry – you wouldn't be the first man to be overwhelmed by my big muscles."

There was a pause.

"I didn't just mean the physical stuff."

"Oh?"

"It's the whole relationship thing – you know how it is."

"You're the second man to claim that today," said Gretchen.

"Grae, you're a fantastic..."

"Don't..."

"Sorry Grae."

There was another pause

"Goodbye Guy."

"Bye."

She placed her phone on the table and leant against a chair. She was pouring herself a glass of water when the managing partner entered the room.

"Gretchen, good afternoon, everything okay?"

Momentarily off guard, she stood upright. "Fine thank you, Stephen."

"Do you have a written agenda?"

"Not for my presentation. I should take an hour thirty five and I've allowed two more hours for questions, then will leave you to the board meeting."

"Good Lord – I doubt if there will be two hours of questions, people will no doubt want to be up town for some fun – you know how it is."

Gretchen winced.

"I don't suppose you could cut your presentation down to forty five minutes could you?" Stephen winked but it was clearly a directive rather than a suggestion.

Gretchen was taken aback. "The report is rather figure heavy."

Stephen scanned the refreshments. "No wine?"

"I thought people would need a clear head to get the best out of the presentation."

"Right I have some sparkly in my office fridge. I'll get that dealt with, you work out a way to chop twenty minutes off the presentation and we'll cut the questions to forty five minutes. I'll chair it. I'm sure it's all in the report anyway. And could you ask young Claudia in IT to hand out the reports." Stephen smiled and left the room.

Gretchen leant against the table trying to take in the last few minutes. "Fun uptown? No – I don't know how it is."

* * * * *

"Mavis, I was wrong and you were right," said Gretchen, rushing back into her office. "Could you ask Claudia if she could spare a few minutes in a quarter of an hour."

"I already took the liberty – just in case."

"Oh. Thanks. Oh and…"

"No calls?"

"Thanks."

While Gretchen waited for her computer to re-open the presentation, she took some long slow calming breaths and looked at a photo on her desk. It was of a man in a string vest sitting on a rock and holding up a thermos flask. "Well," she whispered, "we seem to be alone again."

By the time Gretchen returned to the room it was full of men chattering and laughing, the odd champagne cork popping. For the first time she felt apprehensive. It was a vague and distant feeling which she dismissed as she weaved back to her laptop. Although she knew it would take a moment to upload the changes to her presentation, she couldn't help pausing to take in her audience. At the far corner she could see Stephen talking covertly with the partner from Luton, a man who had constantly lobbied for his own methods and generally been a thorn in her side during the research. In the end she had had to call in old favours just to get accurate data on the Luton operation. There was something conspiratorial in their easy manner and in that instant, Gretchen cancelled the changes.

"Evening, Gretchen, can I give you a hand?" said a man, smiling eagerly.

"Hi, Matthew, thank you but I'm ready to go." Matthew had rather embarrassed himself by the unsolicited amount of help he'd offered during the project.

"Are you ready to meet the enemy?" he asked.

Gretchen wanted to say "I think I'm being set up," but she returned his smile. "I am merely delivering what was asked of me – no more, no less."

Matthew paused. "Hmm," he murmured, examining the floor. "I wonder," he added hesitantly, "if you would like to join a few of us later for dinner? Nothing fancy but... good fun."

"Thanks for the offer, unfortunately I have a day off tomorrow and am travelling tonight."

"Climbing Everest is it?" he asked trying to be agreeable.

"No," Gretchen replied lightly, "I'm doing some work for the army."

"Oh," said Matthew inquisitively, "accounting work?"

"No I'm helping a friend with deer management."

"Oh," Matthew repeated, obviously having no point of reference.

"Stop flirting, Matthew," said the managing partner as he joined them at the front.

"I was doing no such thing, Stephen," said Matthew, his face a deep shade of pink. "Good luck Gretchen, and with the… err tomorrow."

Stephen tapped his glass. "Gentlemen, let's make a start," he said confidently and clearly. "Please find yourselves a place." He waited for most to be seated before carrying on. "You all know that a year ago we committed ourselves to a profitability review…" As he spoke, the words, '*Macaulay Malim – Assessing Value-Added*', appeared on the screen. In his introduction, Stephen explained how they had aggressively recruited Gretchen to undertake such a fundamental review. He outlined her brief but then, it seemed to Gretchen, supplied one or two of his own conclusions.

"So with no more ado, Miss Thorpe will present her report, taking an hour or so and then we should have some time for a few questions." He turned to make eye contact, which Gretchen held until he smiled and offered her the floor. She watched him return to his chair.

"Thank you, Stephen," said Gretchen. "I will probably take an hour thirty to get through the presentation and if we run out of time on questions please feel free to ring my mobile over the weekend." The lights dimmed and on the screen a sequence of carefully constructed images accompanied her opening points.

"Is she joining us tonight?" whispered a man on Matthew's left.

"No," scribbled Matthew on his pad and pushed the note to his neighbour.

Grinning, his neighbour amended the note to "Cos she thinks you're a stalker."

Matthew scribbled defensively, "No – doing something with the army."

"A likely story – stalker." came the reply.

Chapter 3 – Thomas

The surgery waiting room was down to its last few patients. Thomas couldn't remember how long he'd been there. He realised he'd been looking at the same page of *Home and Garden* for nearly ten minutes and returned it to the pile. Another magazine caught his eye. "Hello," he said to himself scanning the motorbikes on the front cover. "'*Chrome ecstasy: a Triumph Retro.*'"

There was a tapping on the glass. Bunty, a short handsome man with a multi-coloured tie stood behind the glass waving slowly at Thomas.

Thomas blew him a kiss.

Bunty didn't respond, only nodded to the door. A message flashed on the screen "Mr Thorpe to Doctor Bunt."

Thomas followed the doctor into the consulting room. "Thank you for seeing me Doctor."

"I had no choice, everyone else has gone. What do you want?" said Bunty.

"Couldn't we do the '*How are you?*' first?"

"No, you forfeited that right when you left me for a pole dancer."

Thomas became defensive. "Now that's factually incorrect. He was a dancer in the Polish National Ballet."

"Hmm," said Bunty, looking through the notes and adding, "Lead in the Nutcracker?"

"Oh, unworthy of you, Doctor."

"Stop calling me Doctor. What do you want?"

"Sorry Bunty. Do you get tax relief for *Home and Garden* and *Bikers Monthly*?" Thomas asked, trying to lighten the tone.

"Seeing someone from the Inland Revenue are we?" replied Bunty, having none of it.

"I have a client who advertises in *Bikers Monthly*."

Bunty sat patiently. "I haven't really got time for this but I will wait."

Thomas drummed his fingers. "Anti-depressants!"

"No. We've been through this before."

"You haven't heard my argument yet."

"I don't need to. You're up to the limit on sleeping tablets and liberally self medicate alcohol, which is why – as you remember – we set up counselling sessions." Bunty scrolled down the computer screen. "Except... I see you aren't attending. Well that was a waste of time. Do I want to hear why?"

"He made a pass at me," Thomas said unconvincingly.

"Reese Jones has four kids and a mistress. I hardly think he would have time for you too."

"He has a mistress?" said Thomas, genuinely distracted. "But he has no sense of humour and appalling dress sense..."

"Ah!" interrupted Bunty, "So I think we've discovered why you've stopped going."

Thomas shifted uncomfortably.

"Oddly, the NHS doesn't have a database field for aesthetics, only clinical excellence."

"I'm depressed."

"I was depressed when you left me. But I got over it. I joined the *Thomas is a Tart* support group, of which, may I say, there are too many members."

Thomas's head began to throb. "You know it's really bad form to drag up the past."

"Yes... 'drag up' being the operative words. How long did the 'Principle Pole' last?"

"I need the pills Doc. I'm really down."

"What you need to do is grow up. You have the emotional maturity of a sixteen year old."

Thomas looked suddenly earnest. "I really mean it. If you don't prescribe them," he shook his head, "I will go to the black market."

Doctor Bunt appraised his erstwhile lover for some time. "Given that a black market to you probably means Jamaicans selling fruit is no real threat but I know any other GP would prescribe just to be rid of you. Fluoxetine will probably do you least harm."

"Thank you Bunty."

"But don't take them with alcohol and sleeping pills. Otherwise I'll have to sit through another rendition of WH Auden's *Stop all the Clocks*."

Bunty handed over the script.

Thomas stood up. "Say hi to Steve for me."

"I will. The grapevine tells me you are seeing John Bentley."

"Well if you heard it through the grapevine..." Thomas thought better of humour. "I am."

"He's a decidedly good chap."

Thomas picked up his coat. "He is indeed. So good in fact he's boating with his two sons this weekend."

"Oh. I didn't know he'd been married."

"Yes, for his sins. Before he saw the light."

"Or the dark."

"Bunty, are you and Steve doing anything tomorrow? I'd like to take you both out for a drink."

"God Tom, I don't think so. Steve's not really one for boozy nights out."

"Well neither am I now I have the pills."

"Still no."

"Well think of it as a chaperone job, that you're saving me from myself; Good Samaritan and all that. Come on, be a good laugh."

"I'll think about it. Now please go or I'll never get home."

"Top man, see you tomorrow."

"I said I'll think about," said Bunty in a loud voice to a closing door.

Chapter 4 – Lulworth

The long army barrack was lit only by the 'EXIT' sign, and Gretchen lay blinking in the gloom, her thoughts still without form. She could recall driving the previous night and arriving at gates ... there were army guards. Her memory cleared. She was in Lulworth, courtesy of the MoD, and had been allocated a large army billet all to herself.

There would be a breakfast at zero-three twenty for a zero-three forty start. Gretchen was not surprised to see that it was only thirty seconds before her alarm was due. She counted down and, in doing so, could feel her pulse rate fall. By the time a knock came on the door, she was dressed and packed. "Come in," she said.

The door remained closed but a deep voice announced, "Breakfast is served in the last room on the right."

Gretchen was pleased to see an old friend already eating.

"Egon," she said brightly.

"Ah, Grae. Good morning to you."

"Good morning, or should I say, guten morgen?"

"Thank you, but now I believe you have exhausted your German vocabulary."

Gretchen bent to kiss the dark-haired man, who half stood in mid-chew proffering one cheek and then the other. "How's the family?" she asked.

"All very well – noisy, muddy, and in constant need of a taxi service."

"Hello, Sperber," said Gretchen, crouching to stroke a large brown dog that responded by lifting one eye and giving a single wag of its tail. "Bit early for you too?" she sympathised.

Egon finished his mouthful. "The army have allowed him here under the special dispensation of 'working dog'. Do the words 'special dispensation' sound too German?"

Gretchen looked bemused. "I have no idea…"

"Because I'm the only Kraut you know, yes?"

"Tom says your sense of humour is too good for a German."

"Ah, how is *ze English Tommy*?"

"Still doesn't like the mud."

"And... no one else with you today?"

Gretchen took a deep breath. "Sorry no."

Egon nodded his understanding.

A large man wearing army fatigues entered the kitchen. "Good morning, Miss Thorpe," he said, and then to Egon. "Good morning, Doctor Borcke."

"Gretchen, do you know Sergeant Beckett?"

"Yes, we met last night, thanks – he very kindly showed me around."

"In civvie town," said Egon, "Sergeant Beckett is Bob but here I have to call him by his rank and he likes to call me Doctor. I'm afraid Bob will call you Miss Thorpe all day so don't argue like you normally do. Isn't that right, Sergeant Bob?"

"That is correct, Doctor Egon. Miss Thorpe, do you have a DPM jacket?"

"That's camouflage to you," said Egon.

"Yes," said Gretchen, gesturing to the coat peg.

The sergeant followed her gaze. "Ah, a *95*, I see. Good, good" Nodding to himself, he left the room.

Egon looked at the door, then the coat, then the door again. "Not a *94* or a *96*. Very important."

Sunrise was at exactly 05:09. Egon remarked that this was so because the army had written it into the schedule. They had all stopped to watch the first rays breach the Purbeck Hills. Though she had seen this event in so many places, Gretchen had never tired of it. Once, after picking Thomas up and driving him home in the early hours, she had pulled the car over as the sky began to pale. She had quietly left her sleeping brother and stood for many minutes in the sharp morning air waiting for the warmth to touch her face. As she restarted the car her brother had stretched and remarked, "So, you do have a soul." She had taken the opportunity to lecture him on the temperature and pressure for the sun's hydrogen to fuse into helium with its resultant electromagnetic radiation. He had fallen asleep fairly speedily but shortly after had mumbled, "Bullshit."

"Sperber!" shouted Egon, and the three of them had turned away and headed toward higher ground, a Bavarian Mountain Dog in tow.

"Okay – listen up," said Sergeant Beckett, addressing his men. "First I want to introduce Doctor Borcke and Miss Thorpe from the Deer Trust. They are here to advise and assist. Our objective today is to fit radio transmitters to six deer. To do this we first have to catch six deer. We will do this by erecting nets and then driving a herd of deer into those nets. You lot have two tasks. One – set up the nets, and two – walk the woodland to drive a herd towards the nets. I will be picking some of you to help this end. Is that clear so far?"

There were no questions.

Sergeant Beckett continued. "Corporals Stones and Pexton have had training in this and you will follow their instructions. I will now show you the map of where the net will go and where the woodland is."

Whilst the sergeant plotted various positions on the map, Egon leant over and whispered to Gretchen, "The Bosch are here, here and here and we are…"

Sergeant Beckett looked back at the men. "Are there any questions?"

"Can't we just shoot them, sergeant?" asked a private at the front.

"Yes we could Private Mate but then the radio trackers would only tell us where the venison sausages went! Any more questions?"

There was silence.

They piled into two army trucks, already full of equipment, and set off along the valley. Within an hour they had established the long V-shaped corral, down which the deer would be driven, and erected the catch nets at the end. Two thirds of the soldiers had then driven off to begin the round-up, leaving nine others to organise the catch.

"Sergeant, that's the most efficient setting-up I've ever seen," said Gretchen, enjoying a mug of tea. "This would normally take at least twice as long with our usual volunteers – willing but hard to lead."

"Thank you. Just clear instructions, that's all. Do you mind me asking, miss, how you come to be doing this?"

Gretchen laughed. "I often ask myself the same question." She closed her eyes in thought. "I joined Egon about… twelve years ago. He'd stuck a note on the wall at college from this charity asking for students to come and relocate deer. I assumed there'd be a rush so put my name on the list early. By the end of the week mine was the only name on it."

"And you're still doing it," observed the sergeant. "Could do with you in the army, nobody volunteers for anything here." He checked his watch. "When do we need to take cover?"

"Half an hour", replied Gretchen, "but better confirm that with Egon."

They walked back towards the others.

As they reached the nets they found Egon trying to explain the details of how to catch the deer to the soldiers, who looked a little nervous and not a little confused. Sergeant Beckett took over. Pointing to three of the privates he barked, "You stand with me, you stand with Miss Thorpe and you stand with Doctor Borcke. You others get into pairs."

"Private Smith!" shouted the sergeant at the soldier moving uncomfortably towards Gretchen.

"Yes, Sarge!" responded the soldier in broad Glaswegian.

"On all fours!"

The private did as he was told.

"If it's a boy deer, it will have antlers," said Sergeant Beckett, getting down and holding onto Private Smith's ears. "Once you have hold of the antlers, do not let them go or they will gore you to death."

The men looked more nervous.

"Then you will lay your whole body on top of them to stop them kicking you to death, like so."

Private Smith collapsed as Sergeant Beckett lay on him.

"When the animal is subdued, your partner will place a hood on the deer like so." Some of the men started to giggle but, seeing the sergeant's expression, thought better of it.

"Finally you will take this, which is called a trawl net and together wrap it around the animal like so. Never, I repeat never, let go of the antlers or feet. Why?"

"To stop us getting gored or kicked to death, Sarge," the soldiers chorused; all except for Private Smith, whose response was inaudible.

Chapter 5 – Bentley and Hacket

"Tara Palmer Tomkinson," said the young interviewee as she looked at the first of the two images. "And... Amy Davis?"

"That is, ah, correct," said Shaun, senior partner of Bentley and Hacket, who had the habit of separating a sentence randomly with either 'um' or 'ah'. He sat opposite the interviewee and checked his question sheet again. "And, um, can you tell me, ah, who they are modelling for?"

"Amy Davis was the size 16 woman modelling for M & S and TPT modelled for Splendor Lingerie."

Thomas sipped his cappuccino and wondered if he should buy a more comfortable leather chair. He and Shaun had been interviewing all morning and this was their tenth candidate; each one of which had glowing reports from school and university. Not that Thomas had read any, Shaun had done all that; analysing them into a matrix of attributes, and then determining those to be seen. All Thomas ever read were their hobbies, which he would then research, allowing a more rounded interview. Unfortunately the present candidate had plenty of 'A stars' but no hobbies and Thomas was struggling to maintain interest. He was, though, quite impressed with her shade of eyeliner, noticing how the light made the turquoise shimmer. As Shaun's questioning 'um'd and ah'd' on he found himself thinking about his own short-lived attempts with eyeliner. The 1980s had plenty of makeup-wearing pop icons but Thomas had worn his in a more subtle manner which, paradoxically, had aroused suspicion. Name-calling had given way to the odd thump and in his last year at school he had been set upon by three boys from the football team. He'd resigned himself to a 'good beating' when suddenly Gretchen had appeared. The last thing he wanted was to be saved by his little sister but he was hardly in a position to give orders. Immediately he'd felt the weight lift off him as one boy fell sideways clutching his thigh. As Thomas pulled his shirt and jumper back down, uncovering his eyes, he saw a boy lunge at his sister. She seemed to move forward, turn underneath him while dropping to her knees. The boy's forward momentum was converted downward such that it would have barely been absorbed by a judo mat; the parquet floor tiles merely reflected it. Although much of the incident was hazy, a moment of clarity that had stayed with him was of the look of calm on Gretchen's face; and his own feelings of utter envy.

"Well I, um, am done," said Shaun. "Tom do you have anything else to, ah, ask Ms Reeve?"

Thomas smiled at the candidate who beamed back. "Yes, though firstly I want to apologise for my colleague's dress sense, his 'symphony of beige' is, I can tell you, just an understated stratagem. Down the Kings Road he is known as *Mr Deceptively Neutral.*"

The young woman suppressed a grin and Shaun gave a wearisome look.

Thomas flashed a winning smile. "Anyway Sarah, to return you to Marks and Sparks, what else can you tell me about the ad?"

The interviewee looked back at the image of the naked *fuller figure* standing on the cliff top. "Well," she began, "it's a Rainey Kelly production and... the model is shouting, 'I am normal!'"

"How did you feel when you first saw it?"

"Surprised."

"Because?"

The young woman shifted uncomfortably. "Well it's daring. I remember thinking M & S had completely lost it."

"And how did *you* feel?" asked Thomas again.

"Well I, I... I'm not sure I understand the question."

Thomas grunted. "Sorry I did rather sound like Tony Blair's therapist. Okay, if you were advising Messers Marks 'n' Spencer, what would be your recommendation?"

"Go with TPT."

"Because?"

"Because sex sells," said the young woman, finding an air of confidence.

Thomas furrowed his brow slightly. "Are you saying that size 16 can't be sexy?"

The young woman's face flushed scarlet, her eyes wide. "Oh no, no, it's just the socio economic... demographic... is not used to... it," she tailed off.

Thomas smiled mischievously as he withdrew a packet of Marlboros, "Tell me, do you shop at M & S?"

The interviewee hesitated. "Well the Per Una line looks good so I may do."

Thomas nodded agreeably and turned to his college. "I'm done Shaun."

"Well er thank you very much Ms Reeves," said Shaun, "we'll erm be in touch."

The young woman stood up. "Thank you Mr Thorpe, thank you Mr Hacket," she said, trying to regain her composure. Both men rose from their seats and nodded.

Thomas opened up his office window and lit up a cigarette. "Well Shaun, thoughts?"

"I, ah, suppose it's pointless to ask that you stop, um, undermining me."

"Absolutely, but sorry my old darling, can't help myself, you are the epitome of an authority figure."

Shaun shook his head.

Thomas exhaled a short burst of smoke out of the window. "Did any of the candidates spark for you?" he asked.

"Not, um, really. I was thinking we should try a different, ah, format for the second interview. Maybe you could lead them in, um, ah, um, group discussion."

"Happy to."

Shaun looked suspiciously at Thomas. "Nothing too, um, *disturbing*."

"Course not – guide's honour."

Chapter 6 – The Army Truck

The gorse bush was surrounded by patches of marsh but provided good cover and an excellent view of the wood. Gretchen lay hidden, scanning the trees for movement. Alongside her in the mud was Private Smith, who had yet to speak. "Tell me, Private," she said eventually in a hushed voice, "what's your first name?"

After an awkward silence, he whispered, "Andrew."

"I'm Gretchen." There was another short silence. "Andrew, I need you to stay close. I'm not that heavy so when I grab a deer I'll get dragged around if you don't add your weight quickly."

"Yes, Miss Thorpe," he replied, adding hesitantly, "how many do you reckon will get caught in the nets?"

"The nets are held up by ten poles. The lead deer will try to jump the net but it's too high. The net will collapse around them and the rest will jump free. I expect to catch eight to ten. We will then run in and tackle one animal per two of us."

"Are they very big?"

"Depends on the type," replied Gretchen. Then a thought occurred to her. "You have seen a deer before?"

"Not for real."

"Oh! Why did you volunteer?"

"We didn't, this was our punishment for being drunk and disorderly."

A herd of deer emerged at the edge of the clearing. There had been no sound to signal their arrival. Gretchen winced when she saw that there were about eighty Sika deer, a relative of the Red and altogether more of a handful than the Fallow. Again, without warning, they began to charge down the race. Though Gretchen had heard and seen this all before, Private Smith, having experienced nothing like it, lay wide-eyed beside her. Within seconds the stags and hinds were past them and crashing into the nets; the lead animals falling, the rest leaping clear, just as Gretchen had predicted.

Egon was the first on the scene and tackled a large black hind. Along the line he could see a young stag back on its feet and beginning to pull free. He shouted but Gretchen was already closing in. She leapt, grabbing an antler and pulling the deer's head down sharply. The animal tried to twist away, which wrenched her shoulder. Gretchen got her other hand on the far antler and the deer fell back on its side, kicking wildly.

"Andrew!" she shouted, gritting her teeth and trying to control the writhing limbs, "Lie on me!"

Alarmed and unsure, the private did as asked. The stag gave a low, indignant whinny, but stopped thrashing.

"You're going to have to do the mask yourself," said Gretchen, her voice tense and her arms twitching with exertion, "I can't slacken my grip."

Though initially fumbling, the soldier quickly gained in confidence under Gretchen's calm instruction. Even as the animal tried to escape there was no sense of panic, Gretchen just held firm and waited until the animal tired. They secured the final drawstring and, after a mutual count of three, they let go. The stag gave a final shake of its antlers before laying still. Gretchen grinned. "Well done Private Smith," she said, "you're a natural."

As they stood back to draw breath, Gretchen scanned the mess of legs, camouflage jackets and upside down nets around them. One corporal hung on grimly to an animal that repeatedly kicked him in the groin, his partner paralyzed with fear. The corporal screamed at him but being shouted at only confused the 'dopey sadistic twat' even more. Gretchen signalled to Private Smith who ran in to help finish the job and save the hapless pair from further harm.

At the far end of the line Egon was checking the animals caught and assembling the transmitters. To one side two soldiers stood empty handed, their expressions a mix of anxiety and shock. Gretchen walked over to them trying to read the situation.

"Problem?" she asked.

It transpired that the catcher had not gripped the small sharp antler tightly enough and, as the pricket flexed its powerful neck, the private had been stabbed through the hand. Both soldiers had rolled away from the danger putting their full weight on the front leg which broke with a sickening snap. The deer then jumped to its feet running on three legs into the woods.

"I'm sorry Miss, I couldn't catch it," said the private tremulously, his hand dripping with blood.

"Okay," replied Gretchen calmly, "these are wild animals, catching is never without casualties," she said, indicating his hand. "Don't worry, we never leave injured animals. I'll go and find it; you go and get some iodine from Doctor Borcke."

"Will the animal suffer Miss?" enquired the other soldier. Gretchen was about to give her 'not as bad as a natural death' reply when she looked into the soldier's eyes. There was a depth of innocence. For a split second she could identify with him but then the reality of the situation reasserted itself. Gretchen looked squarely at the young private and replied reassuringly, "No, not at all." The soldier heaved a great sigh of relief and went to get further orders.

Egon, who was now close by, smiled to himself. Gretchen caught his expression. "Rifle?" she asked.

"In the truck."

Five minutes later she was back with the gun and a dog. Seeing that Egon was once again busy she caught the attention of Sergeant Beckett. "Sergeant, this is Egon's," she said holding up the weapon. "I'm assuming it's a *point two four three?*"

The Sergeant eyed the gun. "Looks like it."

"So," said Gretchen, "just double checking; the magazine in here?"

"Correct and safety button at the end with the red dot."

Gretchen slid the magazine in place, loading a round into the chamber.

"Do you want one of these to accompany you?" he asked, gesturing to the men who were now starting to dismantle the netting.

"Thank you – assuming I can find the deer I could use Private Smith to carry it. My shoulder took a bit of a beating. By the way, is there anyone else on the range today?"

"No we've red-flagged just in case."

The pair entered the wood and Sperber swept back and forward, scanning for movement, sniffing continually. They didn't have far to go before the dog stopped and stared at the injured pricket just ahead of them. The deer jumped up and ran lop-sided for another hundred metres before coming to a halt. Sperber looked at Gretchen who already had the deer in her scope.

Sergeant Beckett was dabbing iodine on the private's wounded hand as a sharp crack rang out from the woods. "Stop blubbing lad," he said quietly. "Christ, if the Iraqis could see what we were sending them, they'd be pissing themselves."

The army trucks began winding their way along the track that would eventually lead them back to base. Egon looked around at Gretchen who was removing her muddy jacket. "That was successful, yes?"

"Could have been a lot worse."

"Damn, I forgot to explore the English negative first," Egon said playfully. "Thank you for helping out, we are always low on numbers weekdays."

"No problem," she yawned, "what are you doing after lunch?"

"Officers' conservation training."

"Can I borrow your dog then?"

"Going tracking?"

"No," said Gretchen, yawning again, "I'm going for a walk down on the beach and could do with the company."

"Just going for a walk? Doesn't sound like you."

"Well, bit of geology."

Egon sniggered. "Sure – Sperber could do with the exercise," he said patting his dog and explaining in German the need to lay off the *eisbein*. "Do you want a meal tonight, Grae?" Not receiving an answer he looked around again to see Gretchen asleep; her rolled up DPM 95 a fitting pillow.

* * * * *

Dust surrounded the converted army lorry as it made its way slowly from the Ngorongoro Crater onto the Serengeti, eventually stopping at a large formal stone and wood building. Below the tin roof, was a sign that read 'Olduvai Gorge – Site Museum of Hominid History'.

The eleven travel-weary passengers disembarked and headed for the shade of the building; two figures hung back, a man seeming to support a young woman as they walked to the side of an open-thatched rondavel. *For a few moments they stared across to the centre of the wide, barren gorge at which point a red obelisk of rock, thirty metres in diameter, rose from a large scree mound. Behind them they could hear the tour guide calling the group to join him at the main building, so they turned and joined their companions.*

"Good morning my white cousins and welcome to the museum," said a small greying black man with a wide grin. "Well," he continued, "I think it's still morning. My father could tell the time by looking at the Sun." He inclined his head, squinting in the brightness. "Me, I have to look at my Casio. Ah yes..." he said, checking his wrist watch, "we are still 'ante meridiem'." The assembled group laughed, checking their own watches. A young woman in the front gazed intently at the man.

"My name," he continued, "is Buck Masios and I have worked here for twenty two years following my qualification as a doctor. Of paleo-anthropology that is, not medicine, so don't ask me to fix your leg or anything." Buck carried on, his enunciation clear though thick with the accent of the Xhosa, his consonants occasionally clicking softly.

The young woman looked out over Buck's shoulder to a large ravine. It was just how her father had described it. The area had been the shore of a huge lake in millennia past until volcanic activity had covered the water and plain with many metres of ash. Some half million years ago a river had diverted its course and slowly cut away layers of prehistory, until the gorge was formed. In the process it had revealed two and a half million years of Hominid activity.

"Does everybody know of Bob Geldof?" Buck asked. "He was here last year and made us all laugh. On hearing that Homo habilis *was present for one million years, he called them 'underachievers'.*" The group laughed out loud and Buck grinned. "He has made you laugh as well. Anyway, Homo habilis *means 'handy man' as he seems to be the first hominid to master cutting tools." Buck's obvious enthusiasm for his subject was infectious and the group hung on his words as he described the wealth of finds in the area and conjectured on the lifestyles this all suggested.*

The young woman raised her hand, "Sorry, Doctor Masios, could I ask a question?" Buck looked across at her, his lined face contrasting with hers.

"Please call me Buck, my dear, and may I ask your name?"

"Gretchen Thorpe," said the woman.

"Please ask away, Miss Thorpe."

"What do you think became of Homo habilis?"

"A good question – I would answer that we are simply in the realms of speculation because history teaches us that all species become extinct sooner or later. Personally I suspect climate change. Maybe habilis *didn't have sufficient skills to acclimatize or maybe other species adapted much quicker. Or, as Mr Geldof says, perhaps they were just underachievers."*

The group took Gretchen's lead, asking a range of questions that encouraged Buck to outline current thinking on the developments that led to modern man, and also entertain his clearly besotted audience.

"Well thank you, Buck," said the tour leader, "I have been here many times but never get tired of this talk."

"Oh, you flatter me, Roger, especially as you know all my jokes."

The group clapped and Buck thanked his audience as they turned to collect their bags.

Gretchen approached the African. "Thank you," she said shaking his hand, "That was very informative."

"My pleasure, Miss Thorpe – are you enjoying your tour around Tanzania?"

"Yes thank you."

"Good – and you have another question for me?"

Gretchen wasn't expecting Buck's directness and hesitated.

"Shall we walk, my dear?" said Buck.

He led her out onto the wooden porch, then down the steps onto the dirt and into the baking sunshine.

"We can go over to the acacia tree – there is shade and a good view of the gorge."

Gretchen walked slowly alongside Buck who pointed out the various soil layers and corresponding dates.

The shade of the tree was a great relief as they both turned and stared across at the arid landscape. "Now what did you want to ask me?"

"Well it's not a question really. My father visited here about eleven years ago and told me all about you. He said the place was full of wonder. He also described you accurately."

Buck looked intrigued.

"My father wrote in his journal that he'd spent a few days with you and that you were very knowledgeable and a gentleman."

"He sounds like a good judge of character," replied the old man with a smile.

"He was."

There was a pause.

"I'm sorry," said Buck, "... you must miss him."

It was a simple and sincere statement yet it triggered a wave of sadness that Gretchen struggled to control. The pair stood in silence for some time until a strange low whistling noise flowed over the escarpment.

"Ah listen," said Buck, his finger touching his ear, "the Whistling Thorn."

Gretchen looked up and took a deep breath. "Oh yes," she replied, looking round but unable to locate the source of the sound. "I'd heard about them, it's another type of acacia isn't it?"

Her companion nodded.

"Buck, I don't suppose you remember my father?"

"I'm sorry; I see many people."

"Of course, I don't know why I asked. Look... thank you very much... you must have other people to see."

"I do I'm afraid, it's my job." Buck began to walk away, then stopped and turned.

"Miss Thorpe, I don't suppose you know if he asked me any questions. I tend to remember questions more than I do people."

"Yes, he did. He asked you what you thought was the cause of increasing brain sizes and you said..."

Buck held up his hand. "That the Hominids were so physically inferior compared with the other animals that err..."

"That natural selection favoured intelligence," finished Gretchen. "He was here."

Buck smiled kindly. "So, Miss Thorpe, you have your answer." He looked down at his watch. "I have to go, and I see a young gentleman is waiting for you."

"Oh that's Sam, he's just a friend."

"Ah, there is nothing 'just' about friendship." Buck extended his hand. "It's been a pleasure to meet you, Miss Thorpe."

For a split second, Gretchen was overcome with a desire to hug the old man but she restrained herself. She shook his hand. "The pleasure has been mine."

* * * * *

Gretchen was aware that the rocking of the truck had stopped and opened her eyes. A large brown dog was staring at her. She patted him on the head then stretched and yawned. "Ah Sperber," she said, "if only you could talk."

Chapter 7 – Soppy Joe's

The taxi slowed halfway along Brewer Street and pulled up onto the kerb. Doctor Bunt got out, looked around and then back at the cab driver who pointed upwards. A second man, Steve – tall, with thinning blonde hair – paid the driver. The bar was located above an Estate Agent and could only be accessed by two flights of steps and the support of two heavily worn handrails. The pair made their way up the steps and into the noisy room. Thomas was already at the bar and watching a television screen mounted above the optics.

"Tom!"

"Bunty!" cried Thomas with a wide smile. He stubbed out his cigarette and stood up.

"I'm here under duress. Steve twisted my arm. We're on our way to eat so can't stay long." Bunty motioned to his partner. "You know each other I believe."

"Yes, yes, good to see you again Steve," replied Thomas, shaking hands. "Sit, sit. What can I get you?"

Bunty retrieved two bar stools.

"What are you having?" asked Steve

"Frascati and some tapas."

"Italian *and* Spanish," noted the doctor loftily.

"All Latin to me, Bunty. A subject that was as impenetrable to me at school as its men are to me now. No pun intended."

"None taken."

"Eh!" said Steve, surveying the bar, "Oh yes, I'll take wine with you."

Bunty nodded and Thomas signalled two more glasses from the barman.

"Any tapas?"

"The good Doctor," said Steve, glancing towards his partner, "advised me not to eat between meals."

"He told me that to, that's why I'm doing it."

"God, I knew this was a mistake," said Bunty wistfully, "I think I'll visit the loo."

Thomas pointed down the bar. "End, turn right."

Steve looked at the video screens around the room, each monitor showing the same movie; the current sequence being a dark-haired woman chasing a tall man down a wide staircase.

"Have you not been to Soppy Joe's before?"

"No, heard about it, something about romantic films."

"Not just romantic," said Thomas, waving a tortilla chip, "the best clips from the best films."

"But no sound."

"No you have to add that yourself. Here." Thomas handed him a pamphlet. "Find the clip and read along or..." he held up his hand to halt Steve from saying anything as they watched the action on screen. The male character turned in close-up.

"*Frankly my dear I don't give a damn,*" echoed a dozen voices in unison.

"Oh, it's *Gone with the Wind,*" hissed Steve. "That's fabulous. What's she saying now?"

Thomas closed his eyes trying to remember. "Something about Tara and its soil, I think."

Steve took a big gulp of wine. "This is a great idea. Who's was it?"

"You're drinking with him," said the man from behind the bar.

Thomas gave a mock grin of immodesty and then nodded to the barman. "Meet Joe," he said.

The barman nodded to Steve and continued serving another customer.

Steve looked back at Thomas. "What you? How did you come up with the idea?"

Thomas held up his finger again for silence.

"*After all, tomorrow is just another day,*" came various high pitched voices followed by some cheers.

"Oh," said Thomas, "I've spent too many hours sitting in bars alone. Joe had another bar; the lease was coming to an end so I shared an idea for lonely drinkers. As it turned out it's just as much fun for groups."

* * * * *

The open window let a cool breeze through into the apartment. As the evening progressed it also let in the shouts of London's revellers.

Gretchen leant back from her desk, stretched her arms high and gingerly rotated her left shoulder. She probed all around the cartilage with the fingers of her right hand, wincing occasionally.

Gretchen closed the window and looked back at a pile of books and flip charts. She drew a long deep breath and walked over to the kitchenette and filled the kettle to the level marked 'one cup'.

* * * * *

Thomas poured more wine. "There's only a couple of lines in this. You two try it; in character. Bunty you be the lady."

Bunty staggered slightly and glanced through the dialogue. "*Where's the cat?*" he said breathlessly.

"*I don't know,*" replied Steve in a soft American voice.

On screen, rain poured on a beautiful dark-haired woman running down an alley.

"*Cat! Cat!*" came sporadic shouts from the drinkers.

The cat appeared from a crate, was scooped up by the woman who then ran into the arms of a man in a raincoat. They kissed passionately.

At the bar a drinker wiped his eyes.

"Gets me too," said Joe handing the drinker a tissue.

Thomas turned to Steve. "You should have been here the night someone brought a harmonica and started playing *Moon River* as they kissed. We were all in tears."

Thomas looked at his watch. "What time's your reservation?"

"Oh fuck it," said Bunty.

"Joe, can we have some more tapas and another bottle?"

Steve was looking up again. "What's this?"

"Ah," said Thomas, "This is the 'Daddy'."

Bunty lifted his reading glasses and squinted at the screen where a man is opening a door.

The well-tailored man hesitantly enters the room while a red-headed woman stares at him over the back of the sofa on which she is resting.

"It's *An Affair to Remember*," said Bunty, through a mouthful of pickles, "with Cary Grant and... and... Deborah Kerr."

Thomas tinged his wine glass. "Correct."

"Come on Steve, you must know it."

Steve filled his glass and shook his head. "Sorry Bunty, what's it about."

The doctor was already reading the script and mouthing the words of both actors in between sips of wine.

"*Is Miss Macka...*" he voiced for the male character.

"*Nickie.*" He alternated for the female.

"*Hello Terry.*"

"*It's good to see you.*"

"*It's good to see you too.*"

"*It's been a long time.*"

"*May I...?*"

"*Please do sit down.*"

"*I bet you're wondering how I got here.*"

"Hello! Bunty's gone," said Thomas watching his friend. "The story," he said, replying to Steve, who was now also following the silent action, "is of Cary and Debs – who fall in love during a cruise despite prior betrothals. They agree to break off their engagements and meet at the top of the Empire State

Building. He turns up but she is run over by a car. Cary thinks Debs must have married the other man."

"*No wedding ring I see,*" continued Bunty, in a deep voice trying to catch the nuance of the on-screen action.

"*No,*" he replied to himself lightly.

"*But I thought...*"

"*No.*"

Thomas scanned the room. Some solo drinkers were watching and reading; other groups were speaking out loud and others again just enjoying the conviviality. He smiled at Joe who replied with a thumbs up.

"*Waiting, waiting, waiting,*" said a man behind Steve, also transfixed to the monitor.

"*And where is he all this time?*" said Bunty in a feminine voice.

"*Waiting,*" replied Thomas.

"What's happening now?" asked Steve, watching the man hand the woman a white crocheted shawl.

"Cary is telling Debs that he once painted a picture of her wearing the shawl and didn't think he could ever part with the painting but one day he was told by his assistant that a women in a wheel chair had come into the gallery and had liked it..."

"*She'd seen in it,*" said Bunty, "*what I'd hoped you'd see in it.*"

"So," explained Thomas, "Cary, not seeing the woman, had told his assistant to give her the picture."

On screen the man stops, a dawning of realisation on his face. He looks at the woman on the sofa. Her face becomes, intense, pleading. He continues talking but looks wildly around the room before opening the bedroom door and there is the painting.

"Oh my God," said Steve.

"Yes, he realises the truth."

"Darling don't look at me like that," said Bunty.

"Why didn't you tell me? If it had to happen to one of us why did it have to be you?" he replied.

"It was nobody's fault but my own. I was looking up; it was the nearest thing to heaven. You were there."

Joe handed the man at the bar another tissue.

Thomas mouthed along without looking at the script until the credits rolled.

"Do you know all the words to these films," asked Steve, draining another glass.

Thomas nodded. "Misspent adolescence." He looked at the empty bottle. "Bunty told me you weren't a boozy boy."

"I wasn't before tonight. My excuse will be your bad influence."

"Ah, does my reputation rather precede?"

"Somewhat."

Thomas shrugged. "Recovered Bunty?"

The doctor cleared his throat. "Don't know what you mean. But I think we should be off."

"Nonsense, the night is young and there are no more weepies. Set 'em up Joe."

On screen a man dressed in a white suit is sitting at a bus-stop and turns to the people on the bench.

The drinkers, almost in unison respond. *"My mamma always said, life is like a box of chocolates..."*

Chapter 8 – Birthdays

David stopped on the spiral staircase, overcome by a sudden lethargy. For several months he'd had occasional symptoms of a cold which failed to develop any further. He put it down to his hectic schedule and would have seen a doctor had he not arrived home on one plane, collected his daughter and headed straight back to the airport. He steadied himself on the wrought iron rail and remembered Yossarian from Catch 22. *'He had a pain in his* liver," David recalled, "that fell just short of jaundice." He smiled and decided that likewise he was destined to never quite have this cold. The moment passed. He could smell warm fresh bread and it reminded him that he was hungry.

The stairway opened out into a breakfast area where four other guests were already eating. They wore climbing clothes and spoke English.

"Hi," David said, "that looks good – where are you guys climbing?"

"Just up the road in the valley," replied one of them. "Are you climbing?"

"Yes, I'm here with my daughter."

They made their introductions. Mark, Robert, Phil and Matt were also taking advantage of the new low cost airlines working the Alicante route. David explained that it was his daughter's thirteenth birthday and this was her birthday present.

"Lucky daughter," said Robert.

Phil laughed. "Robert gives his wife climbing holidays for her birthdays too, but she doesn't climb so he has to go instead."

"Ah is it that obvious?" said Robert to general nods of agreement.

"I can assure you, gentlemen," said David, "this is certainly a present for Gretchen. She is an excellent climber – will be far better than me in a couple of years."

"Where are you climbing?" Mark asked.

"Around here, haven't chosen yet. Nothing too difficult, grade four-ish. Gretchen wants to do her first lead."

"We were at a perfect place yesterday like that," said Phil, "great for acclimatizing – south facing."

"Sounds ideal," David agreed, opening his climbing guide.

"We're moving onto the next crag to look at some harder pitches. Why don't we meet for lunch and we can swap if you want to have a go at something more challenging."

David thought it a good plan and thanked them as Gretchen entered the room wearing her new sweatshirt.

"Is this the birthday girl?" asked Robert, David's expression answering the question. "Happy birthday to you," sang Robert and they all joined in. Gretchen gave a wide, toothy smile and then blushed as they cheered.

From the end of the table David watched his daughter, her long hair flicking one way then the other. In between mouthfuls of toast, she chatted enthusiastically and showed them all her new Leatherman. For the first time in his life David glimpsed the beautiful woman that Gretchen would become and realised that the child was fading quickly.

He felt a sudden pang of regret. Had it really been necessary to leave the house so often before his family awoke or to return after they were asleep? Gretchen's haul of merit badges and sporting medals lovingly placed on his pillow made him proud but also pricked his conscience. He knew from teachers that his son Tom was a gifted storyteller; he'd even managed to read one or two but knew he was losing touch with the boy. David had put down the increasing distance between them to teenage-hood but was that really the case? He made a commitment under his breath that he would resign his charity commitments, scale back his work and from now on, be there for his children.

London was still dozing when Gretchen reached the Serpentine where she stopped to stretch out her calf muscles. She loved this time of day. Hyde Park was empty of people though the wildlife that thrived on their activity was plentiful. Grey squirrels and brown rats froze as she ran by; magpies and rooks called while searching through human detritus. Canada geese, plentiful from a diet of discarded lunches, had started nesting and their downy tufts floated on the warming air. Tits, finches and larks squabbled, busy at their daily feed on bugs that teemed after the spring explosion. Now on her home leg, Gretchen could hear the distant 'clip clop' of horses being exercised. By the time she reached Marylebone, London was stretching and yawning and she had to leap out of the way of a white van, its flanks advertising fresh oysters. She slowed as she reached the top of Primrose Hill, her apartment now only a few minutes away. The hill served her well as a starting point for her run. The painful sprint up the incline prepared her for the rest of the route but, more importantly, the shock to the system repressed lingering dreams still hungry for attention. Gretchen leant against a bench alternately tensing and relaxing her hamstrings. She breathed deeply, surveying the building traffic. Wiping the sweat from her forehead she stretched her arms aloft and began her walk home.

The door of Gretchen's flat creaked as it opened slowly. She didn't look up.

"The door opens slowly to reveal a tall, handsome man in silhouette," said Thomas, "the frame only just wide enough to accommodate his masculine profile. He scans the room. A neatly-made bed, four judo mats, three flip charts, a telescope, a large book case and a desk. A Bluestocking reading a reference book doesn't notice him. The Adonis asks himself, 'Where in God's name am I?' He replaces the chocolates in his pocket and quietly backs out."

Thomas walked in. "Hi, Sis, fabulous morning."

"It is," replied Gretchen turning another page.

"High clouds are sailing, blue sky prevailing. Expect you've already been out for your constitutional."

"I have."

"You'll be amazed to know that even I walked this morning."

"Really?"

"You know, old flesh and blood, when you say 'really' it's rather like being flicked in the face by a wet sandy towel."

Gretchen didn't reply, so Thomas continued. "Anyway, I followed a... What is the collective noun for swallows? A chatter?" Still no response. "Yes, well I followed a chatter of swallows chattering away… chattering about their journey." Warming to his story Thomas acted out the scene, several of the birds swaying on wires, their arms crossed. "Baked over Spain – shot over France – stuck on the M25." Thomas mused thoughtfully, "The terror, the angst, the frustration. And all this just to make Tommy's day. I wonder why I feel so close to them. Do you think they feel close to me?"

"No," she said eventually, still studying her book.

"No? Ah, you are so sexy when you are monosyllabic."

She looked up from her book. "Tom, I've no idea why we should assign human characteristics to them. Their song and posturing is all about mating, territory and resources."

"Oh," said Thomas deflated. "In a short and rather brutal assessment his sister manages completely to extract all the poetry from what he thought a charming scenario."

"Sorry – I thought you were asking me a question."

"I was airing my feelings, dearest of kin, tempting you to resonate with the nuance, be of accord with my new-found sense of wonder, immerse your whole being in my *joie de vivre*. Honestly, anyone would think you had Asparagus syndrome."

"It's Aspergers, and coming from you that is a compliment."

Thomas walked into the kitchen area.

"Hmm, what's simmering?"

"Chutney."

"Bit early in the year for chutney."

"Ali bought in a delivery of cheap tomatoes only to find they were mostly green and un-saleable."

"Bet that didn't stop him from trying to sell them. What else have you got in it?"

"Oh, garlic, chillies, various fruits that were starting to ferment."

"Lovely," said Thomas with a hint of sarcasm. He picked up the kettle. "Coffee?"

"No thanks, I'll have another glass of lime and water though."

Thomas did as asked and then looked around, gurgling noisily. He'd given her an espresso machine last Christmas but guessed it was still in its box somewhere, so settled for 'instant'.

He placed a glass on Gretchen's desk and began toying with her telescope.

"You can't see into any bedrooms with that so please don't move it," she said without turning round.

Thomas took his hands off the mounting and looked over to the flip charts.

"What are you working on now?" he asked as he tried to read his sisters marker penned mind map. "PhD proposal – Traditional valuation methods in a Heu...ris...tic real...?"

Gretchen turned to one of the flip charts, pulling down the leaves. "It's very boring," she replied.

"So, thinking of a doctorate are we?"

"Not really – just playing."

"You never play."

Gretchen frowned and was rationalising a response when her brother asked, "Any feedback on the big presentation yet?"

"Not yet – but I got the feeling that it wasn't what they wanted to hear."

"Now why doesn't that surprise me?"

"Well the analysis was good... but best not say anymore."

"No problem, mum's the word. Talking of which, that's what I came for. It's your birthday next week and Mummy's the week after."

"Yes, I knew that."

"Had you remembered though that it's her sixtieth this year?"

"No, sorry, I had forgotten that bit. Have you arranged anything special?"

"Yes. I thought we could have a small gathering of old friends. I've contacted a couple from her school days, a few from our school years and a couple from the present; about a dozen in all."

"Sounds reasonable. What's the plan?"

"Lunch at *The Olive*."

Gretchen gave a slightly pained expression.

"Don't worry. I've negotiated a good price; thirty pounds excluding wine."

Gretchen nodded. "Do you want a contribution?"

"Ah well," Thomas said, hesitantly, "I have already bought her a new chair for the conservatory."

"So you want me to pick up the tab for the restaurant."

"If you would, lovely."

"Hmm. Twelve at thirty, that's three sixty. Okay."

"Plus Mum and James, me, you and John…"

Gretchen took a deep breath. "So that's over five hundred then," she said looking at her brother who seemed to have taken an interest in the telescope again.

"-ish. I'm afraid so."

Gretchen sighed and took out her cheque book.

"Don't worry about it now," Thomas said.

"No, I'd rather pay now. Then it won't inflate any further as it tends to with your events. And… I might not make it."

"Oh Grae! It's not because of James is it?"

"No, no," said Gretchen defensively, "mother can marry who she wants. I am due some time off and may be abroad."

Thomas tutted. "You and your little outings. Oh well, it can't be helped. I should have told you earlier. On the subject of birthdays, do you want anything in particular?"

"Yes, I broke my watch yesterday so I've ordered and paid for a new one which will be delivered to you to wrap."

"Was that your nobby-know-all watch?"

"The multi-function one, yes."

"I thought it was super roughty-toughty."

"But not stag proof."

"Oh, I'd forgotten you were deer catching yesterday. How's the Hun?"

"If you're referring to Egon, he's very well and asked when you were next joining him."

"Oo, I'll check my diary."

"You might like it. Dad would have loved it."

There was an awkward silence.

Gretchen broke it. "You can tell mum the watch is from her as well. Don't bother about the money."

"I must, darling."

"No seriously, if you must buy me something, get a bottle of gin."

"You don't drink gin."

"But I will have something in for when you come round."

"Now you're talking, this place is drier than the Gobi Desert."

"It's the Atacama."

"What?"

"The Atacama is the driest place on earth, less than one millimetre," she stopped and looked at him, "assuming you were trying to do a comparison joke. Is there anything else?" said Gretchen pulling open her rucksack.

"Not really, I don't think I have the emotional resolve to stay any longer. Thanks though for helping out tonight."

"I'm guessing – because you've asked me – that John is not available."

"He's boating with his sons, a rare moment of bonding so I thought I wouldn't intrude. Can you be at mine before five?"

"Yes, should be able to make it, I've got a meeting in town…"

"Got a meeting in town have we?" interrupted Thomas. "Not the hunk I spied you with the other day. Guy? Was that his name?"

Gretchen continued packing. "That's over."

"Ah."

"Didn't like the mud," said Gretchen as a matter of fact.

"Sounds my kind of chap. Could you get me an introduction?"

Gretchen flashed her brother a look.

"Sorry sis."

"Anyway after my meeting I'm going to the climbing wall but I'll come to you straight from there."

"What about your clothes."

"They'll be okay in the rucksack."

"Lord, I can't wait."

Chapter 9 – John Muir

Through the window of the modest Victorian terrace house Gretchen could see mounds of books, some of them open, others with *Post-Its* sticking out. She guessed she was at the right house and knocked on the green door. It opened to reveal a stooped, smiling gentleman in shirtsleeves and a leather jerkin.

"Hello," said Gretchen, "Jock McBain?"

"Indeed I am. You must be Gretchen, please do come in."

He led her into his study; though the room was large, the working space was not.

"I make no excuses for the state of my room," he said, then adding in a hushed voice, "I have to lock the door or my cleaner may burst in."

Gretchen stood for a second, taking in the number of titles. "Blimey, what a library you have. May I?" she asked, reaching for a familiar book.

He nodded with enthusiasm as she pulled out an early edition of *On the Origin of Species*. She handled it reverently, scanning through the cover pages before returning it.

"Please take a seat my dear, if you can find one that is. Now, I'm intrigued, how did you track me down?"

"The names of ex-trustees still appear on the website," said Gretchen, continuing to take in the magnitude of his collection "and," she added, almost apologetically, "you were in the phone book."

"Ah yes, I don't think I would ever have been recruited by MI5."

Gretchen moved a microscope off a chair, sat down and noticed that she was a foot lower than the adjacent stack of *National Geographic* magazines.

She watched Jock move around the study trying to decide which paperwork to move from which chair. "You need a bigger office," she observed.

"I don't think that would go down well with the housekeeper."

"Is there a Mrs McBain?"

"There is but alas she lives elsewhere."

"Sorry, I didn't mean to intrude."

"Don't be. Her divorce statement accurately cited that 'my interest in and commitment to' my work was somewhat greater than to my marriage."

Unearthing his desk chair, he settled himself and regarded her carefully. "I must say, I can see your father in you."

"Did you know him well?"

"We worked on two or three projects together. I was full time, he only did voluntary work. But we were both members of the Sierra Club."

Gretchen sat forward on her chair.

"Founded by John Muir himself but I expect you know that."

"Yes," replied Gretchen, "I've been up to the Sierra Nevada, I think it was the first environmental movement."

Jock's smile became earnest. "I was very sad to learn about your father's death… I suppose it must be more than ten years ago now."

"It'll be twenty years next Sunday," said Gretchen.

"Will it really? Good Lord *tempus fugit*. He was a lot younger than me of course. I remember him as a man of action and a fabulous sense of humour… Hmm, played some wonderfully wicked pranks."

"He did?"

"Oh yes, you never knew if you'd find a possum in your car or a ferret in your bed."

"Really?" said Gretchen, a puzzled expression on her face.

I remember we were counting bat species in Breckenridge and he told the locals we there to investigate UFOs in the area. Well, we had the radio station out and when I denied it the conspiracy theorists appeared… Chaos! I think I have some photographs somewhere of David around that time, I'll have a look."

"Would you?" Gretchen asked eagerly, "I'd be happy to help you search."

"Sure thing, you better remind me or I'll forget. The mind is willing but…" he grinned. "Anyway you wanted to talk to me about the John Muir Society?"

"Yes, I'd like to become a trustee. I think my experience could be of use and I wanted to ask your advice."

"I'm assuming you are a J.M.S. member?"

"My dad…" Gretchen paused. "My dad bought me a membership for my thirteenth birthday. I didn't find out until after… after. Anyway, I did some research and your name kept cropping up."

"Like a bad penny," said Jock with a snort, picking up several sheets of white paper. "Now," he began, "your résumé is very impressive."

"Thank you."

"Tell me, you seem awfully keen on the Natural Sciences and yet you went into…" Jock looked down again, "Business Consultancy."

"I had no money, and no support; calculated I could make enough from one to continue studying the other."

"Don't know how you had time," he looked down again, scanning the list of names. "I'm afraid I've only heard of Enron."

Gretchen sighed, "Mankind not at his best."

"And tell me about the Deer Trust?"

"It exists to better understand deer ecology, but most of my time is spent on catching and relocating. Unfortunately," she continued, "with no natural predators left we now have more deer than at any time since the Ice Age; the question has become *where to move them?*"

Jock returned her résumé to the folder and scratched his sparse grey hair. "I read the Army have real problems with numbers."

"That's what we're working on at the moment…"

There was a knock at the door. "Mr McBain?" enquired a high pitched voice of indeterminate accent.

Jock put his finger to his lips and looked mischievously at Gretchen.

"Mr McBain, I know you're in there."

Jock cleared his throat. "Miss Cray, I'm entertaining a lady and may be some time."

There was an odd scurrying noise outside the door.

They stayed still.

"What's she doing?" Gretchen whispered.

"Dusting vigorously." Jock whispered back.

"Right," the voice said breaking through the quiet, "I'll be going. Your lunch is in the oven."

"Thank you, Miss Cray."

"It's a little game we play, opportunities for excitement are – shall we say – limited." He looked lost in thought for a second before turning to her. "Anyway, so you want to become a trustee, because…?"

Gretchen gave a brief account of her work and apparent skill at getting to the bottom of things and what she thought she could bring to the trust.

"So," said Jock, "not just because your father was a trustee?"

A brief wave of colour flashed across Gretchen's face.

"Forgive my directness, as I say, time is not my friend." He smiled. "And tell me, at the Deer Trust, what happens when there's no chance of relocating deer."

"Well… Dad taught me to never shy away from responsibility."

"Which means?"

"Well habitat is the most important thing, which means where habitat is being destroyed, we recommend culling."

He took down a box file entitled *Death threats / criticisms* and gave it to her.

"You've had death threats?"

"Hmm, lots of strong feelings when it comes to animal rights," he said sagely, "well, furry animal rights."

"But death threats?" Gretchen opened the lid. "Badgers?" she read.

"Ah yes, dear old Brock," said Jock. "I'd seen what TB did to the badgers, terrible suffering, so I thought we should have a debate about a cull of infected setts. I was on the board of a mammal trust at the time but couldn't even get it on the agenda. So I published a discussion document."

"You must have had some support."

Jock sighed. "Only from the vets because they saw the sickness. The other responses are in that box."

Gretchen looked at typed anonymous letters.

"Now here's the point about governance; do you do the popular thing or the right thing?"

Gretchen looked in the box again. "Mink?"

"Don't look for rationality but, you know, I don't mind the misguided, it's our own executives that need watching. Believe me, some are no better than those you investigate."

"And the J.M.S.?"

"Still good, but human nature will take over; you start out with a well meaning slogan like 'Birds Forever' which invariably gets taken to mean 'Jobs Forever'."

A smoke alarm sounded somewhere in the house.

"Fire?" asked Gretchen.

"No," said Jock pushing himself out of the chair with a grunt, "just our lunch."

Chapter 10 – Tall Black Russian

Gretchen got off the tube at Swiss Cottage and walked along Eton Road. The hawthorns were in bloom, their aroma very noticeable in the afternoon air. The smell had etched itself onto Gretchen's memory, but for mixed reasons. *Crataegus*, as her dad had referred to it, was his favourite tree. But Gretchen also associated hawthorn blossom with the timing of exams, 'O' and 'A' levels, under- and post-graduate. She stopped to peer at a large insect moving up a brick wall ahead. A queen hornet was inspecting the kilned clay, oblivious to the humans that scuttled by or, indeed, the one that regarded her with irrepressible curiosity.

* * * * *

An Ecuadorian tarantula sat on the dinner table facing the oil lamp, transfixed by the insects that flew around it. Inches away from Gretchen's plate of chicken and bread, it seemed unaware of the diners around it, most of whom who had edged themselves away.

"Are you sure it's not dangerous?" one had asked.

Gretchen looked closely at the spider again, the flickering lamp highlighting the spider's iridescent pink and purple markings. "No species of tarantula is really dangerous," she replied. "Especially not this one, it's waiting for supper."

The diners did not appear very reassured.

"No really," Gretchen persisted, "I have a picture of my Dad handling them when he was here."

"I'm sorry Gretchen," said the man opposite in an apologetic manner, "it really is making me feel uncomfortable. Would you mind moving it?"

Gretchen laughed, "Okay," she moved one hand over the carapace and brought the other in front to distract it. The spider visibly hunched and then pushed its forelegs down, exposing the fangs. "Now that is fascinating," she exclaimed, "That's the difference between old world species and the new..." but as she looked up to share her knowledge, everyone else on the table was staring in horror.

* * * * *

The hornet reappeared from a crack and Gretchen blinked and re-focussed. It did one more short inspection before flying upwards to search the eaves.

Gretchen continued on her way, striding past trees and leafy hedges, naming the species she knew and taking note of the ones she didn't. The road was tidy and quiet; greenery gave way to large, sub-divided houses each with its own array of doorbells. She recalled the drudgery of flat-hunting here with her brother back in ninety-two. It had taken much bullying and many dreary meetings with estate agents, Thomas being, in her opinion, overly fussy and reluctant to commit. Eventually though he had given way to Gretchen's reason and put in an offer on a flat in England's Lane. It was only when sorting the conveyance did she realise that Thomas hadn't enough cash for the deposit.

"Tom, I know you had the same as me from Dad's estate. Where," she had asked in utter frustration, "has it gone?"

Thomas prevaricated, twisted and turned but he couldn't escape the fact that he'd largely frittered it away. He tried half-heartedly to blame his mother who, knowing his frailty, had given him the capital. Eventually the truth found its mark and Thomas had recoiled in a sulk. Gretchen agreed to pay the deposit, taking a charge over the property, which turned out to be fortuitous. The value had nearly doubled over the ten years and, while Thomas's friends re-mortgaged to finance their frenetic lifestyles, Gretchen was able to block her brother's attempts at following suit. Having seen his friends struggle with the subsequent repayments he was now thankful for his sister's action though never acknowledged it.

Just opposite his flat was a Seven-Eleven convenience store that had rescued her brother on any number of occasions. Gretchen also frequented the shop and on this occasion had an offer to make to the owner.

"How are you, Gorgeous?" exclaimed the shop owner, loud enough so everyone could hear.

"Fine thank you, Ali, how's the store?"

"It is very good. We only stock local, natural, organic. We are chick yes?"

"You certainly are chic. Do you want some more venison?"

"Is it Halal?" inquired the shop owner, "I can only take Halal."

"Well, it's not the full Zibah, but close."

Ali pulled an expression he took to be shrewd and considered the proposition. "Price the same as last time?" he whispered.

"Yes."

"It's a deal."

Ali's thanks still echoing from the shop, Gretchen walked across the road and buzzed Thomas's flat. The latch clicked several times before opening.

"See you've fixed the latch then?" she said walking through the door.

"Hello sis, no, not yet. I got as far as interviewing the local handy man though."

"And?"

"Well I don't mind hairy men but he looked like Chewbacca."

Gretchen began to ask another question but thought better of it. "I'll do it," she said. "Where are the instructions?"

"Wherever you left them when you installed it," said Thomas, standing back to admire the evening's preparations. "If I say so myself, the food is *bellacuisine*."

"How's the venison? It smells good."

"Divine, darling, two days defrost, two days marinade and it is so tender."

"Should be," shouted Gretchen, extending the screwdriver from her Leatherman, "it was a young..."

Thomas interrupted her. "Don't need to know the provenance *pre mortis*, thank you.

"All done," said Gretchen, walking back into the kitchen, "Can I help?"

"Thank you Poppet, you could tie the hyacinths up."

"Why?"

"What do you mean 'why?' Look at them."

On the table was a pot whose white flowers drooped at forty five degrees, their pink companions having succumbed completely to gravity.

"They smell pleasant enough," said Gretchen.

"Retail my old darling is detail, and I'm trying to give the impression of a man who can deliver on demand, not one in need of Viagra."

"Enough, enough. I'll tie them up."

Gretchen took some white cord from her rucksack.

"Oh," said Thomas.

"What?"

"Green string is in the drawer, perhaps trim the ends off."

Gretchen was going to reply but nodded and did as asked.

"Anything else?"

"Carrot sticks."

"You sure you can trust me."

"Of course," said Thomas. "Try and make them all the same size."

The two busied themselves in the kitchen.

"What's the music?"

"Eminem, do you like it?"

"I've heard of him," Gretchen replied, stopping and listening. "If I had any music this might make the collection."

"I'm sure he'd be honoured. Dennis lent it to me."

"What? Dennis likes Eminem?"

"Gosh yes," said Thomas. "He's even got a beanie, does a great impression."

Gretchen stopped chopping the carrots and frowned. "We are talking about QC Dennis?"

"Yep," Thomas replied. "Straight laced by day, limp-wristed by night."

"But I thought he was into opera, Covent Garden seat-holder et cetera."

"Darling every one I know is a 'seat-holder', doesn't mean they like it. You have never seemed to grasp that London is just a wonderful masquerade, no-one is truly themself, not even the sorts that Dennis sends down or indeed upon which he..." Thomas raised his eyebrows.

"Yes, well, I do not recognise that world and frankly your exaggerations are so monstrous I choose not to believe a word."

"Cross my heart."

"Don't believe it! Right I'm done," said Gretchen, cleaning the sink.

"Wolves, wolves, wolves I cried but she refused to believe," said Thomas in a ghoulish voice and, creeping up behind her, said loudly, "UNTIL THEY GOBBLED HER UP!"

Gretchen dropped her shoulder, pivoted deftly and Thomas found himself held by his windpipe and suspended over his sister's leg.

"Gobble, gobble," he croaked.

She shifted his weight back, releasing him and returned to the sink.

"She drew first blood," drawled Thomas in a husky accent. "All I wanted was some food."

"Was that your Rambo impression?"

"Any good?" he asked, two octaves higher and still rubbing his throat.

"Hmm, I doubt if they'd have called out the National Guard."

"I wonder if they do a pink beret."

Gretchen placed the dish cloth in his hands. "Now do you want me to do anything else?"

"No, poppet," Thomas blustered, still trying to regain his composure, "I might be out of control in life but in the kitchen I am the master."

Gretchen smiled flatly. "Well I'll leave you to your mastery," she said, leaving the kitchen.

Thomas followed her. "The table does need laying."

"Okay, I'll do that and then get changed."

"It's going to be a success tonight, I can feel it," said Thomas, opening the cupboard and carefully removing the china. Inspecting it piece by piece, he handed it to his sister.

"Can I ask why you didn't just take them to a restaurant?"

"Good point, dear sis – mainly because it creates trust. They know my work but they don't know me. I am letting them see me warts and all.

"Are you sure that's wise?"

"Well maybe that's not quite the expression but these relationships tend to be long-lived and starting off with false expectations can be very wearing. They get a chance to sample my fabulous cuisine which is a metaphor for my work. And it also gives me a chance to get to know who I'm working with. I have been known on occasion to back out. I swear, one night, I entertained the Third Reich."

Gretchen's smile regained some of its warmth. "How did that happen?"

Thomas started to giggle. "The principal looked like a young Marlon Brando – how could I *not* ask him to dinner. His associates were lovely too… their ideas not so. It was the first time I've heard the word 'nigger' outside a rap song."

"Oh, how did you get out of that?"

"The penny dropped that I might not share their ideals when one noticed my copy of *The Naked Civil Servant*. They let themselves out. So you see my flat works as a sort of 'screen'."

"I don't know how my flat would work."

"Depends on what you're trying to achieve. Candidates for *The Krypton Factor* may find your abode charming."

Gretchen yawned. "Sorry, tired."

"You know, you have been looking drawn lately. Are you working too much or sleeping too little?"

"I'm fine."

"Ah, evasive as usual."

"No I am fine," she yawned again, inspecting the long mahogany table.

"By the way, Sis, what are you wearing? I hope it's not too bright or we'll clash."

"Tom, when have you ever known me to wear 'bright'?"

"In the mountains dear, I've seen you in orange."

"You've seen me in the mountains?"

"Well, through the lens of a very powerful telescope."

"Really when was that?"

"It was a couple of years ago when we went to Chamonix. I was on the balcony belonging to some chap called Dean, doing a few olives and a Tall Black Russian and you were on some brute of a rock face across the valley. I was so unnerved just watching that I had to de-stress myself in the hot tub."

Gretchen opened the packet marked 'finishing touches' and pulled out ivory coloured table decorations. "Should I ask about the tall, black Russian?" she said, without looking up.

"A TBR, darling, is a vodka cocktail."

"And Dean?" asked Gretchen counting out the napkins.

"He's all man with a hint of animal or is it the other way round. Does your kind of things with ropes and shackles and… widgets."

"Doesn't sound like your usual friends," said Gretchen, moving on to laying the cutlery.

"Oh he's not. A journo friend was doing a piece about him – 'Action Man of the Alps' stocking filler. I simply invited myself along when you went off to play."

Thomas followed Gretchen around the table making small adjustments to the placings his sister had already laid.

Gretchen looked at him.

"Detail, darling, detail – anyway where was I?"

"I have no idea! Chamonix?"

"Oh yes, such a naughty town. Why were you there again?" asked Thomas.

"The Cosmic Arête and the Vallee Blanche."

"Of course you were. Remind me, they are both gin based?"

Gretchen ignored him and picked up her bag. "Off to change," she said, walking out of the door.

Thomas continued adjusting and re-aligning plates and glasses, occasionally taking a couple of steps back to assess the impact. He had contented himself with the overall effect as Gretchen walked back into the room.

"That was quick," he said, and then looking at her top added, "Isn't that your work blouse?"

"Yes, and?"

"Nothing"

"You can't ask a question and then say 'nothing'. I have outdoor gear or work wear unless you want me to borrow something from your wardrobe."

"No that will do. It's not exactly sizzling, makes you look like you've just left school, especially as you never wear any makeup."

"Well, brother, you will just have to sizzle for the both of us."

"Oh I can certainly sizzle. Talking of which I better go and beautify."

"Fine," said Gretchen, surveying the room, "is there anything else you want me to do?"

"No thanks, lovely," replied Thomas, "It's perfect, please don't touch anything. Oh and can you move your rucksack, it looks very… agricultural."

"Agricultural?" said Gretchen to herself. She pulled a mountaineering magazine and some photographs from the side pocket before lifting the bag out of sight. She let out a long slow breath, rubbed her eyes and relaxed on the sofa.

Chapter 11 – Ground Rules

David left his daughter enjoying her birthday breakfast and returned to the room to sort out his climbing gear. He straightened his bedding and emptied his rucksack out on the blanket. The benefit of climbing on 'sport' routes was that climbing bolts were pre-fixed into the rock face, which allowed climbers to shed many kilos of equipment. Some of his friends looked down on this 'continental' style, refusing to climb abroad, but David remained pragmatic, enjoying all forms of climbing.

He laid everything out in order and then followed a mental tick list carefully placing the gear back into his bag. Finally, after clamping the middle section of a coil of rope through the top tether and facing his helmet to the rear, he stood back and took a deep breath. Feeling incredibly hot, he took off his shirt and sat down. Checking his pulse, he found it normal but rested on the bed for a while.

When Gretchen came back she found her dad in his string vest and reading through the guide book. "Do you know where we are going?" she asked.

"Yes, I think we are set."

"The climbers downstairs say they will join us for lunch."

"Sorry, I should have asked, is that okay with you?"

"That's great – they're very nice."

Ten minutes later David and his daughter were heading upwards through the valley, their car muttering as they passed layer upon layer of terraced farming.

"Why do you think the farmers do that?" David asked.

Gretchen thought. "So they can stand level? Or get machinery onto it."

"Seems logical. What about preserving the soil?"

"Oh yes, it will stop the, err..."

"Topsoil?"

"That's it, topsoil from slipping down the hill."

"And for the bonus point," David asked, "what do plants most need?"

"Water! It will hold the water better."

David held up his hand and Gretchen gave him a 'high five'.

As instructed by the guide book, they drove up an unmarked dirt road as far as it went. There was only one other car parked and they slotted in behind it. As Gretchen got out the two things that struck her were the dry heat and the noise of cicadas. The occasional gust of wind that kicked up white dust would drop the temperature by a couple of degrees, but otherwise the cloudless sky indicated 'a scorcher'.

David tied his climbing shirt around his waist and applied some suntan cream first to Gretchen and then himself. The walk-in took them along a well trodden path that led up to the crags through scrub and high gorse bushes. Occasionally they paused to look at insects or birds, the latter invariably raptors enjoying the early morning thermals. An odd clump of trees caught David's attention and he scrambled down, beckoning Gretchen to follow him.

"Now this is interesting," said David, running his hand over the base of the trunk that had had its bark stripped away. "What do you think?"

Gretchen ran her hand over the trunk. "It feels spongy," she said.

"Good and what about the leaves?"

"They feel like holly, sort of prickly and waxy."

"Yes," agreed David scrunching up the leaves. "And what's lying on the ground?"

"Acorns," she said picking up a handful and then dropping them when she saw a large black ant appear. Is it an oak tree?"

"Well done, it is – an evergreen oak tree. Any thoughts on the spongy bark?"

For a moment Gretchen was silent, thinking, but then shook her head.

"What do you stick in the tops of wine bottles?" he prompted.

"Cork! The bark makes cork."

"Amazing isn't it."

The last section upwards was very steep, almost a scramble, and David was sweating heavily with the exertion.

"Not fit, Daddy," said Gretchen who had, it seemed, barely perspired.

"You are right there, lovely, but I'm not feeling brilliant today. I've had a cold for ages; just can't shake it."

David put on his helmet and Gretchen followed suit. "Dad, why is this limestone a different colour from the white stuff down there?" she asked, pointing to the farm land.

David looked at the rock face, a mix of salmon pinks and light terracotta. "I don't know but it's a great question."

Gretchen silently thrilled to this commendation. "Could it be," she hastily guessed, "That the animal bones that laid down this section were pink like shrimps?"

"I like your thinking but I doubt it. Shellfish are greeny brown, only going pink when they are cooked. And why would all of them happen to stack up here. Um…"

David picked up another piece of rock from the floor and struck it against wall. The impact took several jagged flakes from the surface to reveal a milkier under colour.

"Oh," said Gretchen, "it's just the surface."

David picked the fragments up, turning them over. He dropped the shards of limestone into Gretchen's outstretched hand. "It would seem so," he said, "but I'm still none the wiser. There's a question for you to look up when you get home."

Thomas appeared wearing a dark blue Paul Smith shirt with ivory cufflinks and cream chinos chosen to match the table furnishings, the crocodile leather strap of his Rolex matching his shoes. Gretchen was sound asleep on the sofa so he crept into the kitchen and filled the kettle.

"Oh sweet," he said as his sister twitched and occasionally muttered. "You are a lot easier to handle like this," he said quietly from the doorway. "Grae!" he said a little louder. She did not move but muttered a little more. "Grae!" he said, louder still.

She awoke and immediately began to straighten up as he approached.

"Sleepy?"

"Yes, a little."

"Here," said Thomas, handing her a mug of tea. "I know you like the hard stuff before a night out."

"Sorry, tough session at the wall this afternoon – trying to clear my head."

"And is it clear now?"

"I think so," she said as the last wisps of her dream fragmented then vaporised.

"Oh," said Thomas, picking up Jock's photos from her lap. "My God, that's Dad. He must be our age. Where did you get them?"

"I had lunch with a man today who used to know him." Gretchen held out her hand.

Thomas gave them one last look and returned them. "Anyway, I want to go through some ground rules for tonight," he said.

"Ground rules?"

"Well, guidance really. I would like you just to be pretty and pleasant and please go easy on them. I am trying to land them as clients, not interview them for the space programme." Thomas poured a healthy measure of gin into his glass.

"I love that, Tom, I agree to help you out and then have to submit to mental bondage."

"Welcome to the world of a woman, darling. And that's another thing – I wouldn't let on you shot the main course. Some people are a little funny…"

"About reality."

"Gretchen, that is exactly the type of comment not to make. The golden rule is 'play it by ear', one has to ebb and flow with one's guests, make them feel special."

She took a deep breath. "Actually, I think Egon shot that deer but, alright, I won't mention it. What about the wild mushrooms, shall I mention them?"

"Again, only if they lead that way. I really think you'll like them – Tim and Max are climbers."

"Really?" asked Gretchen suddenly showing interest.

"Yes, did that Three Peaks thing last year – sounds divine."

"That's not climbing. It's fell walking."

"Picky, picky. Same thing in my book, Sis, you've done it which to me says 'adventure'. I think they did it in a good time so they must be quite fit. Tonic?" Thomas asked, holding up the bottle.

"When I've finished my tea."

Thomas poured a small measure of tonic into his glass and a large measure into Gretchen's glass which he put down next to her.

"So, to recap 'ebb and flow', if things are getting sticky, ask them a question. Cheers!" he said, holding up his glass.

"Cheers," replied Gretchen, holding up her mug.

Chapter 12 – Hors d'oeuvres

Thomas was in the kitchen when the entry-phone buzzed. "Grae, can you get that?" he shouted.

"Okay", she replied, crossing the room to press the release button. Gretchen waited until she could hear footsteps in the corridor and opened the door to a tall, middle aged man. With him was an immaculately dressed woman of similar height to Gretchen.

The couple looked somewhat surprised until Gretchen introduced herself. "Hi, I'm Tom's sister, Gretchen."

"How do you do," replied the man, shaking her hand, "I'm Max and this is my wife Louise."

"Call me Lou, everyone does," clipped the woman self-assuredly.

"Do come in, Tom is just in the kitchen at a crucial moment with the food. Did you manage to get a parking space?"

"Good girl – neutral question," thought Thomas, pleased to hear that his advice was being heeded.

"It was a struggle," said Louise, 'mind you everywhere is a struggle in a Range Rover. How do you manage?"

"I have a bike," said Gretchen.

"Good Lord."

"Very noble," added Max.

Gretchen was taking their coats as Tom emerged wiping his hands on a towel.

"Hello, hello. You are bang on time, well done, well done."

"Thomas, good to see you," said Max handing over a gift box of wine and, gesturing towards his wife, added, "my wife Lou."

"How do you do," said Tom, offering his hand, "and, may I say, I love that jacket. I think I saw something like it in the Knightsbridge Prada."

"I wouldn't know where it came from," replied Louise. "It was an anniversary gift."

"Well lucky you," said Thomas, opening the box and cooing at the wine in appreciation. "I keep trying to get Gretchen into boutiques but I can't get her past Marks and Spencer."

"Not a priority, Tom, don't go there," shouted Gretchen from the cloakroom.

"I *don't* go there darling, that's my point."

"I wouldn't knock Marks and Spencer, Tom," commented Max, "I shop there all the time – besides Gretchen has too wonderful a figure to worry about clothes."

"Lord, don't encourage her, or next time she'll be in woad."

Max laughed at this, a response not echoed by his wife.

The buzzer sounded again. "Please go through," said Thomas, handing the wine back to Louise. "That'll be perfect with the main course, could you ask Grae to let it breathe."

Max followed his wife through to where Gretchen was bringing in hors d'oeuvres.

"Ah Rochforte," said Louise inspecting the food.

"Is it?" said Gretchen, "I thought it was Stilton. I'm afraid it's all Tom's work. And I'm not sure what this pâté is."

"Foie Gras!" shouted Thomas from the hall.

"Sorry, hopeless on food," smiled Gretchen, putting down the silver tray.

"Wonderful," said Max, "I hear your brother is just as creative on the media front."

"I hear that too," replied Gretchen.

Louise handed Gretchen the wine. "Could you let this breathe, dear – that means you'll need to open it."

"Sure," replied Gretchen. Max winced slightly.

"Tim and Fi," announced Tom, showing another couple into the room. The man was of similar build and height to Max; Fiona, though shorter than Lou, was equally well-dressed. "No introductions necessary except the schoolgirl holding the canapés who is my little sister Gretchen."

Thomas watched the couples complete their usual greetings before offering drinks. "There is Champagne, freshly squeezed orange juice or a mix."

"Oh excellent, I'll go for the mix," said Max. Fi and Tim followed suit, Louise opting for Champagne and Gretchen for the orange.

"I noticed some roller blades in the hall, Thomas – are they yours?" asked Max.

"Well, I do own them but I think they'd disown me. I visited San Francisco and was thoroughly beguiled by the natives – they glide so effortlessly along the sunny beachfront boulevards," Thomas sighed. "When I got home I made the classic mistake of trying to recapture the holiday feeling. I bought the CD *Hotel California*, a pair of roller blades and drove straight to the park."

Thomas took a sip of his drink, his audience clearly intrigued. "It went badly from the start, I clung to the rails for so long a dog stopped to pee on my leg."

Fi gave a giggle.

"So I let go and though the incline was slight, let me assure you, ladies and gentlemen, the acceleration was brisk."

Max too was beginning to laugh. "I assume you have brakes?"

"Alas no. Brakes on roller blades are rather ugly, my dears, but aesthetics were the last of my worries. I careered toward a bandstand from which issued a medley of Carpenters' songs."

Thomas took another sip. "It struck me – shortly before a row of chairs did – that pride had truly cometh before the fall and I must have looked like a dying swan as I pirouetted into the Trombone section."

Even Gretchen – who knew the story – chuckled quietly.

"If I looked like a cultural suicide bomber my attack would have been in vain as I failed to halt a single beat; as in all disasters, the band played on. In conclusion, I will say this – tarmac at speed is painful but does not begin to approach a tuba playing *A Kind of Hush*."

His audience laughed appreciatively. Thomas knew to 'leave them wanting' and excused himself.

Max turned to Fi asking after the family, and Tim to Gretchen. "So Gretchen," he asked, "do you work in the City or are you just staying with Tom?"

"Well that depends who's employing me. Generally I do short contract work."

"Ah the old temping game, I remember that," said Louise.

Gretchen smiled.

"And what do you temp at?" asked Tim.

"I work in accounting," replied Gretchen.

"I have eight accounts staff working for me," said Louise, "don't know how they make ends meet."

"What line of work are you in, Tim?" asked Gretchen.

Thomas listened intently from the kitchen.

"Well Max and I run a finance company, we broker deals between big lenders and retailers. The pickings have been good but it's getting quite competitive now, which is why we are considering marketing a little more seriously to raise our profile."

Gretchen knew the business model but followed her brother's advice. She kept asking pertinent questions and was surprised by Tim's candour. Louise had drifted away to talk to Max and Fi as Thomas brought in the first course and called everyone to his seating plan. "Now apparently there are no dislikes so plenty of variety tonight."

"Fabulous," said Fi, eyeing the dish, "Caesar salad with…?"

"Rocket and Cos, anchovies, parmesan, egg and garlic and other things I can't remember," Thomas fibbed, knowing exactly what went into it.

It looks delicious, just like the one I make," said Louise. "Is it a 'Roux Brothers'?"

"No this is a Delia."

"Ah, the old standby."

Louise, Fi and Thomas began discussing whose cookery books were in vogue.

"Gretchen is a temping accountant," Tim said to Max.

"Oh really, who are you working for at the moment, anyone we'd know?"

"Macaulay Malim."

"Oh Max plays golf with a partner of Macaulay Malim; Andy Byrne, do you know him?" asked Louise, switching conversations.

"Not socially, partners don't really mix with employees."

"No," drawled Louise, "I suppose it's not really the done thing."

"Andy was telling me," said Max, "probably confidentially, that they are undergoing a full strategic review, got some hot-shot Cambridge graduate in, scaring everyone to death – pulling apart systems, interviewing staff about billing, sounds our kind of bloke."

"I agree darling," said Louise, "your employees need a kick up the rear."

Gretchen relaxed, the moment of difficulty having passed. She wondered though, had Andy Byrne said she was a man or had Max naturally assumed the 'hot-shot' was a man.

"Do you know this guy?" asked Max.

Gretchen shook her head.

"Ah well, why would you want to get bogged down with all that, you are probably too busy staying in shape."

Gretchen was rather trapped for a reply so again followed her brother's advice and asked a question. "Do you do any sports?"

"Well golf has replaced squash but Tim and I did the Three Peaks last year, have you heard of it, Tom?" asked Max.

"Remind me," he replied attentively.

"Well," said Max, now animated, "The challenge was to the climb the highest peaks in Wales, Scotland and England in twenty four hours. After a particularly gruelling board meeting and the requisite alcohol, somebody brought up the idea and when you've had a few, suddenly the impossible seems possible."

"Don't I know it," agreed Thomas.

Max continued. "So Tim and I became expedition leaders and…"

For the next ten minutes Max, with excited additions from Tim, described the trials of getting a corporate event moving, the politics and the physical hardship. "Great fun," he said, rounding off the story.

Tim agreed. "What I miss," he said, "is that sense of camaraderie – the training together and bringing the group home in twenty four hours."

"You should try it, Tom," said Fi, clearly impressed with her husband's achievement.

"Good Lord no, climbing a mountain to me is an advertising metaphor not a physical event."

They all laughed.

Louise watched Gretchen smile at her brother's declaration. "Have you done it, Gretchen?" she asked.

"Yes I had a go."

"Oh, what was your time?" she enquired.

"Three and a half days."

"Oh bad luck," said Louise.

Gretchen shrugged.

"Oh well," Max said generously, "it is all about the team."

"That's right, the slowest member of the team," Louise added.

"Was yours a corporate do?" asked Fi.

"Oh nothing as grand as that," Gretchen replied evasively. She rose from her chair. "Would anybody care for more wine?"

"Group of friends was it?" persisted Fi.

Gretchen started topping up empty glasses. "No... I couldn't find anyone to do it with me."

"Oh dear!" said Louise.

"Ah," said Tim, "hence the time. It certainly was our camaraderie that kept me going but above all it was our two drivers that made the job possible."

"Now darling don't be modest," said Fi.

"I'm really not, Fi. We slept soundly on the bus while our drivers took it in turn to deliver us from place to place. Did you drive it yourself, Gretchen?"

Gretchen glanced at her brother. "Sort of, I... cycled."

"What? You cycled! In three days!" exclaimed Max. "Well that's crapped in our salad, Tim," he added with a laugh.

Gretchen wasn't sure how to proceed. "It's really no big deal," she said, immediately regretting it.

"No big deal!" exclaimed Tim, "I wonder what a big deal is to you?" he asked in some bewilderment.

Gretchen thought franticly. "Being able to lead a team less fit than myself? I failed a team building course for that very thing."

Thomas held his breath.

Max thought for a second. "I guess that's a point, Tim, most of us thought the trip would not succeed and most of the problems were not our fitness but motivating the team. After all we are all career businessmen, not athletes like Gretchen here."

"Hear, hear," interjected Thomas, "Grae will tell you, she is obsessive on the fitness front – running today, yesterday and I dare say the day before that, weren't you, poppet."

"I dare say," echoed Gretchen, agitated by the word 'obsessive'.

"I used to be fairly fit," said Tim, still slightly crestfallen.

"Fairly fit?" said Fi, "*Very* I'd say. You were always down the squash club or out on the tennis courts."

Louise continued to eye Gretchen who opened another bottle of white.

Chapter 13 – Just Desserts

Thomas and Gretchen carried the main course to the table, the vegetables still sizzling.

"And what do we have here?" asked Tim.

"Venison and wild mushrooms."

"Wow," said Fi, "is *this* a 'Delia'?"

"No, this is a 'make it up as you go along'. We have yams, *dauphin noir* and a host of other veggies as you can see. We are, I should tell you, heavy on the garlic tonight so careful who you snog. Please dig in."

Gretchen watched in fascination as her brother deftly handled compliments about his cooking. She noted how he moved the subject back to others and only interjected when the conversation lulled.

"Now I want you all to try Lou and Max's Grand Cru," declared Thomas, pouring the wine into clean glasses. "It certainly is a cut above my *Saint Emilion*."

Louise launched into a demonstration of how *good red wine* had 'legs' or 'sears' that clung to the side of the glass. There was a short silence as she replaced the glass decisively on the coaster. Thomas thanked her for the tip before telling an anecdote about his visit to the wine area of Reims.

"The name of the first vineyard, I pronounced with difficulty, later on I pronounced everything with difficulty..."

Gretchen watched Thomas make the case and play the fool. The vignette had him swallowing when he should have gargled and spitting the wine into an ice bucket when he should have made a toast. The tale ended with him waking, fully dressed and sat on a toilet.

Thomas looked at his guests in bemusement, a hapless victim of excess as they laughed and clapped.

Main course became second helpings and Louise began a long story of how she had become involved in genealogy. She had employed a researcher to track her family tree and found that she was related to the House of Lancaster. Gretchen, having little knowledge of modern history, was surreptitiously reading the wine label. The name, *Le Saussois* in Burgundy, seemed familiar and then she realised she had been there for a climbing competition. Instantly she was transported back. She could feel the heat of the afternoon, the limestone that bit into her fingers, the chirrup of the cicadas, the limestone that bit into her fingers, climbing a tough overhang, the limestone that.... Her fingers, what was it about her fingers? Gretchen realised that she was staring manically at them. She glanced around the table but no-one had noticed. She focused on her breathing, calming herself while Louise continued.

Thomas had noticed though.

"That is amazing," he said to Louise as she finished her story, "sounds like you have a fascinating ancestry."

"Well, one tries."

"There's nothing in my line," said Tim morosely. "I've looked as well. What about you Gretchen?"

"What?" she said slightly dazed.

Have you any blue blood?"

"Err, I guess we must have."

Louise looked at her. "Oh?"

"Hell," Gretchen thought, "here we go again." She could feel Thomas willing her to but couldn't think of a question. "Well the numbers... the numbers make it so – for me and everyone," she said, hoping this was self evident. Their silence suggested it wasn't. The puzzle unfolded almost immediately in Gretchen's mind. "Okay," she asked Louise, "when was your ancestor living?"

"Fourteen fifty," Louise shot back smartly.

Well, let's think. Five and a half centuries multiplied by four generations is... twenty two generations," Gretchen muttered to herself. "Two parents to the power twenty is one million so to twenty two," she cleared her throat, "is potentially four million ancestors. What was the population back then?"

"About four million," said Tim.

Gretchen nearly said 'QED' but thought better of it.

"So are you saying," Tim continued, "That all of us are related to everyone back then."

"Not quite, because we inbreed; hence why the population gets smaller as you go back in time not bigger, all the way to Eve."

"Sounds like you need to look a bit harder then, Tim," said Max while his wife quietly seethed.

"Talking of Eve," said Thomas, lifting the silence, "reminds me of a cross dresser I used to know who visited a salon called 'Adam *as* Eve'."

"I know the place," said Max suddenly.

"You *know* the place?" repeated Thomas.

"I didn't say I was a customer."

"Ah, methinks the lady doth protest too much."

Max held his hands up in defeat while Thomas continued his tale.

Thomas joined Gretchen in the kitchen as she scraped the plates into the bin. "You okay?"

"Hmm fine."

"No you're not."

It was true. Gretchen wanted to be elsewhere.

"She's just trying to goad you," said Thomas, taking a guess at what was wrong.

"She's doing a pretty good job," said Gretchen.

"Have you read Harry Potter?"

"No."

"Well you should do. Whenever Lou says something barbed, just think, 'Riddikulus'."

"Ridiculous."

"No you must pronouce the consonants clearly," he said demonstrating the spell.

Gretchen said it again

"You've got it."

Gretchen carried out the last course, a display of various fresh fruits and Greek yogurt which, she had to admit, looked like the result of a lot of work. "If this was a metaphor," she thought, "then his work must be both detailed and imaginative."

"Once again," she said, "I'm afraid I have had no hand in this."
As she put the heavy tray down, Max noticed her wince in pain and rub her shoulder.

"Overdoing the tennis?"

"No I... fell when I was running."

"Chased by a dog were we?" baited Louise.

Thomas entered with Tim and Fi's dessert wine.

"Tom you've outdone yourself again,' said Max.

"Sweet of you but they're just desserts,' said Thomas with a wink. "Okay, we have twelve fruits for you to identify. If you win you get the honour of been the first ever to do so."

After some time of touching, tasting with and without yogurt and washing down with Muscat, seven fruits were identified, five remained.

"What in God's name?" said Tim, pulling a contorted face as he bit into a yellow fruit.

"You should have eaten that with a *runcible spoon,*" said Thomas.

"Quince." Shouted Max

"They are kind of familiar," said Fi.

Gretchen waited until everyone had given their ideas. "I think I've seen these two – pawpaw and gogi-berry?"

"Two more down," said Thomas, "last two?"

"Goodness, Gretchen," said Fi, "I bet you go to the new Chelsea Healthstore."

Max reappeared from the loo. "No," he said, "I suspect she's seen them in the wild."

"Done the gap year travel?" said Tim, looking closely at some small purple fruits shaped like acorns.

"I couldn't afford to," Gretchen replied, "I have only travelled when I've saved the cash, using annual leave or time between jobs."

"Sounds very hit and miss," said Louise.

"Yes, my tent has blown away occasionally. Have you guys travelled much?"

As port was served, Louise held court on the virtue of five star cruises as Thomas played up to the extravagance. Tim joined with their favourite holiday, an Abercrombie and Kent safari. All the time, Max kept throwing Gretchen puzzled glances. "What about you Gretchen – favourite holiday?" he asked.

"Difficult to say, nothing like yours. I always have a tent on my back."

"Goodness, I know temp work is poorly paid but can't your boyfriends stretch to a hotel occasionally?" said Louise.

"I don't have a boyfriend."

Louise gave a tiny raise of the eyebrows.

"Sometimes I might splash out on a hostel. What can I say – I'm a very boring accountant." Gretchen poked the red waxy skin of one of the fruits and looked at her brother. "No idea, Bro."

"Mountain Apples and Java Plums," revealed Thomas, "I win."

"Oh," said Fi, "I thought I recognised the apple, I saw them in the new whole-food store, erm... Organic Vega."

Gretchen gave a slight frown which Louise seized upon. "Would that not be a shop you visited?"

Thomas could see that Gretchen was really tiring of this game. Acquiescing was not her. Not her at all. She rubbed her temples. "I'm not sure that it's possible to be both vegan and organic, that would seem contradictory."

"I don't understand," said Fi, looking at Louise.

Gretchen sensed trouble but went on. "Organic production needs animals in the system in some shape or form. If there are animals it can't be vegan."

"But the animals are eaten by someone else" said Fi.

"Well I think you would have to be a particularly short-sighted vegan who used animals but then justified it because someone else drank the milk or ate the meat."

Max settled down in his chair as if watching a tennis match and Thomas kept quiet, knowing better than to explain the concept as a brand.

"I hadn't thought of it like that," said Fi. "Oh well, as long as it's organic it doesn't really matter. We call 'organic' the holy trinity, don't we, Lou?"

"We certainly do, tastes better, better for the environment and better for one."

Gretchen didn't respond but Louise persisted, "Surely you can't disagree with that?"

"I wasn't aware of any blind tasting that favoured organic," Gretchen began, "and I wasn't aware of any evidence that it was better for health. The last time the world was organic, man's longevity was twenty years less than today. On the environment..." She pondered, searching her memory but finding nothing specific. "I would be very interested to see the benefit demonstrated. Organic production yields roughly half that of modern methods therefore needing twice the area, which in itself impacts on habitat."

Fi jumped straight back in. "At least it's free of genetically modified food, you must be against that."

"It depends," Gretchen reasoned. "If I was diabetic, I wouldn't be alive without it…"

"But that's produced in the laboratory," interrupted Louise, wagging her finger, "NOT in the field. One intuitively knows it's wrong to go meddling about with nature. We might have a Frankenstein catastrophe. Nature understands…" Louise searched for the word. "Nature understands *balance*," she said, implying this was the final word.

There were nods of approval from Thomas, Fi and Tim. Max knew his wife had not succeeded.

"I agree," said Gretchen, "natural selection does eventually bring a state of equilibrium or 'balance' though occasionally we have something like the meteor that wiped out the dinosaurs."

"Well that's Mother Nature which is *natural*," said Louise, once more trying to end the discussion.

Again nods from Fi and Tim. Thomas began throwing mental daggers at his sister but knew it was pointless. Max continued to keep score, trying not to grin.

"So, Louise, just to clarify," said Gretchen, leaning forward, "what you are saying is that, if a similar meteor was detected speeding towards Earth and we could somehow stop it, we shouldn't because it would be…" Gretchen matched Louise's cadence, "*unnatural?*"

"Come on, Grae," Thomas broke in, still trying to be jolly and save the day, "I know you're an avid greenie and not against organic food." He'd seen her demolish a poorly-made argument before and knew she was raising the axe.

"Its fine as long as it's not a panacea for easing a conscience. If it's part of whole approach, I can see the merit." Gretchen could see her brother's pleading looks but couldn't stop herself. "Otherwise it's just absolution for the middle classes."

Chapter 14 – Primrose Hill

The early morning sun was rich yellow as a small Nissan Micra made its way along Santa Monica Boulevard and left onto the San Diego Freeway. Gretchen recognised names from childhood television: Bel Air, Beverly Hills, Hollywood.

Her early start had been designed to catch the sunrise over the Pacific and to miss the traffic. Only the former was successful and now many other motorists had joined her, some in combative mood. Still suffering from jet lag, she had to concentrate fully to navigate, drive on the right and avoid the swerving drivers.

The week had been manic. Gretchen, having just sat her accountancy finals, was supposed to have flown out the previous Thursday but ill-timed problems with her brother had meant deferring her departure.

Interstate 5 was even busier with traffic, slowing to a standstill at points, until it breached the Los Angeles boundary and headed up over the Tehachapi Mountains. As the road climbed, Gretchen began to relax, realising she had an hour before her next turn off. An angry airhorn sounded as a large wagon came up close behind and she realised she'd slowed to thirty. She tried to accelerate but the small car had very little power for going uphill. Having eventually pulled away from the disgruntled trucker she pushed the function button on her watch and looked at the altimeter. It only read two hundred and ninty metres. Gretchen knew that she would be driving at ten times that height and that the car would really struggle. She regretted not taking the advice of the rental man who she assumed was just trying to rent her a more expensive model.

The climb plateauxed and Gretchen caught glimpses of the countryside. She had expected some cacti but it was mostly low scrub and rocks with the thinnest covering of grasses. These hills were the southern end of a ring of high ground surrounding California's entire central valley. Gretchen knew a little about this area after researching a talk on 'evolution'. Her mum had asked her to explain the subject to the local Women's Institute and Gretchen had decided to use the example of the salamanders found in this high area. The salamanders had first established a colony in the hills five hundred miles to the north and had very slowly spread out – going both clockwise and anti clockwise following the high ground. The two paths had given the salamanders different challenges: predators, food, shelter and so on. Those that survived these challenges passed on their better adapted genes; that is, they were selected by nature hence 'evolution by natural selection'. By the time, probably tens of thousands of years later, the two groups met up again at the southern end of California, their different journeys had made them so different, that they had become two separate distinct species. The ladies of Rockdale WI had sat impassively through her pre-amble wondering what her point was. She went on, "What makes this case so unusual is that all the way around the rim of the valley, colonies of those intermediate stages still exist so we can see the evolutionary adaptations with our own eyes right back to the common ancestor at the north end." Gretchen drew crosses on the flip chart around the circle. "What usually happens over a longer time-frame is that intermediate stages becoming extinct and we have to piece ancestry together by fossils."

Some of the ladies had begun to nod their understanding.

"In the case of us humans, we share a common ancestor with chimpanzees that lived some seven million years ago but the intermediate stages are no longer living to tell us the whole story. If they were this whole subject wouldn't be so controversial and Richard Dawkins wouldn't have to keep writing books."

Some of the audience smiled at the remark and Gretchen felt that she had gained rapport.

"Tell me Gretchen," said the voice of her brother from the back of the hall, "Hasn't Richard Dawkins been put here by God to test our faith?"

The audience had then been treated to Thomas making jokes with his sister trying to keep on-subject. The ladies' entertainment of the sibling rivalry was at the topic's expense and any knowledge imparted was lost by the end. The talk however was still seen to be one of the most memorable.

The Nissan Micra passed a large yellow sign, the legend Runaway Truck Ramp *caching Gretchen's attention. Beyond it the San Joaquin valley opened up before her. Gretchen headed right onto Route 99 which sliced through broad acres of intensive horticulture. As she turned north, grape vines filled the vista; a sign hailing* The California Raisin *indicated the fruit's destination.*

The die-straight roads added no interesting features so Gretchen turned on the radio. The news channel was full of tributes to the actor Christopher Reeve, who had broken his neck the previous week. Other than that, the news was local and she found herself giggling as listeners rang in to complain about the lack of rainfall and too many Mexican migrants; one caller referred to the new arrivals as communists.

The tracts of grapes accompanied Gretchen as she cut off at Tulare along the 63 and she recalled the John Steinbeck novel that she had studied for her English 'O' level. She pulled over to stretch her legs and eat a sandwich. She tried to imagine Steinbeck's desperate workers. What struck her most though, sitting on the bonnet surrounded by a landscape of would-be raisins, was the absence of nature: no trees, hedges, wild flowers, no birds, no bugs. She had read that the nearby town of Fresno had the largest number of crack cocaine addicts. Maybe, she mused there was a link with this sterile landscape. Maybe these were the true Grapes of Wrath.

The ground began to rise as she approached a T-junction. It was signed 'Kings Canyon Park 27' and she felt a thrill at seeing the name. She was now driving by memory from her father's journal that sat on the seat next to her. "The East Kings Canyon Road," he'd written, "becomes the General's Highway and as you wind higher there is the tell-tale sight of red bark."

The car spluttered and Gretchen dropped down to second gear, then first. "Sorry," she said as it struggled to build up speed so that she could re-try for second. There by the side of the road she recognised a tree, small but unmistakably a sequoia. The car coughed again but Gretchen no longer registered its protestations as the sequoias, accompanying the road, increased in size.

Finally she was there, surrounded by groves of the enormous red trees. Transfixed by the spectacle it seemed to her inconceivable that all this would ever have been under threat; to suffer the same fate of the valley below. "Thank God for the intervention of John Muir and Co," she thought.

She stood before the General Grant Tree and read the stats, 'Height, two hundred and sixty eight feet; girth, one hundred and seven feet; volume, forty seven thousand cubic feet'. The sense of awe in the place was palpable. John Muir had said that in these National Parks could be found 'rest, inspiration, and prayer' and indeed all the visitors spoke in hushed voices. Gretchen certainly felt it. She had seen sequoias before but not like these. Being made to feel small was something she had experienced many times but usually from exposure on a rock face or gazing into the night sky. To stand under something so overwhelming yet living was different again. She noted that her father had resisted superlatives by just quoting Muir: "Any writing is a weak instrument for the reality it wishes to convey."

Gretchen climbed over a small wooden fence and laid her palms on the tree's bark. It was as her Dad had said, 'fibrous and yielding'. She lent forward and placed her forehead against it.

A ranger watched her but said nothing.

She took a step back and looked up. Only the cirrus clouds caught in the jet stream seemed high enough to clear the upper branches; the illusion made her head swim.

"Ma'am?" said a voice in a quiet West Coast accent.

Gretchen turned to see the ranger, a young man barely eighteen or so.

"You okay, Ma'am?"

"Yes," replied Gretchen weakly clearing her throat, "fine, thank you for asking."

The ranger looked indecisive.

Gretchen smiled. "You're going to tell me I'm on the wrong side of the railing?"

"Well Ma'am, we have millions of visitors and if they all went your side..." he broke off. "You understand?"

"Of course. I apologise, it's my birthday and I got carried away."

"Happy Birthday, Ma'am. You sound a long way from home."

"Do I? I feel strangely at home."

The ranger tried to explain. "Well the accent and all. It sounds English."

"Oh my accent, yes, I live in London."

The ranger looked unsure and Gretchen wondered if this was because he didn't know where London was or didn't know how to react to her transgression.

Gretchen patted the tree then put her hands on the top rail and vaulted back onto the path. She looked at the ranger's name badge and extended her hand. "I'm Gretchen Thorpe and I see you are Ranger Lawrence."

"That's correct, Ma'am."

"Do you mind me asking about your job here?"

The ranger, seeing no other visitors, told her all about his role in protecting the national park. As they walked the route through the sequoias, he enthused about the wildlife and answered questions about the trees. Gretchen complimented him on his knowledge at which he blushed.

"Where are you from?" asked Gretchen.

"A little place in the valley called Maricopa."

"Is there anything interesting about Maricopa?"

"No Ma'am, nothing happens there. Well except for the San Andreas fault."

Gretchen stopped. "That's pretty interesting."

"Really?" said the ranger, looking pleased.

"Where is it?"

"About eight miles through town on 33, turn right at an old gas station. Soda Lake Road."

Gretchen repeated the details. "Eight miles through Maricopa on 33, right at old gas station, Soda Lake Road. Hmm, if I get time on the way back, I'll go and explore. Thanks."

"Where are you headed now?"

"Yosemite."

Some other visitors were climbing over the barrier. Gretchen nodded, "I see you're needed, thanks for your time."

Ranger Lawrence turned to go. "My pleasure," he said and tipped his hat. "You take care, Ma'am."

* * * * *

Gretchen smiled at the memory, which had been a pleasant distraction. She sat on the bench at the top of Primrose Hill, which was as far as she had got. This morning even the searing pain in her thighs and lungs from sprinting those first few hundred yards couldn't 'lift the fog'. The blue devils responsible for months of restless sleep had been joined by the acid drip of conscience. The dinner party had been a disaster, Thomas would surely lose the account and it was her fault.

Snatches of engine roar reached her and she looked up. Airliners from all over the world circled high above waiting for the magic time of 06:02 which signified daytime. Gretchen pushed her mind down this path of knowledge and she forced a laugh as she recalled the reason for this un-virtuous state of affairs; a pressure group had successfully stopped night landing; the net result being that planes had to waste hundreds of tonnes of fuel waiting for 'daytime' to begin. "The ironies of environmentalism," she yawned to herself.

Gretchen stood up, the perspiration down her back absorbing the chill from the air. She shivered and ran the options for the day through her mind.

1) Go back to bed – who am I kidding, I'll never sleep
2) Work
3) Natural History Museum

"Okay," she alloud, "if the next bird I see is a finch or tit I will work today, anything else and it's the National History Museum."

She was pleased to see a blackbird pecking at a worm.

Chapter 15 – John

Andre sat at the reception of Bentley and Hacket. On the desk was a recent self portrait, its glass surface a perfect mirror in which he could alternatively practise a smoulder and then a pout. Even before answering the phone Andre would check his handsome reflection and, in a studied manner, carelessly run his fingers through his hair. Occasionally, when executing a moderate task, his well groomed eyebrows would meet in the middle, but since he was rarely challenged beyond the very basic, his classical looks were the first thing to meet callers at B & H head office.

When John Bentley entered the office he found Andre on the phone. 'The most beautiful receptionist in the world' – an epithet provided by Thomas – continued to chat as John checked his in-box and withdrew a pile of letters. John picked up a hand written note with childlike handwriting, attempted to read it and gave up. Only after John had cleared his throat for a second time did the telephone call end.

"Good morning, Andre."

"Ciao, boss, and welcome back. Did you have a nice holiday?" asked Andre, with what he took to be a knowing smile.

"I did, thank you, Andre." He held up the paper, "Your hand writing, sorry I can't read it."

Andre took the paper and looked at it for some time, his eyebrows converging. "I think it was a message from Tommy but he's in so you can ask him."

"Right," John replied slowly, "okay, well thank you anyway. Oh and you needn't call me boss anymore; I'm just a mere freelance."

"Oh, right," said Andre, staring blankly.

"A freelance means you will only see me occasionally and I should be calling you boss."

"Really?"

"It's true."

"Gosh," said Andre, his beautiful eyes sparkling. "Well in that case," he beamed as a thought suddenly struck him, "could you get everyone a coffee? I'm sweet enough but Philip has it…"

"Andre stop, stop," interrupted John holding up his hand. "A freelance is different from a tea boy."

"Oh I get it," said Andre in a tone suggesting that he clearly had not.

"See you later Andre."

"Ciao baby."

"Hello, Tom," said John, approaching Thomas's desk.

"Hey you," replied Thomas affectionately. "My, aren't we tanned."

"Yes, lots of weather."

"Can't wait to hear all about it."

"I'll save holiday stories for the weekend. You need to store up conversation topics for boating." John adopted a serious tone. "Now, Thomas," he said.

"Oh dear, he uses my full appellation, here comes a reprimand."

John looked around and lowered his voice. "About Andre..."

"Dreamy isn't he?"

"Well I don't doubt he lives in a dream world."

"Stop right there, Mr Self-Employed," said Thomas grinning.

"You are aware the staff are getting a little fed up with him?"

"The clients love him, like a little pet furry dog with highlights."

John could sense defiance. He held up the note. "Did you leave me a message? 'Sister' was the only word I could read"

"I did, and I need a favour."

John eyed him suspiciously. "I've fallen for your favours too many times. Let me hear before I commit."

"It's nothing too onerous – Gretchen is popping in and then we are going for lunch."

"Ah, my chance for a formal introduction."

"Well not quite – you'll have to introduce yourself. I have a meeting with the Bell brothers shortly and I wondered if you could give her a quick tour and tell her I'll meet her for lunch."

"Has she really never been here?"

"Nope."

"Why now?"

"Oh bridge building, I guess."

"Of course, the dinner party, you mentioned on the phone," John said chuckling. "'Absolution for the middle classes'; good aphorism, she could work for us."

"Not a chance, she couldn't argue a case she didn't believe in." Thomas gathered his papers and stood up. "Thinking about it, I better choose the restaurant otherwise we'll end up with homemade sandwiches on a bench in the park."

"What about 'Greens', that's fairly wholesome."

"No she'd find it pretentious."

"Err, *Peter's Place?*"

Thomas laughed. "You know she used to work there."

"I didn't."

"I thought I'd told you the story. Oh priceless. I got her the job. I've know Peter from way back when. Grae was an undergraduate and hard up, I told Peter about her being diligent, presentable et cetera, et cetera but the problem with Gretchen is that she's well… too good."

"Too good?"

"Well, too goody goody. It's difficult to put your finger on it. Anyway *Peter's Place* – firstly, despite wearing shirts, jeans and trainers, she has a physical confidence that unsettled the diners. Also she doesn't understand flirting. So when men tried it on she replied like a lawyer interviewing a dodgy witness. Her put-downs were all the more demeaning because she wasn't trying to."

"Ah."

"Because of this," Thomas continued, "she got very few tips which, as they were pooled, pissed off the other waiting staff. And then she rewrote some sort of accounting programme which upset the manager."

"Oh Lord, how did Peter take it?" asked John.

"He was really good humoured, gave her a few hundred quid towards her college fees and suggested that the service industries were not really her thing. To this day she doesn't understand what she had done wrong."

"Hmm, 'too good' would be a difficult basis for a tribunal."

"Well," sighed Thomas, "people go out to escape."

"And yet knowing all this, you asked her to dinner with clients."

"I know, I know. What was I thinking? There is a still a persistent rumour," said Thomas, "that she refused to give a northern family a dessert menu on the grounds that they had 'had enough'. Peter swears by it but I'm sure it's apocryphal."

John laughed as his friend acted out the scene.

Thomas looked up through the glass partition to see two well-dressed men in conversation with Andre. "Fuck, I'd better save my clients before Andre emulsifies their brains."

"What about the restaurant?"

"You choose."

John was busy working at Thomas's desk reading through some proofs when he became aware of a slightly reduced noise level in the room. He glanced up to see Clinton, another freelance, staring across the room to reception.

The phone flashed and John picked it up.

"Tommy, there's a woman here who claims to be your sister, though she can't be because she doesn't look like you, more like a Power Ranger."

"Andre, it's John, don't worry I'm coming over."

"Hi," said John extending his hand, "I'm John; we have met briefly a couple of times over the years."

"Oh hi," replied Gretchen, "yes and I've heard a lot about you."

"It's all true I'm afraid – unless it came from your brother, in which case none of it is."

She laughed. "Yes, I know what you mean."

"I'm entertaining you for half an hour, Tom's got clients with him and will join you at the eatery."

"Fine," said Gretchen looking around at the framed adverts that covered the walls. "So, this is where it all happens. I've never been here."

"That is surprising."

"Well not really, neither of us really understands the other's job so we leave it at that. What are you working on at the moment?"

"Ha, straight to the point, that's how Tom described you."

"Sorry."

"It's okay. Well the project is confidential, so, strictly content-free, Tom's working for a client who produces motor bikes and wants a cool campaign."

"How's it going?"

"Well stalling a little," said John. "They produce something called *four stroke* motor bikes."

"I know what four stroke means."

"You do? Good lord, that's a first in this office, anyway we used a simple technique of undermining the competition, the competition being the super-bikes, which are two stoke."

"And?"

"Well super-bikes are tuned to gain attention; similar to the pitch as a baby crying."

"Is that true?" asked Gretchen suspiciously.

"Well…" John gave a polite laugh. "Truth… Hmm. What advertisers do is shape perception and as perception is reality… besides," he added earnestly, "one doesn't wear red leathers and drive yellow plastic to go unnoticed."

Gretchen nodded her understanding.

"So the strategy for our bike is based around a modern day Marlboro man – black leathers, quiet engine, understated yet powerful and we've contrasted this with the *two strokers'* clear display of low self esteem."

"So why is it stalling?"

"Well, the magazines won't carry the ad as it will offend most of their readers."

"Who already drive red bikes in yellow leathers?"

"That's right, so we are having a rethink, without much success. Clinton wants to keep the black leather but on naked women which has rather upset your brother."

"I didn't think my brother was prudish."

"He's not; he just liked the idea of finding an iconic Marlboro Man and doing the same for the bikes as Nick Kamen did for jeans."

"Who?"

"Nick Kamen? He was a model in a brilliant jeans ad made by our competitors BBH. Don't you remember the laundrette and the guy taking his jeans off?"

"Oh yes, all the girls fancied him. In fact your receptionist is the spitting image of him."

"Yes," said John, heaving a sigh, "and that is another story."

"Is my brother any good at this stuff?"

"Yes indeed. When he's on form he can really read the zeitgeist."

"The what?"

"Oh... zeitgeist, it means 'the sprit of the times'. We had a guy walk in about four years ago, name of Rory Fox, a big bluff metal worker from Lancashire. He'd had a decent redundancy package and told us he wanted to open a restaurant. The account was smaller than we would normally touch but Tom sensed there was something worth looking at. Anyway, the guy was absolutely passionate about home-cooking, *toad in the hole, summer pudding* and the like. He kept using the word 'honest' which Tom picked up on and then the guy said in this wonderful accent, 'I were crap at school but I could allus cook'. Tom asked what 'O' levels he'd got and Rory replied 'four Cs'."

"My God," said Gretchen, interrupting "I've seen the 4Cs logo, was that Tom?"

"Pretty much. In three characters he encompassed provenance and mission – really clever. The owner deserves the credit for the product and the graft but Tom, or rather 'that great puff' as Rory calls him, was a major part of the success. There are three of them now and I suspect a fourth is on the way."

"Wow, I'm impressed, I really am."

"Can I get you a drink of some sort?" John asked.

Gretchen checked her watch. "A cup of tea would be very welcome thank you."

John buzzed reception to find it engaged; looking across the office, he could see Andre on the phone tossing his hair back. "Better come with me to the kitchen," John sighed, "I'm the tea boy."

Chapter 16 – Spin

Thomas was on time and Gretchen looked up and smiled, her shoulders rising slightly as an act of contrition. "Hi," she said, "sorry about Saturday, I am a fool."

"No problem, my old," replied Thomas, placing the palm of one hand on top of her head and thumping it lightly with the other. "It's my fault, wrong mix."

Thomas caught the eye of the waiter and held his gaze a moment too long. He grinned as he sat down.

"What?" asked Gretchen, seeing his expression.

"Oh, nothing, lovely."

"John seems a really decent guy, different to your previous boyfriends."

"What because he goes to church?"

"Does he? He didn't mention that. How does that work with you?"

"Well let's just say there are three of us in the marriage so it can get a little overcrowded."

Gretchen looked puzzled. "Sorry, you've lost me again."

"Lady Diana dear," said Thomas with a hint of exasperation, "Pop culture really is wasted on you."

"John was very complimentary about your work. I didn't know you were behind the 4Cs."

"Well, you never ask about my work because you think it's pointless."

"No I don't, really I just… I just don't get it. Tell me about the 4Cs."

"That's easy," he replied, "for once I need not embellish a single soupçon. You know it was based on his 'O' level results?"

"John said."

"I liked Rory Fox from the start though he was a little wary of me. He knew exactly what his product was and how to present it. His plan was simplicity and excellence, only four options per course, on basic tables but with good linen napkins and top quality glassware. We explained that the jargon for his approach would be referred to as his *unique selling point or…*"

"USP," said Gretchen.

"Which was great to hear said in a butch Lancashire accent making the 'U' sound 'yoo'. After a couple of weeks he suddenly said to me. 'Look! You're a puftah and I'm not very bright but I reckon we can make *Shepherd's Pie* together'. Well I mean, what can one say? Guess what the wine was?"

Gretchen shrugged.

"House red or house white."

"That doesn't seem like a good choice – does it?"

"Well that's what we thought but Rory explained that," Thomas tried a Lancashire accent, "'as most folk don't know 'owt about wine, any road, I'll get Gilly Gooolden to choose an out-stand-ing pair ev'ry munth.'"

"And it worked?"

"Amazingly well. Although his dishes are very traditional sausage-and-mash fare, Rory has an excellent quality control on every plate that leaves the kitchen and, believe me darling, they are always sumptuous. However he won't be 'messed about with'. I was in there once when a lady, sounding a might too 'lardy-Mayfair-dah', asked for her Cumberland Sausage to be replaced. She had already made a fuss about the restricted wine list. Rory came out and asked about the problem. She said, rather patronisingly, that she expected 'more than just sausages'. Well you could hear a pin drop." Thomas once more affected the accent. "'I won't be charging you or your group for anything you've eaten or drunk but I will ask you to leave my premises'. The poor woman's friends could see he wasn't joking so they crept out – one even apologised for the fuss. Then Rory turned to the rest of us and asked loudly, 'How's the food?' to which we all replied with gusto, 'Fine, Rory' and fell about laughing. He just cracked the tiniest of smiles, nodded and disappeared back to the kitchen."

"I don't often eat out but I will go and see for myself." Gretchen thought for a moment. "About Saturday, have I really messed it up for you?"

Thomas took a deep breath and leaned forward roguishly. "Well, my dear, as it happens Max 'big in the pants' Pickering, rang me this morning to say he and Timbo had had a hoot of a time and had found your directness 'most refreshing'. Of course their wives will never speak to me again but they don't write the cheques do they? So it's 'all's well that ends well'."

"Oh," sighed Gretchen with relief. "That's fabulous, Tom, I was so worried. I really did try to 'ebb and flow'. I managed to avoid revealing my job."

"Yes, they clearly thought you were in itinerant bookkeeper. Except that Max had sussed you out. He'd seen your picture on my toilet wall, the one of you in your gowns and recognised Cambridge in the background. Anyway, as I said, Sis, it really was my fault – I'm paid to understand this stuff. I just don't think London is ready for a twenty first century Thomas Moore."

"I'm not that bad, am I? People ask my opinion…"

"But don't want to know the real answer. It's like Alistair Campbell and my new washing machine."

"Sorry?"

"All spin. But 'twas ever thus." Thomas felt for his Marlboros and then thought better of it. "They were even at it in the fifteenth century – that's when the Jesus on canvas made a miraculous transformation from small, dark, pious Jew to a figure resembling Arnold Schwarzenegger; such a physique I almost converted."

Gretchen finished her wine and refilled her glass with tap water. "And that doesn't strike you as wrong?"

"Depends on your viewpoint but most of us are such willing victims. Bentley Hacket work for the cosmetic industry, which is continually undergoing some exposé or other but it all falls on deaf ears. You, yourself, tell me that anti-ageing creams can't work, yet sales rise every year. Whether they soothe the skin is irrelevant as long as they soothe the soul. Coco Channel had a line for it." Thomas closed his eyes. "'Luxury is a necessity that starts where necessity stops'. Boy, I wish I could write lines like that."

"Isn't that selling snake oil?"

"I call it selling hope. The higher the price, the more hope we buy."

"So you're saying it's not deception if the deceived want it."

Thomas drummed his fingers on the table as he considered the alternatives. "So the fabric of truth is a little, shall we say, 'threadbare' but, nobody wants to know that the Emperor is actually naked."

"What like… a wilful blindness, that's ridiculous."

"No it's just human, exclude yourself if you must."

Gretchen continued to look perplexed, pained even.

Thomas shifted uncomfortably. "Look," he said, "it may be true what you said the other night about organic food – but you must know that you committed absolute heresy in saying it, at that moment, in that place?"

"That's more or less what John said this morning. 'zeitgeist' is it?"

Thomas nodded. "That's right. Remember when I started with Bentley Hacket we had the *millennium bug* going on and you told me it was rubbish."

"And I was right."

"And you were right, but it would have been commercial suicide to go against the zeitgeist. There was serious money to be made and in the end only Margaret Beckett got left with egg on her face; kind of a win:win."

Gretchen sighed and leaned back. "Tom, I will never understand people." She picked up the menu but didn't look at it.

"Nowt so queer as folk, sis," said Tom with a wink. "Oh! Tell me, what did the great Macaulay Malim think of your grand plan?"

"Oh yes," said Gretchen, fixing a smile, "they fired me."

"What!"

"They fired me. I turned up this morning to be greeted by Reg, the security guard. He was looking rather sheepish. When he referred to me as 'Miss Thorpe' even I recognised something was wrong. He handed me an envelope containing a brief note..." Gretchen took a drink of water, "thanking me for my services, that they were no longer needed, and that a bonus would be paid in six months contingent upon me not contacting employees of the company."

"No!"

"Yes. Actually I felt a bit sorry for Reg because we both knew I could throw him through the glass door if he tried to stop me entering the building."

Thomas regarded his sister. Had he just witnessed a hint of bravado? Had the ice cool mantle fractured, be it hairline, allowing a small glimpse of emotion. "My God," he thought, there is hope for her yet. "Are you all right?" he asked.

"Oh yes, It's come at the right time because I want to do a bit of exploring, some climbing, some 'chilling'."

Again, Thomas noticed her eyes too bright, her smile too wide. "Grae, I've never known you chill," he said, "but you had worked so hard to produce the report. I really am sorry."

"Well don't be. Look I bought us these." Gretchen unfolded a piece of paper.

"*An Evening with Stephen Fry,*" he read. "Excellent. How did you get them?"

Gretchen shrugged. "Oh a friend of a friend."

Thomas suspected this was not the case and that effort and full price were involved. "You are amazing." A thought suddenly struck him. "Wait a minute; you're not at work then."

"Apparently not."

"I'm going up to John's boat for the weekend; you must join us for your birthday. I'm driving up Thursday morning."

"How could I refuse? Ah," said Gretchen, as a black tee-shirted figure approached the table, "here's your gorgeous waiter, let's order."

Tom looked again into the eyes of the waiter. "Good lord, are the portions as big as your biceps?"

Chapter 17 – Grey Notebook

The trees of Hyde Park were usually a tonic for Gretchen but as she wandered through the bright foliage her mood was at best neutral. She was so relieved the dinner party worked out well but random images, some boyfriends, others jobs, others indeterminate, kept appearing, each vying for attention. All, she tried to repress since she'd found that giving energy to feelings resolved little. In her work she was renowned for being able to track a complex audit trail yet in her private life the trails always petered out. "Get a grip," she said quietly to herself as she crossed the busy road. And for a few streets the activities of London's shoppers proved a welcome distraction. Entering Regents Park however, introspection returned. She imagined these discordant thoughts as bubbles trapped in some magma chamber where pressure was imperceptibly rising. In turn, temperature would increase causing more liquid to become gas further raising the pressure. At some point the old bedrock would... "GET A GRIP," she said aloud, causing a young couple lying on the grass to roll off each other.

Gretchen closed the door of her flat and stared into her main open plan room. One wall was covered in maps and photographs, the other lined with books but otherwise Thomas's description of 'monk's cell' had a ring of truth. She had very few possessions by London standards but owning stuff for stuff's sake seemed a little futile. She let out a long sigh and walked over to her desk. Reaching onto the shelf Gretchen retrieved a tattered grey notebook.

She couldn't remember when she started reading her father's journal. In her early teens she guessed. It had become more than a source of support, almost a talisman. Thomas had accused her of taking drugs, it being the only explanation for her constant even-temperament. His response to the lows of adolescence had been epic tantrums. Gretchen however could maintain a calm exterior so long as she could commune regularly with her father's words and consequently the notebook was always with her. There had been a point though, at the end of her 'A' levels, where the magic seemed to be wearing. A friend had died, she'd fallen out with her mum and after several days hiding in her bedroom, she hit on the idea of following her father's footsteps; to actually bring the journal to life. And slowly a plan came together. The first trip had been to a wood near Loughborough where, after a hike through the undergrowth, she had found the subject of the journal's entry; a group of pre-Cambrian fossils. Running her hands over the rocks at the same time reading her father's notes had improved her spirits markedly and the quest had began.

Reclining her chair, she put her feet up on the desk and opened the notebook. Her dad's handwriting was so familiar; the style full of information, 'un-flowery' he had called it.

There were twenty seven separate entries and the only structure was date order. Some were about the things he had seen, others about things he had done; over half in the UK and the rest all over the world.

Gretchen opened a page at random; the entry was dated '20th March 1979' and was headed, 'Catching adders in Hampshire'. It was an account of helping to record the species and her dad had caught five in the early morning. '...before the sun had brought their bodies up to temperature'. Even though her dad's descriptions were largely a chronicle of each event, his excitement shone through in phrases like 'tailing my first adult', and 'bloody painful' after been bitten by a hatchling. Many years later she had followed suit, helping to collate the national data.

Gretchen read his words over, the images that formed around them made richer by the addition of her own experience. However, an unsettling consequence was that, as these merged, she was sometimes unsure as to whose experience she was bringing to mind. Being bitten though, she happily reflected, was uniquely her father's.

She made a hot chocolate and continued reading. The next entry was dated '11th December 1979' and was headed 'High diving in Crystal Cascades'. It chronicled the first part of her father's trip to Queensland, a hike from the lodge where he was staying to a renowned local swimming hole.

Fifteen years later, Gretchen had checked into that same pub, *The Red Beret*, and made her way up the same road in a similar oppressive humidity. The long walk-in was mentioned in the journal. However she doubted that the road was as busy or unpleasant all those years before, so she crossed to a smaller, windier route that roughly tracked Freshwater Creek. The way soon became sheltered by trees in amongst which, she recognised, stood the odd 'Morton Bay Fig'. Cars passed her on the way up, two stopping to ask if she needed a lift; one of them, full of boys, had driven off to a cacophony of cheers and wolf whistles.

The walk was not steep but it had taken another half hour to reach the secluded series of rock pools. The boys that had passed her in the car were all swimming and jumping from the left hand cliff into the main pool; none, she noted, jumped from the right cliff. Some other young people were sunbathing next to a sign which read *No Crocs Allowed*.

Gretchen took a sip of her hot chocolate, a warm feeling spreading through her as she read her dad's comment, 'It all looked idyllic'. She also remembered it this way: sun glinting through the canopy onto clear water, low crags on each side, waterfall in the background with the whole domain framed by tropical rainforest.

As she walked by she had acknowledged the boys with a small wave. According to his journal, this was as far as her father had got, having dived straight in, but Gretchen wanted to explore further and continued along the path that accompanied the creek. The sounds of humans soon gave way to those of the rainforest. The insects were both plentiful and inquisitive and she stopped to apply some repellent. Checking a suitable rock for an absence of wildlife, she sat down. After the long walk her water and sandwiches were a welcome relief and she dined in a state of rhapsody watching butterflies alight on the damp sand. She couldn't identify the source of any of the squeaks, clicks, buzzes or cackles; in fact Gretchen had little knowledge of this environment. She tried to guess the approaching animal from the sound of its footsteps which lumbered through the leaf-litter. A huge monitor lizard, dark grey with yellow cross stripes and around two metres in length, appeared providing the answer. It looked intimidating. Gretchen believed them to be docile but still prepared to leap onto the rock if it got within four paces. At five paces it stopped. Its long tongue tasted the air and it looked Gretchen up and down.

"What?" she asked.

By the time she returned to the pool, the boys had gone and now a group of middle-aged tourists sat on a nearby log. 'I climbed the left hand cliff', Gretchen read, 'and then pushed off hard to avoid the rocks below.' She closed her eyes and remembered her own dive. It had been a perfect swallow hitting the cleansing water as the onlookers all clapped. 'Then I climbed my way up the right hand cliff, known locally as *No Fear*. The pool looked small below and as I leapt, I felt like Tarzan.' Gretchen had stood on the same cliff, her bare feet standing where his bare feet had stood, their senses joined through time. She felt, in those fleeting seconds, that he was falling with her.

Gretchen's hot chocolate had gone cold. She closed the book and looked over at her wall maps. They were covered with coloured pins and lines and she stood to get a closer look. To date she had followed twenty five of her father's adventures, following his footsteps as carefully as possible. There were two left, both in the UK. Eyes lined by curiosity, she traced her finger over the map. Happy with her decision, she nodded and picked up the phone.

Chapter 18 – Malvern

According to a feature in *Scientific American,* life on earth did not begin with the energy of the Sun's rays, but in the black, sulphur-rich world at the bottom of the oceans. Gretchen's copy of the article lay open next to her bed along side a half-drunk cup of tea; evidence of another night's broken sleep. Gretchen awoke thinking about the arguments that favoured chemosynthesis over photosynthesis. It seemed intuitive that the mineral soup surrounding the hydrothermal vents was, for billions of years, the more stable environment but her background had taught her to be wary of intuition.

She breathed in deeply just as her alarm sounded. She glanced briefly at the article again, made a mental note to investigate further, and began preparing for the day.

Gretchen cycled to Camden Town tube station to catch the first train north to High Barnet. From there she had another three mile cycle to pick up her car which was garaged on a farm. She went straight to the barn and pulled back the dust sheet to reveal an old Land Rover. "Hello," she said, patting the bonnet.

Over the years the '1974 Series Two' had provoked a number of derisive comments embodied by the response; "you are joking?" The Land Rover had been in the family since it was new but Thomas still questioned his sister's sanity in taking it on. Gretchen defended her action, telling her brother that she could demonstrate mathematically that it was cost effective to run. However she could also remember being with her father in it – bumping over some hillside hunting butterflies or sleeping in the back of it waiting for the dawn chorus. One never knew what treat the glove compartment may conceal; a slow worm, a raft spider, always entertaining for an unsuspecting passenger.

For its twenty-fifth anniversary Gretchen had commissioned and helped to rebuild the car and though the ride was much improved it was still noisy. On long runs she'd taken to wearing ear defenders and in so doing had given Thomas an excuse to avoid it altogether declaring ear defenders to be 'so last year'.

After removing the mousetraps from the engine compartment and checking the oil, she headed slowly west. After two hours, Gretchen picked up the A417 north to Ledbury where she stopped, took the map from the car and looked for somewhere to breakfast. Sitting in a tea room that doubled as an iron mongers, Gretchen realised that, for once, her car did not look out of place. An even older Land Rover had passed by, Collie dog barking from the open back, and an Austin Cambridge was lodged opposite. After a fabulous home-cooked breakfast – quoted to her at 'three pounds ten' – Gretchen took the A449 north which soon rose into the Malvern Hills. She noticed that on the OS map, the hills looked like a prostrate dinosaur. "A plesiosaur perhaps," she thought, as she drove across what would be the upper neck.

Parking in Great Malvern, she followed signs to St Anne's Well. The path was steep but short and she stopped at the Victorian building to 'take the water'. Gretchen had read that the famous elixir started as rain taking thirty days to filter through the rocks trickling out virtually distilled. It struck her that the celebrated 'restorative powers' were then just those of clean water; a miracle in itself in Victorian Britain.

From here she could see her destination, the Benedictine monastery, but she decided to delay her visit and continued upwards. The lower forestry soon dwindled leaving no protection from the wind and drizzle.

Standing at the top next to the trig point Gretchen slowly turned three hundred and sixty degrees. The cover of rain clouds was far from uniform and she watched as the sun broke through, was thwarted and escaped again. The result of all this activity was randomly changing shades of light on the farmland below, an effect her brother had once described as 'disco lighting for old people'.

Returning to the town, she crossed the road towards ivy-covered houses and walked into the quiet gardens of The Priory. The path cut the grounds in half on both sides of which were graves that ranged from the old to the ancient. Gretchen was there to find one grave in particular but wasn't sure how. She sat on a wet bench and pulled out the journal thinking it might offer her a clue. Then she noticed a man standing under a Cedar of Lebanon, staring at a headstone. Unaware that he was being watched, he took a photograph of the stone and stood a while longer. Gretchen guessed that her search was over before it had begun and flicked to the page titled 'Annie's grave'.

Her dad's journal entry for his visit to this place was unusual. It wasn't just the location that seemed unadventurous it was more her father's tone. It started with a quote from Charles Darwin, 'Oh that she could now know how deeply, how tenderly we do still and shall ever love her dear joyous face.' Under that, he'd written a short description of Anne Darwin. It all seemed so much more sober, serious even.

Gretchen was aware that the young girl's death had destroyed Charles Darwin's remaining religious faith. Freed from those constraints he'd finally published the book which ultimately changed the course of history. Was that why her father was drawn to this place? And to record it in his journal? Seeing that the man with the camera had left, Gretchen approached the grave from the canopy of the cedar tree. The headstone was a modest, dark grey curved stone, leaning slightly to one side. It read 'ANNE ELIZABETH DARWIN, A DEAR AND GOOD CHILD'.

"Why am I here, dad?" she whispered to herself.

Gretchen noticed her fellow visitor returning and, on the spur of the moment, addressed him.

"Excuse me, are you a researcher?"

The man stopped.

Gretchen pointed to the grave, "I saw you…"

He smiled, "Sort of, doing a science Masters."

"Ah, I know this sounds odd but is it something to do with Anne's death and the loss of religious conviction?"

The man gave a friendly chortle, "Nothing so clever, I have a daughter the same age... the poignancy of this stone, knowing so much about Darwin…" he searched for a word but failed. "I feel for the man," he shrugged. "Look here's my daughter now."

A girl appeared and was accompanied, Gretchen assumed, by her mother. The man said, "Goodbye," and left to join his family.

A thought slowly emerged. She moved further under the tree out of the rain and opened the journal again. The journal entry was dated 'July 15th 1980'. Gretchen would have been just over ten. Looking back at the headstone she read 'BORN MARCH 2 1841 DIED APRIL 23 1851'.

Gretchen finally understood. Her dad had visited the grave when Gretchen was exactly the same age as Annie was when she died. The entry marked the link of one father with another. Like the man with the camera, her own dad had recognised a simple human connection and been moved.

She laughed at herself, so analytical yet so dumb. Gretchen turned her head up to the rain, enjoying the sensation as it hit her face. "Oh, Dad," she whispered with amusement, "I am a fool!"

Chapter 19 – Homo Erectus

The surge of rush hour was over but there was still a steady stream of people leaving the tube station. Although the commuters moved with certainty the tourists tended to meander or even stop without warning. Small eddies of brief cases formed and cups of takeaway coffee were held aloft to prevent spillage. To avoid holding up the flow, Gretchen stepped into a shop doorway and dropped the heavy rucksack from her shoulder. Tying her hair into a ponytail, she pulled out a pair of sunglasses and placed them on her forehead. She grasped the rucksack and, in a well-practiced move, heaved it vertically dropping her shoulder to catch the weight. Several men in a nearby bus queue stared at her as she flicked the seventy-litre pack around her other shoulder, pulled down the straps and, now ready, rejoined the stream.

Thomas waited at the interchange of Hawley Road and Kentish Town Road, singing along to a David Gray song. Seeing no obvious gap, he slowly edged his Saab forward until the passing traffic had to give way. Moving out he raised his hand and mouthed "Thank you" to a driver who did not respond. In his mirror he could see the man was only several feet from his bumper. *"Please forgive me if I act a little strange,"* he sang, and dabbed his brakes. The car dropped back a little and Thomas could see the driver mouth a profanity. *"Feels like lightning running through my veins*, ooh, bitchy." He pressed two buttons on his phone.

"Hi Tom," answered the voice.

"Hi, poppet, where are you?" shouted Thomas above the music.

"At the Garage, where are you?"

"Just on my way, traffic as usual, should be there in ten. Could you be a love and get me a muffin from the shop. Bit on the drag this morning."

"Sorry, what? 'This morning?'" she said trying to hear him above the music.

"On the drag – going to be late!"

"Nothing new there. Will do."

Thomas could see his sister from a distance. It wasn't just the rucksack and hiking boots that made her stand out. She seemed much taller than her five foot seven, her posture unapologetic. He indicated and flashed his lights.

The Saab pulled onto the forecourt followed by several other cars and Gretchen, despite the rucksack, got in in one fluid movement. She lent across and kissed her brother's cheek as he began pulling away.

Thomas turned the music volume down but continued to mumble the odd lyric as they remained captive in the traffic. Reaching the North Circular, they began to move more freely.

"New car?" Gretchen asked, sliding her chair back to allow room for her rucksack on the floor.

Thomas looked across with some irritation. "Yes it is. Do you want to put that in the back, you'll scratch the leather."

"I'll be very careful with your upholstery – I need to go through my stuff." Gretchen looked at the backseat where four cool-boxes and two baskets were placed. "Travelling light, I see," she said.

Thomas turned the music down. "Just a few things I rustled up."

"It's a lovely car, Tom, is it different from the last one?"

"I have no idea, he was such a gorgeous salesman, how could a girl say no?"

"By saying no perhaps," she replied, opening her digital organiser.

"Speaking of new toys..." Thomas nodded toward the gadget.

"It's the new PDA from Compaq."

"My god, a brand, she's a consumer."

Gretchen ignored him, it's called an IPAQ – diary, dictionary, encyclopaedia – that sort of thing," she explained.

"And I thought all you girls needed was a lippy in your handbags. Where've you been the last two days by the way? I've tried you twenty times."

"A place called Malvern and then Snowdonia. I didn't get back until late last night."

"Shopping expedition was it?"

"Something like that. Where are we going today?" she asked, tapping the menu button and selecting *ROUTE* function.

"The Backwaters, darling."

"And the Backwaters are...?"

Thomas passed her the address. "Apparently men of letters refer to it as the Eastern Amazon, such is its bio... society. The river voles take morning coffee with badgers then luncheon with deer. Coypus are, of course, excluded on account of their clumsiness."

Gretchen tapped in the coordinates. "Coypus were eradicated in the eighties," she recalled.

"Well that's just charming, lack a jaw line and a few social graces and it's bloody genocide."

Thomas glanced across and caught a smile around his sister's mouth as she continued scrolling through her PDA.

"Oh," she said, "it's near Walton-on-the-Naze."

"That's right, do you know it?"

"I went there years ago, collecting sharks' teeth."

"How wonderful," said Thomas, feigning excitement, "Great White or... the other one?"

"Difficult to tell when they are fifty million years old so let's go with the 'other one'. Do you have directions?" she asked, "Or do you want me to do the honours?"

"Err," Thomas began as he joined the busy lane marked A1. "No thanks, been there a couple of times in the early spring to help with hull repairs."

Gretchen stared at her brother. "You? Manual work?"

"Well I confess I managed to make good tea and a mess of everything else. Luckily John took pity on my less-than-able ship-mating and instead plank-walked me to the chandlery."

"Plank-walked? Is that the term?"

"No, I was just trying to maintain sailor-speak. Anyway the chandlery is full of straps and shackles very similar to a shop in Soho I know. John did get annoyed when I kept trying them on and seeking his opinion in front of the locals... Don't think there's a very big *scene* on the Naze."

"Tell me about the countryside?" Gretchen asked, intrigued by the term 'Eastern Amazon'.

"More birds than... Blair's Babes."

"What does that mean?"

"Lots."

"In total or different species?"

"Does it matter?"

"Absolutely – if there's a diversity of species it means a diverse ecosystem, that's good news. If there are just loads of Canada geese, we could be in Hyde Park."

"It certainly isn't Hyde Park. As far as I could see from the shore wall it was all inlets, outlets and mud, mud inglorious mud."

"That does sound interesting."

"We had a walk around the fauna and flora. John laughed at my anecdotes but must think me a bit of an eco-numpty."

"Well you are," agreed Gretchen.

"I'm not that bad," Thomas replied plaintively. "... I know the sound of a cuckoo."

"Changing the subject, how religious is John?"

"Hard to tell. He does believe in God, well I think he does. At the same time he seems to know so much and as far as he tells it, it's all contradictory. I can't really work him out. If I were you I'd just stay off the subject."

They fell silent. Gretchen began searching for anything on the Backwaters while her brother tapped along to the CD.

"Did you get me a muffin?" Thomas asked as they filtered onto the M25.

Gretchen un-wrapped the cake and handed it over without taking her eyes off the IPAQ.

Thomas looked over at Gretchen, her face a picture of concentration, as he devoured the muffin. "Life of the mind and life of the stomach," he mused, trying to weigh them equally as an indulgence.

Thomas took the exit for the A12. "Did you get any feedback from Macaulay Malim?"

"Yes a little. A partner who seems to think he's in love with me rang, full of apologies and wanting to meet up. He told me in the strictest confidence that it was the Luton partner who rubbished my methods and canvassed everyone to have me fired."

"Did you expect the attack from him?"

"I thought the report on his branch was fair. It ranked Luton about midway by standard measures but, after my 'value-added adjustment', it dropped to near bottom."

"Ah!"

"I could have been far more damming if I had been asked for a qualitative document."

"Why, shagging his secretary was he?"

"In a manner of speaking, his girlfriend was his PA and they ran it like a fiefdom; drinks parties that were obligatory, employees having to curry favour, strong personalities forced out. There were all the signs that I had learnt to look out for from my experience with Enron."

"What did you say to the partner who rang you?"

"Oh I let him down gently and then he said something very sweet and very sad."

"Which was?"

"He said I reminded him of the life he never had."

"Ouch! Poor man. What did you say?"

"Nothing. I thanked him and wished him good luck with the business."

"Will you take it any further?"

"God, no! Out of the hundred or so partners, there were only a few who I liked. I'd rather work with voluntary organisations. By the way, although I'm no longer an employee, I am discreet so keep this to yourself."

"Cross my heart and hope to go bald."

"Clacton-on-Sea," said Gretchen, reading a road sign. "Know anything about Clacton-on-Sea?"

"Oh, roller bladers and hunky surfers, sunny skies and dellie culture..."

"You don't know anything about it do you?"

"No."

"So you were in describing…"

"San Francisco."

"I see."

"Probably a mistake," admitted Thomas. "Hmm, 'Only in America, Never in Clacton,' I could use that."

"Ah," said Gretchen reading and interrupting her brother. "*Clactonian man, four hundred thousand years, named after flint tools that were found in Clacton-on-Sea, Essex*". I had no idea *Homo erectus* was here that long ago."

"Ah, we've been around a long time."

"*Homo erectus* not homosexual."

"Yes, yes. Big hairy men."

"No, Neanderthals."

"Neanderthals, yes, I've had the odd close encounter,"

Gretchen sighed. "Of the third kind?" she asked, resigned to her brother's game.

"Fourth actually; afterwards I would take them home to meet mother."

Gretchen gave up and returned to her research.

The busy rural traffic dwindled through villages until, eventually, they were on their own and turning down a single lane track signed 'Hamford Marina'. The road snaked through low-lying pastures bounded by the grass banks of sea walls and a forest of sailing masts.

Thomas drove around the car park twice.

"Where are we going?" asked Gretchen.

"I want to park next to the smartest cars so there's less chance of getting mine scratched."

"We could have come in my Land Rover."

"I couldn't possibly be seen in an antiquity," said Thomas.

"Is it the age or the discomfort?"

"Both, darling. In the OED, under the word 'discordant', it says, 'see Thomas in Gretchen's car'."

Chapter 20 – Backwaters

"I better just phone the office," Thomas said, turning off the engine. "Who knows when we'll next get a signal?" Gretchen wandered up to the sea wall and looked across the salt marsh. The scene was awash with bird life, their wings flashing against the dark mosaic of greens and fawns. The marina itself was a mix of pontoons and jetties moored to which were hundreds of motor and sail boats, the latter providing the mass clinking sound of halyard on mast. There was an unmistakable smell of sea air and Gretchen breathed in deeply. Looking back to the car, she saw her brother still on his phone so walked across to the store, emerging five minutes later with a small book.

"Ahoy there, scurvy mates, I bear gifts rich in vitamin…" Thomas searched his memory.

"C?" suggested Gretchen.

"C," exclaimed Thomas, "and also breadfruit to stave off rickets."

Gretchen decided to let it go.

"We are the Swiss Family Thorpe, bound for adventure. I like swallows and she's been to the Amazon…"

Boat-owners along the pontoon stared at the man and woman who walked past, both laden with cool-boxes; the man a barrage of maritime banter, the woman a picture of bemused resignation.

At the end of the jetty a large sloop was at berth and John sat on its roof. He watched his friend salute the other berths, whistle as if piping himself aboard and hop on one leg while squawking 'pieces of eight'. John raised his eyebrows as Thomas stopped by the bow.

"What?" said Thomas innocently.

"Hi John," said Gretchen, smiling as she glanced around the boat. "I would say, 'permission to come aboard' but I sense my brother may beat me to it."

"Permission," said Thomas, with great pathos and in a deep Cornish accent, "to come aboard?"

"Granted."

Gretchen cleared the gunwale in a graceful bound. She turned to her brother, "Cool-boxes please, Captain Birdseye."

"My goodness, mildly amusing," he replied, handing over the cache of foodstuffs.

John looked quizzically at the boxes as they mounted up. "Did you think we were sailing around Cape Horn?"

"One can never be sure of the distance to the nearest lemon and you did say 'come prepared'."

"I rather meant waterproofs and sun-cream but now you mention it, a slice of lemon in a cold G & T would be welcome."

Thomas held up a flask, his eyes flashing.

"Tea?"

"Smell."

"Good Lord. G and T."

"I know a pre-mix is like a clip-on bowtie," said Thomas, "but adventure demands some sacrifice."

Gretchen looked around the boat. "So this is *Bexsy*. I didn't know what to imagine; she's very impressive. I'm afraid my knowledge of boating is limited to school dinghy sailing."

"Fear not. John will tell you which rope to pull. But better jump to it mind," he said disappearing into the galley and, once more affecting a loud Cornish accent, "or it be the *keel haul*."

"The fact that we indulge his behaviour probably says more about us," said John.

"True," replied Gretchen, "What's the plan?"

"Well, we are going to get off straight away while we've still got the tide and moor up in a small quiet creek not far away. I know you like exploring so thought we could take the kayaks out round the islands and see if we can find the seals. Your brother can read and practise his nautical phrases."

"Sounds perfect, what can I do?"

John pointed forward. "I need you to untie that rope and push the bow out when I say."

John started the engines, untied the stern, increased the engine revs and nodded to Gretchen.

The boat slowly moved away from the landing stage, Gretchen hopped back aboard and they headed into the channel. *Bexsy* chugged slowly to minimise the wash, which fanned out behind them, gently lapping the banks of the salt marsh. Gretchen coiled the rope and joined John at the wheel. He looked more relaxed and, at the same time, more vibrant since last they had met.

"You look at home behind the wheel."

"Thank you. *Bexsy* and I are the best of friends. It's the most productive relationship I've ever had with a female."

"She's beautiful."

John patted the wheel. "She is but I need to tell you that she's been around, the little minx."

John explained that *Bexsy* had originally been a lifeboat first launched from Cowes in 1930. She had been christened the *Shirley Anne* after her patron and had worked the busy coastline from Dorset to Devon but her crowning moment had been in May-June, 1940.

"What happened then?" Gretchen asked.

"I said Grae didn't know anything about history," shouted Thomas.

"It was Dunkirk; the little ships."

"Sorry, of course I've heard of Dunkirk. And *Bexsy* took part?"

"By all accounts she was there seven days out of the nine, constantly ferrying between beach and destroyer."

"That's some provenance."

"You're sailing in history, sister," said Thomas.

The channel, bordered by a myriad of creeks, was opening up into a bay. A few other boats passed them, heading for the marina, giving Thomas the opportunity to salute. To the east of the bay lay the North Sea and several cargo vessels were visible as they approached Harwich. John brought *Bexsy* around and they headed inland.

"How long have you had her?" Gretchen asked.

"Father found her in the 1960s. The euphemism is 'project boat'."

"Not my sort of euphemism," piped Thomas. The others ignored him.

"For years I remember him restoring her. He made much of value-for-money but I knew it was more than that."

Gretchen thought about her car. "Will we get the sails up?" she asked, changing the subject.

"Not today, we're tight for tide; we're aiming for a fairly shallow creek."

"It's a large boat," said Gretchen, "will we get far up a creek?"

"Now that's a euphemism," said Thomas approvingly.

John suppressed a smile. "She has a very shallow draft," he said, looking at the depth gauge, "despite her thirty tonnes."

Brent geese flew unusually low over the boat, the engine noise drowning out the sound of their calls. As *Bexsy* made her way down a series of progressively smaller creeks, Gretchen could see turrets of mud, some topped with grasses, broaching the surface. The sediment made it impossible to judge the depth and, within a hundred metres of a small quay and a series of houses, the hull found the bed. "I guess we have landed," said John and cut the engines.

The silence was abrupt and nobody spoke. Across the creek they could hear the squabbling of thousands of water fowl arriving as the approaching low tide exposed their feeding grounds.

Gretchen had already found the cabin binoculars and trained them across to the widening foreshore. "Can I do anything, John?" she asked, without removing the glasses.

"No, I've just got to get us anchored and I'm sure Tom has the lunch sorted."

"*Sort* infers *unimaginative*," said Thomas, "I don't *sort*. I arrange, create, concoct, or even compose."

"Great, well when I've composed the anchor let's eat."

John tasted the chilled Sauvignon Blanc while Thomas looked on. "Excellent, Tom."

"Yes, it does somehow say 'yippee' to the sundried tomatoes."

Gretchen sipped at the wine. "It's really good, Tom, but do you mind if I have a softy – lunch and alcohol and all that."

"Philistine," he replied, wearily. "softies in red cool-box... and anyway, you don't do alcohol at anytime."

Gretchen raised her plastic beaker. "Well cheers all, here's to... where are we?"

"You are in Hensie Creek but the world knows it as 'The Secret Water'."

Gretchen looked blank.

"As in *Swallows and Amazons*," added Thomas.

Gretchen still looked blank.

"You see, John, I told you – popular culture – complete mystery."

"I do know about *Swallows and Amazons* but I thought it was set up north in The Lakes."

"The first one was," affirmed John, "but they were a series and one of them was set here and it's called *The Secret Water*."

"Well then," said Gretchen, again raising her plastic beaker, "here's to Secret Water."

"Secret Water," they repeated.

"And who wrote it again?" asked Gretchen.

"Arthur Ransom," said John. "I used to have the book here in the cabin but it went overboard near Skippers Island. I grabbed for it but as its dog-eared pages slowly submerged, it suddenly felt a fitting place to rest. So I let it go."

"You can see why I love him," said Thomas and seeing John's glance added, "turn of phrase, darling."

"What was it about?" asked Gretchen.

"Oh the usual," replied John. "1930-something children's adventure. The father marooned them on an island and told them to chart it all before he returned. In the meantime other children with boats arrived… It was really about the values of the age, self reliance and resourcefulness. I doubt today's children could relate."

Thomas re-filled his glass. "Hmmm, it still forms the basis of most ads though – I could really do something with this place but John won't let me come near it."

"Too bloody true, I'd hate it to become the *not very* secret water."

Thomas viewed the marshes through his outstretched hands. "Panning shot picks out apprehensive children with rowing boat waving Arran sweaters," he said. "Large white sloop retreats, parents waving, tears in their eyes, until out of sight they break open New Zealand wine and Italian food. Both parents heave a sigh of relief. 'Give them a week?' suggests one. 'Agreed,' replies the other. Cue relaxing music and voice over, 'Cabernet Sauvignon. Give yourselves a break'."

"Cliché," said John.

"Effective though."

"I love it," said Gretchen, "but I think the final shot should be of the children; one saying, 'Give them a month?' and the other replying, 'Make it a year'."

"Never work."

"Why not?"

"Children don't buy wine."

"Should be a public information broadcast then," protested Gretchen.

For the next twenty minutes Thomas and John traded shots on the merits of filming in such a unique setting. Gretchen retreated to a comfortable padded corner of the wheelhouse and opened her new book, *The Geology of Essex*. She flicked through the pages reading the chapter headings before going back to the beginning.

"The geological story of Essex starts with rocks that are between 440 and 360 million years old. Dating from the Silurian and Devonian periods these rocks consist of mudstones, sandstone, and hard slatey shale..."

* * * * *

Gretchen stood amongst the shale. Around her the huge expanse of this Canadian reserve was a single shade of light grey; evidence of the uniform conditions at the time of its creation. As well as lacking colour, the quarry was without plant and animal life yet none of this dampened Gretchen's enthusiasm or those that accompanied her. The group had only formed hours earlier down the valley in the briefing room, yet a common passion for fossils had made for lively interaction which had continued all the way up through vibrant green pines of the mountain slopes. Against a backdrop of animated banter and clanging of rocks, Gretchen found herself smiling, knowing the collective name her brother would apply; 'a nerd'. The Burgess Shale had been one of the most important finds in palaeontology giving a much clearer picture of life half a billion years ago. Gretchen felt at home sharing her thoughts with the fellow rock hounds as they pondered the weird and wonderful creatures that existed on earth. She continued in good spirits all the way back down to the information centre where she checked a few facts but then preceded to her most important task; the purchase of a blue cotton tee-shirt, boldly inscribed with five white trilobites.

Chapter 21 – Lady Di

"Balls, darling balls!" Gretchen heard Thomas cry. "Sounds like you must have reached checkmate, John," she said.

"No, just Mornington Crescent," said Thomas.

"I never asked," said Gretchen, "just how did you two get together?"

"Well," John began, "we first met over seven years ago when Shaun – who's the Hacket in Bentley and Hacket – and I had just started the business. We were looking for creative people and I happened to be in a restaurant with some friends and on the next table sat your brother. He appeared to have his whole party in hysterics recounting some anecdote… about confusing big band jazz for a local swingers' club."

Gretchen nodded, recognising the story.

"Well my dinner companions were rather dull, so I spent the night ear-wigging his conversations. I gathered by his rhetoric that he was in advertising so slipped him my card."

"Yes, I thought the saucy old devil was trying to pick me up," said Thomas.

"Well I was, in a manner of speaking."

John continued. "He came to see us at our humble address."

"God! Was it humble…" remembered Thomas.

"Yes, I recall our formal introductions with clarity. "Hi, I'm Thomas, Christ these offices are crap!"

"Did he really say that?" Gretchen laughed.

"Yep, Shaun and I really were in two minds but the clients loved him. So he stayed. Completely re-energised me. After the responsibility of working in newspapers, I felt liberated… youthful again. Shaun played dad and often looked disapprovingly when the merriment got out of hand."

"Listen, um, you two," said Thomas imitating Shaun, "we have a, ah, business to, um, run."

"Did Tom tell you about the tea contract?" asked John.

"No, don't think I've heard this."

"Oh it's legend. Tom did this pitch to a very conservative English Tea company called Kenning's; an account we had little chance of signing."

Thomas began sniggering at the memory.

"They wanted to make a play on the fact that their tea was a stimulating beverage. Tom had recently read an article," John hesitated delicately, "mythologizing the *G spot* and, as only he could do, substituted *Tea spot*. Within an hour he had the ad storyboarded with a very English version of the Meg Ryan café scene – a woman drinking the tea while suppressing an orgasm. The strap-line was, of course, 'Kennings, hits the T spot'. I was sitting in with him during the pitch and the more their delegation sat po-faced the more Thomas let rip. I could hardly control myself. As Tom wound up with an impression of Meg Ryan I could feel myself beginning to choke. When he crossed his eyes and purred like a jaguar, I thought I would never breathe again."

They all laughed, John wiping the tears from his eyes.

"I don't suppose you got the account?" asked Gretchen.

"No – surprisingly, though one of the directors left and we did get work from his new tea company. Oh boy, we had some fun which reminds me, time to put the kettle on. Coffee I'm assuming for you, Tom?" John went below still smirking at the memory.

Gretchen called after John. "I'll have some squash if you have it,"

"Of course we have it," said Thomas, "I'm on the culinary case now."

Gretchen squinted at a flock of light brown birds that flashed their white undersides as one.

"Thank you," said Thomas, as John placed the his cup and saucer down.

"Best thing the English has done for the world, tea," said John. "Here's to Kenning's." he said raising his coffee mug.

"Wasn't it India who started the tea trade?" asked Gretchen.

"China originally," said John, "but the British made it their own and re-exported it – led to the Opium Wars."

"And the loss of America," added Thomas. He took a sip of his coffee and remembered the original question. "John says he always fancied me but I never got the slightest hint."

John shifted uncomfortably. "Old fashioned values I'm afraid. I didn't think it professional for staff to date and anyway, we were both already in relationships."

"I can't tell you Grae, how dull some of his 'friends' were – so old."

John started as if to take exception but then reasoned, "Well Philip was fifteen years older than me but good company and a fine mind – punned in Greek."

Thomas took a deep breath. "I think I upset him. I suggested one night he join us in the *scene*. He was visibly shocked!"

"I'm not surprised," said John. "You have to bear in mind that Philip was born during the war and pretty much had to live his entire life in the closet. He told me that he could never be himself while his parents were alive. Don't forget, one of our greatest war heroes was hounded to suicide because he was queer."

"By the way," asked Gretchen, "is 'queer' the right word now? Tom uses it as often as 'gay'."

"Seems to be," said John. "Peter Tatchell says so, and who'd dare disagree. Personally, my identity is first and foremost in my work and hobbies – I never found much solace or substance in the *scene*. The last time I was in a presence of thousands of queers was... not since we were out in the Mall together, that bizarre day six years ago.

Thomas frowned and then suddenly picked up the reference. "It was not a gay scene!" he barked. "That's a shitty thing to say."

"Okay there were many others there but the majority of men I saw were 'in the club'."

Gretchen was confused. "Sorry I'm lost, what happened?"

"You may well ask. It was the funeral of Diana. I... well we all seemed swept along in the tide of... something, I don't know."

"It was called grief," cried Thomas. "It was grief."

"But why?" protested John. "What were we grieving for, the lack of copy? We didn't know her. We..."

Thomas put down his drink with a clatter and walked to the bow.

"I'm sorry, Tom," said John, raising his voice, "I am allowed to express how I feel on this one. I was there too."

John turned to Gretchen. "How did you feel about it?"

"Feel?" said Gretchen and then added, almost apologetically, "I didn't. I thought Tom might have told you, my reading is pretty dull; mostly scientific journals. Not too many celebrities in there," she added with an appeasing smile. "Although I did read a piece in *Nature.*"

"And what did such an esteemed journal think?"

"It was more about the phenomenon of mass hysteria."

"Any conclusions about us lot?"

"I think it was something about guilt. Unconscious... collective? Err." Gretchen closed her eyes as she tried to remember. "I think the point was that the masses partly knew they were to blame, the corollary being: no readers no paper, no paper no Paparazzi...'"

"So no readers, no tragedy. Yes I'm aware of that old chestnut though it would have been suicide to print it. Perhaps that's why we directed the fire elsewhere."

John looked up at the mast and stroked his chin. "I'm sure Tom would agree that a good headline writer can shape public opinion – well he would if he wasn't having a strop. I would have said then – in mock humility – that we only reflect the public mood but really we revelled in our power. It was uncanny, following Diana's death, the degree to which the man on the street was repeating phrases from the previous day's copy. Even I, who knew the machine, succumbed and was calling for the Monarchy to 'show us you care'." John sighed. "I feel ashamed looking back. The Queen's own grief must have been... well. But as we editors say 'if it bleeds, it leads'."

"Is that why you left journalism?" asked Gretchen.

"It was all sorts of things. I'd had a great time as a cub reporter; got a rush from seeing myself in print. Pride I know but I did start to wince when I got it wrong. By the time editorship was upon me, I was having sleepless nights."

"Tell Grae about *The Fisher King*," interrupted Thomas, walking back up the boat.

John half smiled in embarrassment. "Well it's not that important," he responded.

"Tish and Pish."

"Well a little, perhaps... call it a catalyst. There was a film in the early nineties," John said, "called *The Fisher King*. Do you know it?"

"No," said Gretchen.

John continued. "It was a comedy but at its heart was a fatal shooting caused by the glib remark of a radio DJ. I suddenly saw myself causing that kind of incident and couldn't live with the thought."

Gretchen was puzzled. "I find it hard to believe that we are that taken in."

John sighed. "Yes I try not to analyze but I do wonder. Why otherwise perfectly rational beings get carried away. I'm assuming you have heard of Joseph Goebbels."

Gretchen nodded.

"Everybody's heard of him because he's the arch bad guy – propaganda minister. But he was only partly responsible for the mass hatred of the Jews – it was the editor of the then tabloid, *Der Stürmer*, who was the real culprit. Just as mad as the rest but where he scored – not sure if that's the right phrase – is that he understood the masses.

"What happened to him?" asked Gretchen.

"Luckily, the Nuremburg court realised his part and he was executed."

"Fitting I guess."

"Then and now."

"What a lot of pretentious bollocks," said Thomas, pouring another glass of wine.

"On that note," said John, "I think it's time to go and explore."

Gretchen stirred herself. "Sounds good to me," she said collecting the plates from the table.

"Oh crikey, you might find a treasure map and foil the Nazi spies," said Thomas in an enthusiastic child's voice. Then adding in a weary voice, "Don't worry, sis, leave the plates to Cinders."

"If any men call about a shoe, don't try it on," said John, untying the kayaks.

"Well if he is a prince, I may have no choice." Thomas fluttered his eyelashes.

"Are you sure you don't want to join us?" asked Gretchen.

"You're joking," said Thomas waving a copy of *OK*. "I'm going to paint my toes and read my horoscope. You take lover boy here to find the walruses."

Chapter 22 – The Abbey

Gretchen was already in her kayak and paddling in a circle by the time John climbed down the rope ladder and eased himself into his seat with a wince and a grunt. "Old man!" came the cry from the cabin.

"We'll be back in about four hours," shouted John, pulling away from the hull with clean strokes. "And lay off the sauce."

"You kids have fun, ya hear," drawled Thomas, waving a tea towel in one hand and a wine bottle in the other.

The tide was dropping so they barely scraped through the first creek but it was fairly easy going on the whole. The top layer of silt was so yielding that it was only the occasional waft of swamp gas that alerted the pair that they were in fact paddling through ooze.

"Mud, mud, glorious mud," sang John to himself as he slowed and pulled out a map.

"Are we on course?" asked Gretchen.

"I am never sure around here. 'Probably' is the best I can come up with."

Gretchen stopped paddling and looked around, taking in the sound and smells of the marshes. "This is fantastic," she said, "I've not been here before. Tom said it was called the 'Amazon of the East'."

John looked into the distance and then back to the map. "Yes, I think I told him that. Lacking a bit of jungle though."

"I'm guessing it's the sheer diversity of plants and animals."

They continued to drift, soaking in the afternoon sun.

"Tom tells me you climb," said John.

"When I get the chance."

"There are some cliffs further round at Walton, though not very high."

Gretchen shook her head. "They're made of Red Crag."

"I feel honoured that you would assume I know what that is?"

"It's too soft to be rock, lacked the time or pressure to complete the job." She turned to meet the tide.

"I see," said John, "sort of grit with aspirations."

Gretchen smiled, "Great for fossil hunters I bet, I'll certainly go and have a look."

"Ah, into geology are you?"

"All of nature really, but only when I have time; last week I happened to be in South Dorset, so went to check out something called the KT boundary, you know… the meteor strike and the end of the dinosaurs."

Gretchen explained about the layer in the rock sediments, below which are dinosaur fossils, above which are not.

"Oh," said John, "so that's when the Tertiary Age starts?"

Gretchen nodded, pleased that John seemed genuinely to be interested as opposed to merely polite. The tide took them slowly past an island teeming with gulls. The noise was tolerable but prevented further conversation. They made their way northeast, doubling back occasionally when inlets turned out to be dead ends.

"What's that?" asked John pointing to a large white bird.

"Little Egret."

"Never seen one before."

"It's related to the heron," said Gretchen, shading her eyes from the sun as she followed the bird. "The bittern is on its way out, the egret on its way in."

"Is that good or bad?"

"Neither, it's just change, though I'd get grief from the RSPB for saying so."

"You know Tom did a pitch to the RSPB?"

Gretchen looked surprised. "No I didn't."

"It featured a sweet grandmother listening to the dawn chorus and then being chemically sprayed by a farmer; the soundtrack switching from melody to punk rock. Shaun said it couldn't have been more un-subtle had the farmer been sporting a Nazi uniform and insane cackle, though Tom swore he was just following their brief." John thought about his friend back on the boat. "I wonder what your brother's up to."

"Drinking I expect."

"Hmmm," John mused. "Yes fond of his drink. He mentioned you helped him when he was… 'a patient' at The Abbey."

"I don't think I helped him out much. In fact my efforts have become another of his celebrated anecdotes. It must be seven years ago now. I was just finishing my finals and about to fly off to Yosemite."

John had heard the detail but held back from saying so.

Gretchen heaved a sigh. "I was worse than useless, really. I thought most of the patients were being self indulgent, including Tom. I had to sit in the group sessions and listen to the addicts talk about their heroin, their alcohol, their shopping… and how it was affecting them."

"And you were supposed to be in America?"

"Yes, climbing in sunny California. I'm afraid I was not very sympathetic. Then I found out The Abbey were charging five thousand pounds a week. I couldn't contain myself, in the middle of a session I told them all it was pointless and offered to take them, for free, to the top of a mountain but they couldn't come down again until they stopped crying. It didn't go down well."

They drifted in silence.

"You know your outburst gave Tom the strength to leave the next day."

"Yes he did phone. I was already in L.A. having lost half my annual leave but still feeling guilty for abandoning him."

"And the week after that, he was working for me," said John.

"Oh, I didn't realise. Well a happy accident then."

"Yes it would even be appropriate to use the word serend…"

"Peregrine"

"What?"

"Peregrine falcon," said Gretchen, pointing to a high silhouette.

"Oh, so that's what they look like. Bigger than I expected."

They watched the other birds scatter as it dropped quickly in pursuit, rising further along the creek; the chase unsuccessful.

Another movement caught Gretchen's attention. "I think we have company," she whispered.

John slowly lowered the glasses and turned.

Twenty metres to their starboard was a seal, its head visible down to the nostrils which it flared as it filled its lungs. As quietly as it appeared, it sank out of sight.

They cleared a tangle of marsh plants, disturbing three more seals basking on the exposed mud. The seals lifted their upper torsos and slipped into the water.

"Interesting," said Gretchen. "Look at the red staining on the skin, I wonder if it's the Red Cragg leaching into the water; iron oxide or something."

Gretchen's kayak grounded and she used the oar as a punt to push back into the channel.

Greylag geese flew in their direction barking intermittently, changing course as John lifted his yellow paddle. They continued to be pulled along as the basin emptied its contents into the North Sea. The seals followed, persisting in their vigil, grey and black heads continually emerging and submerging.

"I think they are two types, see the different shape of their faces."

"Yes," said John slowly, comparing those that remained visible long enough.

"I'm guessing one would be Grey and one Common."

"You know, popular stuff aside, you do seem to know a lot."

"My father had an enquiring mind," said Gretchen thoughtfully. "He said a few facts were like fixings on a map, you know, that helped you navigate the rest."

"And has it?"

"What?"

"Helped?"

"No," Gretchen said without hesitation, "but I don't have enough facts yet."

At that moment two small heads appeared and Gretchen was relieved to deflect the conversation. "Look pups, better leave them in peace."

"We need to be going, anyway," said John,

"Where are we heading?"

"Well, if it's still deep enough, we'll cut through between New Island and Peewit. There's a small beach on the other side and I guarantee we'll have it to ourselves."

Chapter 23 – The Baker

They reached the cut in five minutes and managed to get three quarters of the way through before running out of water.

"Better not walk on the salt marsh. I once had a slap on the wrist from the nice warden for disturbing the birds so we'll bare-foot along the channel to the beach," John smiled.

Gretchen trod gingerly, wary of cutting her feet, but soon the bog gave way to sand and they were easily able to pull the kayaks through.

"The last time I was on a beach like this was a sandy cay off the Barrier Reef," said Gretchen, washing her feet.

"Tom said you had travelled widely."

"Not as much as some – I couldn't afford a gap year. I started work the day after my exams finished."

"Really, that was very commendable."

"I had a debt to clear – I finished on the Tuesday at four and by Wednesday at nine I was at a desk."

"No parties at all?"

"I doubt if I was missed – I didn't really socialise.

John pulled a twig from the marsh grasses, planted it at the water's edge and joined Gretchen who was already seated.

"My two boys are at college at the moment," he said, "but I doubt if they have once stopped to think about debts."

"You must have had them young."

"Yes, I married Clara at twenty two and the boys were born one and three years after that. Clara was a few years older than me. She had this plan," he said, sitting down next to her, "to marry an Oxford graduate – anyone would do – and then rear the children to go to Oxbridge, thereby joining what she thought of as society. I was still hapless and stunned as her plot was hatched."

"Why did you marry her?" Gretchen asked, raising a bottle of water to her lips.

"I don't know really, she wasn't what you call attractive. She just did all the running, closed all my escape routes and, in the end, I thought it impolite not to."

Gretchen nearly choked on the water she was drinking.

"Ah you find that amusing, I wonder how many marriages get started that way – one has an agenda and the other just acquiesces."

"Sorry, I didn't mean…"

"Its okay, anyway after the boys were born marital relations came to an end, which was a blessing, probably for both of us. Instead, though, we had these ghastly parties. Clara actively pursued the upper classes, even if they were complete grizzlies. I can't tell you how I loathed them. It was a merry-go-round of backbiting and intrigue. If I hadn't realised I was gay and therefore been handed an exeat, Lord knows what I would have done."

"When did you realise you were gay?"

"Off and on through my teens, similar to Tom, but as I was going to a single-sex school I was never sure if it was just the lack of girls. Even after a few years of marriage I wasn't sure because I had a sort of crush on a woman called Sally in a house nearby. Like us, she had two boys but, unlike us, she was so much fun, seemed to do everything contra to Clara's values."

"That must have upset your wife."

"Oh yes. Clara would work her parties specifically around Sally being away. The only fun I had in my marriage was seeing my wife's annoyance when Sally turned up. Clara would try to undermine her but, as Sally laughed hardest at herself, it was impossible to," John chuckled, thinking back. "Clara had this saying when discussing delicate matters, 'What if the baker were to hear?' You could have understood her paranoia if 'the baker' was the code name of a Soviet spy and we were discussing national secrets. But the baker was just the baker, and all that really concerned Clara was just a slip of the façade. Typically, Sally cottoned on to this expression, after which it became the phrase to represent absolute social disgrace."

Gretchen recalled some of her college protocols. "Did your wife catch on?" she asked.

"No, but I would thank God for the breath of fresh air that Sally had brought."

"Why didn't you leave Clara to find a 'sally'?"

"Old fashioned values. I felt that once I had children I was committed until they were at college. So I decided that I would forego the next fifteen years of my life and then leave."

"What happened?"

"Oh, several things at once. Firstly the children went away to boarding school so my father-skills weren't really required. Then I found out that Sally was moving so I would have to face the parties alone. And, thirdly, I found myself 'cottaging'. I confess I'm not proud of it and it wasn't the sex. I just wanted to feel alive. My priest, father Luke, gave me a long list of 'Hail Marys' and that would have been that. But we were under surveillance would you believe?"

"Not the baker!" laughed Gretchen.

"To quote your brother, wouldn't that have been 'delicious'? No, I'm afraid it was just a photographer from the local paper who thought he'd advance his career by waiting inside the bushes and 'outing' all the men visiting the toilets. I pity any poor sod who merely wanted a pee. Working in the industry, I knew it would make great copy for him so decided to tell my nearest and dearest first. Luckily I found support I never realised I'd had. Work practically celebrated it."

"And at home?"

"Oh we could have lived with one more elephant in the room, we had a herd already but…"

"The baker couldn't find out?" said Gretchen knowingly.

"Correct."

"And did he?"

"Well," John replied sheepishly, "in the whole affair, it was my one act of defiance. After receiving a fax from Clara's solicitor, I packed my bags, closed my own door for the last time… and drove to the bakers."

"You didn't! What did he say?"

They both began to giggle.

"Well obviously, the baker hadn't a clue what I was talking about," John said, holding back the laughter, "or why I was telling him. I bought a dozen doughnuts and shook his hand." He laughed openly now, big wholesome guffaws.

Gretchen was laughing too now, enjoying the rapport. "You are funny," she said.

"I know," he gasped, "I don't eat doughnuts!"

Out in the bay five large tankers lined up in solemn convey unaware of the two humans that regarded them, giggling uncontrollably.

John got up and moved the stick a couple of inches further out.

"But at least you were free," observed Gretchen.

"Not quite, for hell hath no fury. Clara spent so lavishly on the boys' education that I have effectively been impoverished for the last fifteen years. However, good cheer is nigh as my last payment ever is due very shortly."

"Hence your resignation from the partnership."

"Partly the reason, you know, it's common for parents of our ilk to celebrate the last education payment, the joke always being that it's down at the soup kitchen. I hope you can join me for my last payment supper."

"What at the soup kitchen?"

"No, I think we should go to Rory's," said John, with an air of release, "and book the whole place for the afternoon." He lay back in the sand and looked up at the early evening sky. "You know, there were several ironies about this saga. My priest, dear old Father Luke, whom I did like, was also caught cottaging. And then, the reporter that shopped us all ended up working for me."

"Oh dear, did you make his life hell?"

"No, unlike my ex-wife, I'm not the vindictive sort. Unfortunately for him, my employers were not so kind. I think he sells cars now."

The latent warmth of the day met the light on-shore breeze and the two adventurers watched herring gulls drift lazily overhead.

"The final irony, though," reflected John, "was that my boys, Edward and George, with the best education money can buy, did not get into Oxbridge. Sally's, on the other hand, who were mostly state-educated, did. I'm proud to say, my boys were okay with it and we all had a great laugh together. Kids are smart – they knew Clara saw them mainly as accessories."

"Are you and your boys close?"

"We are now. I like to think they realise that my love is unconditional. In fact we were all sitting on this spot just last week."

"They are very lucky to have a dad like you."

"Thank you."

"You know, you are the same age my dad was when he died. I remember having chats with him like we've had this afternoon."

John waited for Gretchen to say more but she didn't. He looked at the stick again and noticed its base was covered in water. "Tide's turned," he said getting up.

They began to paddle back into the main channel, the setting sun on their faces, the current and breeze speeding them home.

The paddle back took less than half the time going out but it was still nearly eight o'clock as they silently approached *Bexsy*. Tom's canvass deck shoes protruded above the stern railings.

"Is that snoring I hear?" inquired John.

"Oh dear, I hope he's just tired."

"Hmm," said John, thoughtfully, "tired and emotional."

"I heard that," said a voice from above. "Where have you been? Holland?"

"Sorry," said Gretchen as she sprung up the ladder. "It's amazing wildlife."

"Did you find any treasure or did you just club a walrus?"

Gretchen smiled at John as she leant down and steadied his canoe.

"Sorry we're late Tom, entirely my fault," said John sincerely.

"I hope you guys are hungry," said Thomas.

"Could eat a walrus," replied John.

Chapter 24 – The Gospel according to Versace

A leveret was sitting upright and still in a field adjacent to the creek. Approaching it, Gretchen could see through the binoculars, was a woman whose black Labrador was nose down and on the scent. As they drew closer, the young hare flattened its ears and then itself. Only when the dog had nearly touched its quarry did it accelerate away. The young Labrador gave chase but gave up after only thirty metres or so. Gretchen watched the hare course gracefully to a safe distance but then bounce uncontrollably as it slowed. The hare may have evolved the capacity to run fast she thought, remembering an article somewhere, but it's still struggling with slowing down. Gretchen remembered watching a young springbok being beaten on a turn by a cheetah, the cheetah having a far greater capacity to absorb…

"Grae… Hello, hello," waved Thomas.

"What? Sorry?" said Gretchen.

"You were gone, Grae."

"Was I?"

"Supper?"

"Yes please," said Gretchen, blinking. She looked round at the table. "My God, a roast. How on earth?"

"A little something I rustled up," said Thomas smugly.

"All from a little galley no less," added John.

"Well the kayaking has certainly given me an appetite," said Gretchen. "Must have burned two thousand calories."

"Let's not use the 'C' word at the dinner table please."

"Sorry, Tom. Well cheers once again."

"Cheers again," said John.

"Bon appétit," said Thomas.

"Look at this," said Gretchen in wonder, turning over meats to reveal various trimmings. "Did you have a good afternoon Bro?"

"Fabulous darling, slaved over the dinner obviously…"

"Obviously," repeated Gretchen.

"But also found time to play with some poetry."

"Anything good?" asked Gretchen, sawing a potato in half.

"Hmm, some prospects. I was reading John's sailing terminology…"

"Ah," said John, "hence why the words…" He picked up the *OK* magazine and looked at the cover, "'Spindrift, privateer and extremis' are written on the front. I thought it seemed a little out of context. But then you've written rowlocks, futtocks, spanker and bottomry."

"Well the flow wasn't there, so puerility took over."

"Bottomry? That's not a nautical term!"

"Au contraire Captain Bligh, there you be wrong or call me Mr Christian. Bottomry or *Bottinage* is when a captain offers his ship…"

John waved a Brussels sprout by way of appeasement, "I believe, I believe."

Gretchen cut into a sausage. "Bro," she asked, "what's the story with Andre?"

"What's John been saying?"

"Nothing at all, I assure you," coughed John, trying not to laugh.

Thomas eyed him suspiciously. "Well, what can one say? He is my picture perfect. Admittedly, education rather passed him by. You know," he snorted, suddenly remembering, "my team was doing some work on the Gospels and, guessing that Andre wouldn't know who wrote them, rather cruelly asked him to look up Matthew, Mark, Luke and Bob."

"That was rather cruel," agreed Gretchen.

"Completely backfired though when he asked, 'What are Gospels'?"

John shook his head and looked skyward.

"Still – he answers the phone and adds a certain 'je ne sais quoi'," said Thomas staring at John and daring him to reply. He put a forkful of beef in his mouth, gave a gesture indicating he'd forgotten something and swung back down into the galley.

"Which client wanted to know about the Gospels?" asked Gretchen. "Surely you are not branding Christ?"

"Far too late," said John, that was pretty much done by the fourth century,".

"Bloody hell, sis," Thomas called from the galley, still chewing the beef, "I told you not to mention God!"

John held up his hands, waiting for Gretchen's reaction.

"Don't listen to my brother, please carry on."

"Creep!" shouted Thomas, returning with horseradish.

"Yes please," said John, seeing the bottle. "Have you heard of the Council of Nicaea?"

"No."

"Well it was a sort of a regulatory body set up to decide what *we* believe and what *we* do not. Classic branding. Amongst other things, was the issue of which Gospels to champion and which to suppress. Everything in, *gospel*, everything out, *heresy*. Matthew, Mark, Luke and John were the only four to make it."

"I didn't know there were anymore."

"Oh yes, there was James, Thomas, Philip, at least one Peter, can't remember the rest."

"Why did they just pick four?"

"It just seemed a good number; four corners of the earth and all that. They also roughly corroborated each other. It became a race to suppress the others and to be fair the council did a good job. Only in the last half century have scholars started piecing together... a more rounded story. By then the 'New' Testament was the brand leader."

"What about the Gospels left out, were they wrong?" asked Gretchen, now genuinely interested.

John shrugged. "Different interpretations. If I remember rightly, Thomas forgot to mention God. And there was a Marcion who was an influential writer ..."

"God this is my worst nightmare," interrupted Thomas, "someone who asks too many questions and another that knows all the answers."

Gretchen ignored her brother. "You were saying?"

"Yes, Marcion... thought the disparity between Old and New Testament so great there must be two gods."

"And that didn't go down well?"

"Like a gay kiss in Mecca, I imagine," interrupted Thomas. "By the way, is anyone enjoying the dish I've slaved over?"

"Absolutely," said John, "an incredible achievement."

"Very good, bro, sorry."

"Okay, you may talk again. Cinders is going below again for some Pouilly-Fuissé, which she knows she put somewhere."

Gretchen looked back to John. "Two gods not good?" she whispered.

John thought for a second. "Well, in antiquity there had always been several gods but, I suspect, too much time and energy had been invested in the new notion. And we still kind of have the Devil, which makes two." He pushed a piece of stuffing through the rich gravy. "Tom, I would wager that this *is* the most scrumptious meal ever to be served on this boat."

Gretchen, her mouth full, nodded vigorously. "Umm," she swallowed, "you could be one of those new celebrity cooks."

"Hear, hear," said John, "the show could be called *From the Galley.*"

"And you could be my helper, 'Roger – the Cabin boy'," Thomas's voice rang out from the galley.

Gretchen looked puzzled.

"Children's cartoons," said John, by way of explanation, "before your time. Cheers!" he said, raising his glass again and finishing the last drops. "Are you coming out, Tom?"

"What are you trying to say?" said Thomas, reappearing waving a bottle. "Seek and ye shall find – I assume the ugly sisters want some."

"Yes please," they said in unison, not daring to decline.

"So what do Bentley and Hacket want with the Gospels?" asked Gretchen.

"You may well ask," said John, glancing across at Thomas who was busy with the wine. "We are pitching to an Italian clothing company who are known to be quite provocative, and your brother has come up with the idea of archaeologists discovering yet another set of papyrus scrolls, that is another Gospel which reveals Jesus as a *trendy dude*."

"Not a 'Gospel according to Versace'?"

"Not far off."

"Isn't that blasphemy or something?"

"I agree – it's far too controversial."

"For the demographic we are aiming at," said Thomas, "there is no such thing."

"We are about to go to war in the Gulf, which is already being seen as a crusade and… "

"It's a winner and you know it," interrupted Thomas.

"I'm sure it is. That's why I'm worried."

"Oh please! Pot, kettle, black," cried Thomas. "In your day, you were twice as audacious!"

John sighed but did not reply.

Thomas took a long sip of the white Burgundy and let out a gasp of admiration. "Such a dry, flinty taste!" He turned to his sister. "I told you not to ask him about theology."

Chapter 25 – Numbers

"Thanks for today, you guys," Gretchen said, raising her glass of wine without drinking. "I've really enjoyed it – done and seen a lot."

"Eaten and drank a lot too," said John.

"Talked balls a lot too," reflected Thomas.

"Well one tries," said John, flatly not rising to the bait.

"You will notice, Sis, that John never gets upset. I'm not sure if it's his public school background or his God."

"Both, I'd say," said John.

"Really?" said Gretchen. "Forgive me, but you don't give the impression of being religious."

"I may not believe the religious stories but that doesn't mean I don't believe in God."

"Sorry, I thought they were the same."

John shrugged apologetically. "I don't see it that way."

Gretchen scratched her head, continuing to look puzzled.

John took a deep breath. "It seems to me that man has been trying to fill in the blanks since year dot. The Aborigines believe we came from a rainbow; the Thais, from a milky sea; and a tribe in the Middle East, from dust. My faith happens to derive from the latter. It dawned on me quite early that, if my parents converted before I was born I could be anything and be none the wiser. But this has never diminished my feeling of a constant presence – a presence I know as God."

"Oh," said Gretchen, her tone unsure.

John smiled. "You're not with me on this are you?"

"Not really," replied Gretchen hoping not to sound offensive.

"Okay, the point is this – I don't feel the need for an explanation. I have faith. To me, the more people feel the need to shout about their faith, the more I doubt their conviction."

"Is that how others interpret it?" asked Gretchen.

John thought for a second. "In the age of enlightenment it's difficult to ignore man's fingerprints."

"Right," said Gretchen, "Well I'm not sure that leaves room for debate."

"Should it have to? I think the need to commune is very strong; just because it can't be quantified doesn't mean it doesn't exist."

"Don't worry Sis," said Thomas who was reclining with a cigarette. "I've been round and round with the old sod on this one. The more I put a case together, the serener he becomes. Maddening but at the same time enviable. It's the kind of brand loyalty I spend a lifetime dreaming about."

"Brand loyalty that you can't put a price on," offered John.

"The Vatican does," said Thomas provocatively.

John smiled, affecting serenity. "Do you want to have a go at my school now, or are you okay to conjure up a pudding."

"Who said there is a pudding?"

"If there is no pudding, then I charge you with being an impostor," said John playfully, glad of the diversion.

"Well as you put it so sweetly, I did happen to make a fruit crumble."

"You offer us *ersatz*?"

"There's nothing *ersatz* about my fruit crumble."

"*Ersatz*?" asked Gretchen, wondering if she had heard correctly.

"It means substitute; prisoners of war were given fake coffee – *ersatz* coffee. The word came home with them to a country still in rationing. Fruit crumble was only invented to save on pastry. Isn't that right, Tom?"

"So they say."

"Can you remember rationing, John?" asked Gretchen.

Thomas laughed.

John chuckled. "I was born in fifty nine, rationing stopped by fifty seven so you weren't far out. I certainly remember my parents in raptures at having meat when they wanted."

"I have only ever known plenty."

"Said as if a bad thing?" queried John.

"I don't think my thoughts on energy consumption would go down well at dinner."

"Hear, hear," said Thomas, pouring another glass of wine.

"Tom, how many glasses have you had today?" asked Gretchen.

"Ooh ten, fifteen but who's counting, Miss Goody... Goody."

John winced. Tom's capacity for drinking, though large, was not inexhaustible. Too often he'd seen his friend cross the fine line from virtue to vice. He would have to tread carefully. "No doubt we all consume too much," he offered by way of appeasement.

"Speak for yourself temperance boy." said Thomas. "By the way, who wants custard?"

All hands went up.

"This is excellent, Tom," said John, tucking in. What's the filling?"

"Strawberry and peach. The secret of the crumble is to rub the butter into the flour gently so the texture is like breadcrumbs. What do you think, Grae?"

"Hmm, nice."

Thomas took a deep breath. "Nice!" he repeated sarcastically. He turned to John. "She is such a food philistine. Sometimes, I think I could give her boiled rice and plain fish for ever and she'd be fine."

Gretchen considered the statement. "Throw in some veg and fruit and, yes, I see nothing wrong with that."

"It's boring!" cried Thomas.

"Depends where in the world you're living and what resources..."

"Do you like my fucking crumble or not?"

"I love it, Tom, sorry."

Gretchen finished her bowl, got up and started clearing away. "Who's for coffee?" Only John put his hand up.

After about ten minutes, Gretchen returned with three cups. "I assumed you wanted one, Bro."

Thomas nodded as Gretchen handed them through the hatch.

John had turned the lights on and Thomas sat in the corner flicking through a *Vogue*. Gretchen sat back at the table.

"No moon-shine tonight," said John indicating the lights.

They both looked up to the tiny rim of the waning moon.

"I hear you do a bit of star gazing," said John.

"It's a hobby. The numbers are mind boggling. Do you know there are more stars in the universe than grains of sand on all the beaches in the world?"

"Numbers aren't a hobby," cut in Thomas, looking at his magazine, "they're a form of punishment."

"I never could get my brain around light years," said John. "Do you actually like numbers?"

"Well they are a lot easier than people think."

"I'm not sure the population as a whole would agree. Did it click early for you?"

"No but Dad was a really good teacher."

"I don't recall that," challenged Thomas.

Gretchen was about to respond but John managed to catch her eye, giving a tiny shake of his head.

"Maths," said Gretchen, her brother's comments still needling her, "began for me when 'powers' clicked. I learnt this equation." She scribbled '$x=y(1+r)^n$' on some newspaper. "It was a compounding formula for a savings deposit but I could see how by doing this…" She re-wrote '$\sqrt[n]{x/y} -1 = r$'. "…I could find the interest rate. I would love going shopping with friends and exposing store-card rip offs."

"Oh, was she a bundle of joy to go shopping with," said Thomas sarcastically, "she would take out her calculator and salesmen would tremble."

Gretchen pressed on. "How much interest do you think you would owe if you borrowed thirty thousand pounds at twelve per cent to be paid back in twenty five years?"

"Hell," said John, "I don't know. Sixty or seventy thousand?"

"Nearly half a million," enthused Gretchen. "Imagine that."

"Imagine," echoed Thomas.

Gretchen was quite animated now. "How high do you think a stack of paper would be if you took a single sheet and doubled it fifty times?" Gretchen half waited for a guess from John but continued. "Most guess a few metres but it's actually one hundred and forty *million* kilometres; the same as from here to the sun."

John looked suspiciously at Gretchen, "It just can't be."

"You too!" said Gretchen laughing. "Apparently our minds are programmed to think in proportion not progression; that's why we have to beware of intuition."

"Fancy," said Thomas.

John had his eyes closed trying to see the numbers but then shook his head.

"When you get home try it on a calculator," said Gretchen. "I'll give you a start, after three folds, the paper is about a millimetre thick, just keep doubling another forty seven times."

"Darling Sister, you have no idea how dull that is."

"Maybe," said Gretchen, "but it is true."

"This may come as a shock to you," said Thomas sharply, "but winning arguments does not win friends."

"It's not about winning arguments, it's about getting to the truth... That's what Dad always taught us."

"You maybe – *Daddy* was never there to teach me!"

"That's not fair – he always worked so hard."

"At what?"

"His work – he was trying to provide for us. And he did so much charity work too."

"Ah yes his *charity work*."

"What is that supposed to mean?"

Thomas threw his head back. "Oh, you tell me darling, I thought charity began at home."

Gretchen struggled to answer this. Though fuming inside, she knew her brother had drunk too much and it was best to keep calm. "Well if that's what you think, clearly you didn't know him."

"Ain't that the truth, darling."

Any remaining joy left Gretchen's eyes and she was silent.

John wanted to intervene but he sensed that he couldn't heal the fissure that had just opened up. It was a short, sharp exchange that hinted at long-held hurt at least on Tom's part. Gretchen took the remaining dishes below and went to clean her teeth. By the time she emerged, Thomas was in his cabin and John was laying out the cushions on deck.

"Are you sure you want to sleep up here?" he asked.

"Oh, yes, I love the stars," replied Gretchen. "Sorry about all that," she added.

"Please don't apologise, I've known Tom long enough to focus on his considerable good points."

"Thanks for everything today, John," Gretchen said, leaning forward to kiss him on the cheek.

"Oh," John said, taken aback. "Well, see you in the morning."

"Goodnight."

Chapter 26 – The Stowaway

As John disappeared through the hatchway, Gretchen checked her watch, picked up her mobile and began texting. She then looked at John's local map and started taking notes. Staring through the dark she could just make out from the reflections that the incoming tide had reached the quay. Her phone bleeped an incoming text which she read and made some more notes. After attaching a piece of paper to the wheel, Gretchen began rummaging through her rucksack.

Ghostly figures, navigating by moonlight and accompanied only by the sound of their wing beats, skimmed the water's surface. Gretchen watched the pair of mute swans fly by as she stood naked on the side of the boat. She checked the watertight seal on the bag and gently lowered her rucksack into the water. "Eureka," she said quietly and in honour of an experiment done centuries before, as it bobbed on the surface. She scooped her hair back and wound it into a bun before taking a few deep breaths and slowly lowering herself into the creek. The water temperature had not yet had the benefit of the summer and Gretchen nearly cried out. She stayed still for a minute, letting her nerves acclimatize to the cold. Pushing the bag in front of her, she kicked quietly towards the quay. She controlled her breathing and kept her stroke easy but felt an absolute sense of freedom. The open sky and the stillness combined with the temperature of the water were revitalising and she stopped twice to prolong the feeling.

At the wood-fronted quayside, the buffer tyres provided an easy purchase and Gretchen hauled herself and then the rucksack onto dry land. The stones cut into her bare feet and she sat on the wooden jetty. She quickly dried and dressed taking particular care over her feet and dried each toe carefully, a walker's habit that had served her well.

An outside light came on behind her. "Can I help you?" asked an elderly gentleman, leaning on a stick.

Gretchen, closed her rucksack and, swinging it on to her back, walked up the path to him. "I'm sorry," she said, adding warmly "did I disturb you?"

"My dear thing", replied the gentleman, "for fifty years I've waited for such a vision."

"Well," she said charitably, "I'm pleased that your wait is over."

"I assume you are a stowaway, jumping ship."

"I am," Gretchen replied putting her finger to her lips. "Could you tell me how far the nearest village is?"

The old man pointed and said, "About two miles," adding as an afterthought, "I can take you if you'd like."

"That's kind but I've been on a boat and my legs could do with a stretch." Gretchen looked down the long dark track and then back to the old man. "Well, good bye," she said with a wave.

The man held up his hand but didn't say anything. He blinked, watching the strong, youthful frame stride off. He blinked again, the lighter colour of her jeans still visible and he stood for some time staring at the spot where he had last seen her, his eyes eventually glazing over. Back inside his house he caught sight of the phone and hesitated briefly. "They'd never believe me anyway," he smiled.

Chapter 27 – Jem

John emerged around seven. He always slept well onboard but the previous night's exchange had tested even *Bexsy's* restful magic. He lit the stove and quietly placed the tin kettle on the flame before carefully opening the hatch and climbing on deck. He was met by the sight and sound of thousands of waterfowl and waders exploring the mudflats. A curlew caught his attention, its signature call never ceasing to touch his heart. It was some moments before he realised that Gretchen was not there. He checked back in the cabin and saw her rucksack was also gone. Seeing that the boat's tender was still bobbing at the end of its line, he started to panic. Then he noticed the paper tied to the wheel. It read:

> *Dear John, thanks for a great day. In need of some exercise so have gone to see a man about a mountain. Give my love to Bro when he wakes up.*
>
> G x x

John stared at the note. "Probably for the best," he told himself.

After making his coffee he settled down with his book. He had read the *Riddle of the Sands* before but sitting on deck in the sea breeze gave an added connection to the maritime thriller. It was only as the sun rose above the upper deck and John found himself trying to shade his eyes that he became aware of the passage of time. He glanced at his watch. "Tom, are you moving your carcass yet?"

There was no reply. "Thomas!"

Still no reply.

John swung down into the Galley. "Tom?"

He knocked on the cabin door and entered.

In an instant he took in the scene, the deathly white arm hanging from the bunk, pills scattered on the floor. He was running forward shouting "No, no, no, no, no, no!" He grabbed the arm which was cold to the touch and flung it into the bed. "THOMAS!"

"What, what?" shouted Thomas with a start, then, "OW, my fucking arm!"

"What the fuck! What do mean your fucking arm, what the fuck have you done?"

"What? OW!" wailed Thomas again, cradling his arm.

"What the fuck?" exclaimed John again, seeing more pills in the bed.

"Pins and needles," said Thomas through gritted teeth.

"The pills! What's up with the pills?"

Thomas looked around him and gently laid his arm down with a wince.

"They're even stuck to your skin," said John pulling two blue pills from his back.

Thomas pulled a face of concentration. "Err… I remember taking a couple a sleeping tablets." He looked around him. "Oh, I must have spilled my anti-depressants."

"Are you sure you didn't take any?" John was regaining his composure. "Think!"

"I don't want to think about last night, I know it was grim."

John started collecting the blue pills and returning them to the pot.

"I'll give you fucking pins and needles," said John and left.

It was another half an hour before Thomas emerged on deck looking a little sheepish. He looked around furtively before lighting a cigarette.

"Where's Grae?"

"She's gone." John put his newspaper down with a smack. "You gave me a hell of a scare back there."

"Sorry, but you gave me a hell of a scare too. I thought we were sinking."

"I rang Bunty."

"Oh you didn't! What for?" said Thomas with a whine.

"I wanted to know how many anti-depressants he'd prescribed you so I could calculate if you'd taken any. You're missing nine."

"That's one a day for the week and there were two more in my bed… What did the good doctor say?"

"He called you a cunt. And I agreed."

"Bit strong. I only spilled a bottle of pills."

"He meant it in the general sense and I agreed in the general sense. And your sleeping pill instruction was 'a half tablet – not with alcohol' not two tablets with twenty units; no wonder you slept well." John took a deep breath, pleased to get all that off his chest. "How's your arm?"

"Painful."

"I'll get you a coffee."

Thomas followed his friend into the galley. "Sorry, I was just agitated after last night so thought I'd disappear into the land of nod."

"Well, let's just forget it."

"Yes please," said Thomas, waggling his fingers before clenching and unclenching his fist.

"So where's Grae gone?" asked Thomas.

John passed him the paper.

"'Gone to see a man about a mountain'," read Thomas. "Oh well, saves me apologising." He flopped down into a canvas chair exhaling a long plume of smoke. "Was I a shit last night?"

"I think you were lucky not to be thrown overboard."

Thomas grew defensive, "You have no idea how hard it is to have somebody in the family so… so fucking perfect." He looked at John for some response but none came. "The most annoying thing is that she doesn't seem to realise that it's 'she' who is out of step. She…" Thomas began, his voice loaded with tension, but then changed subject. "Did she say which mountain?"

"No, gone before I was up, though she mentioned a place yesterday."

"Snowdon?"

"No that wasn't it. Somewhere in Skye."

"Christ!" said Thomas, coughing out a lungful of smoke. "She's gone to climb the Cuillins."

"Why, is it difficult?"

Thomas thought. "I vaguely recall Dad saying it was the hardest thing he had done. I even remember going to wave him off… from a car park I think. All a bit of a blur, to be honest. There was swirling mist, a baron moor, not to mention three toothless hags cackling… or was that a *Hammer House of Horror* film?" Thomas shivered, pushed the plunger down in the coffee maker and poured a drink. "Well I suppose Grae had to try sooner or later," he reflected. "That would explain her trips to Wales and the Pandora's Box of a backpack – couldn't get it off her. I told her she'd never get anywhere looking like Quasimodo."

"Aren't you intrigued to know how she got off the boat?" interrupted John.

Thomas sipped his drink and was about to shrug his shoulders but he could see John was genuinely concerned. He narrowed his eyes. "I would say, Watson, that we are dealing with a cunning adversary." He sniffed the air and stepped up onto the deck. "Hmm, well it wasn't the butler."

John watched his friend cast about the deck, inclining his ear to the sound of a distant motorbike and tilt his head to view the mast. Thomas looked at the tender, then across to the small quay and nodded his head. "She swam across last night at high tide."

"How do you know?"

"Previous form," said Thomas. "Very resourceful girl. Wouldn't give that short swim a second thought."

"And her rucksack, Holmes?"

"Hum," replied Thomas. "Fashioned a raft from passing drift wood."

"How would she have got from here to the nearest transport?"

"Elementary. Shanks's Pony. She'd far rather rely on her own legs. I've known her walk twenty miles when the tubes were on strike. Grae's life is one long challenge." Thomas took a long draw on his cigarette and exhaled as he spoke. "She's a nightmare to live with."

John recalled Gretchen's comments about the Abbey patients. "Is that the reason for no permanent boyfriend?" he asked casually.

"Hmm?" murmured Tom, pretending to read.

"You can't deny it, she is a striking girl."

Thomas, put down his paper. "Yes, yes, yes – and you are only the ten thousandth person to tell me. Pursued by many men but it never lasts for all sorts of reasons. One left after a debate about lottery tickets. Apparently Grae used her white board to prove the illogic of playing a lottery then she was surprised when he wrote on the same white board 'ice queen bitch'."

"Cracking physique too," said John, feeling Thomas deserved it.

"Again not that I need reminding for some reason she inherited an arse, suitable for perching on bar stools and I was handed down a derriere, suitable only for *chaise-longues*. Her suitors must feel like… oh who's the bloke that has to complete a series of tasks?"

"Hercules?"

"Was it? I thought it was Sinbad. Anyway – catching wild animals, scaling peaks – must be bloody tiring."

John chuckled at the imagery, pleased to see his friend's sense of humour returning.

"Hmm, glad you find it amusing. Led to some tensions when we were growing up, let me tell you, Johnny Boy. For a start, we both fancied the same guys and obviously they always chose her over me."

John cleared his throat. "Well the odds were – and are still come to think of it – about twenty to one that those guys would be straight," he reasoned.

"Now you sound like Grae. Please don't apply logic to the affairs of the heart, I was just a love-sick puppy." He drained his coffee and began to pace.

* * * * *

In the early evening sun a group of figures stretched and flexed. Thomas had long since decided that, amongst the athletic fraternity, sprinters were singularly aloof and narcissistic. From his vantage point in the discus area, he could see the odd envious glance from the other disciplines. The sprinters had hungrily adopted 'spandex' which, Thomas felt, sculpted their thighs and deliciously enhanced their allure. "I hate my shorts", he had told his perplexed mother, "they are so nineteen sixties."

Thomas prided himself on being able to recognise most of the sprinters from their running style alone. However, that evening, it was an unknown figure who pulled away from the cohort, 'ran the bend' smoothly and effortlessly and flowed into the straight with a cadence later recalled by Thomas as 'ill-measured by time alone'. This vision then accelerated past Thomas who watched until it became a silhouette etched against the sun. The main group of sprinters were stationary now, stooping from the effort as their bodies recouped oxygen. A lone ebony figure walked slowly up the track, his back to the stadium. Thomas felt like a condemned man awaiting sentence without remission. "Oh God help me," he whispered, as the approaching sprinter emerged from shadows. The apparition was more beautiful than Thomas could have believed possible. He suddenly realised he'd been openly staring and looked away.

Thomas got unsteadily to his feet and wandered back to the pavilion. A javelin landed twenty metres to his left. "Look out, twat", someone shouted but he walked on oblivious. The changing rooms were empty and he sat for a while in stupefied silence. But for a shout from his sister he would have missed the bus and he had to scramble to collect his kit together.

"What's up, Tom? You're awfully quiet," asked Gretchen when he dropped down beside her on the top deck.

"Nothing. Just tired," he lied, avoiding eye contact.

"Did you see that new black guy?"

"Uh?" Thomas mumbled awkwardly.

"The sprinter? He's just joined us. He's a first year from Leeds Uni."

Thomas was looking out of the window so she continued. "He transferred from South Africa because of the apartheid thing. His name sounds like Jeremiah but people call him Jem."

"Jem, Jem, Jem," repeated Tom silently.

"Runs a sub twenty two – really impressive. He's good looking too."

* * * * *

"Good looking she said... and Mozart's Requiem was a nice fucking tune." Thomas looked at John for a reaction. "Sorry. I am not normally so, you know..." Thomas searched for the word.

"Honest?" suggested John.

"Maudlin," countered Thomas. "I just hadn't realised it would be so grim. I was expecting an arrow from Cupid not a dagger from Brutus. I know now I got off lightly but you try explaining that to your teenage self." Again John remained silent. "Well anyway, the languor set in, and I wrote some dreadful poetry and that would have been that. Except..." Thomas stubbed out his cigarette, "the following spring, 'the vision' appeared at our house. The inevitable had happened and he had asked Grae out."

John tried to remain impassive but his expression gave away his reaction.

"Yes, 'ouch'," said Thomas. "I can still remember the very moment he appeared; grey polo shirt, mid blue 501s and white Nike trainers to match his teeth. And his eyes..." Thomas breathed in deeply. "Anyway, as you can imagine, the family dynamics were somewhat strained. Since Dad's death, the three of us had sort of become a unit. Suddenly there's this other person in the house. Someone that Grae fancied, that Mum liked. And poor Thomas... well he was, as the song goes, bewitched, bothered and bewildered."

John laid a hand on Thomas's shoulder and gave a squeeze.

"Oh, people get it much worse so I can hardly make a fuss. But then things went really weird."

Thomas started pacing again, eventually settling on the transom.

"I got in to Sheffield Poly, more to get away than to read History. Meanwhile, Grae had been given a conditional place at Cambridge and was studying like a woman possessed. Jem decided it was a prudent time to return home to South Africa. Communications weren't that good back then and Grae didn't really worry that weeks had gone by with no word. Then I got a message from Mum to come home immediately and when I got there she was pale and shaking, clutching an old Telegraph."

Thomas stood and looked out across the marshes. "You know its like the 'where were you when Diana died?' You know the way trauma etches the memory. '18th May 1988 – United Air DC Douglas crashes in Africa killing all'; its all still so vivid. I told Mum it was probably unrelated but there was a pit already forming in my stomach. Reading the article, the pit became a chasm – I realised the date and flight from Bloemfontein to Johannesburg fitted Jem's movements.

"Oh no," moaned John.

"We simply did not know what to do. Later that day we received a phone call back from his cousin in England to confirm the worst. The plane had gone down in a place called Hennenman, a fire on board apparently. No survivors. I tried not to go to pieces but really wasn't much help to Mum – she was wondering how to tell Grae. We didn't really know what her feelings were for Jem but there were all the hellish memories of Dad and the most important exams of her life in ten days."

"What did your mum do?"

"She decided to lie and began a cover up which had to endure for three whole miserable weeks."

"How on earth did you manage?"

"Well I didn't. I went to stay with some friends. Mother, bless her, lied like a trooper and made up excuses to keep Grae away from all the places and people that knew Jem. There were no mobiles back then but Mum had to monitor all phone calls and letters. She replied on Grae's behalf and sent flowers to the grave et cetera. Worse, to head off Grae's occasional concerns, she lied that Jem had rung to wish her luck with her exams. That was a real act of self sacrifice on Mum's part because she could guess the consequence." Thomas shook his head. "And a real act of cowardice on mine for staying away. I did however turn up on the day Grae's exams finished and was there when Mum told her. It was bad, it was very bad. She just turned round and went to her room. While all the other high achievers went out to celebrate the end of their schooling, Grae stayed upstairs with the door locked. Not coming out the next day or the next. Eventually she let me in. I was expecting some kind of self pity but her only words were, "I'll never forgive her."

John winced.

"I pleaded with her that mum had done it for her but she was adamant that she could have handled it. And that's all that was said on the subject. It's possible she had no real feelings for Jem, I really don't know. She seemed to just move on."

"And you?"

Thomas considered the question. "I can't say that I'm upset any more. Time heals and all that. Jem was my *visione amorosa*. You know?"

John frowned. "Not really. Do you mean the old 'rose tinted spectacles'?"

"Hmm. More than that. I mean you choose rose-tinted glasses don't you. You choose to see something in a good light. I didn't get a choice.

John watched his friend struggling to articulate his feelings.

"Imagine," said Thomas, "being hit in the gut – but not knowing where the punch came from – or why. I think we need to make sense of the pain to stop it hurting more deeply. I was too young and confused to work out what was happening to me – stunned even, by the sight of him to ever get the chance to find out his limitations. He just stayed on the pedestal, the poor sod."

John dimly saw what Thomas was driving at, "In *The Great Gatsby*," he began slowly, trying to recall his schooling, "Gatsby saw in Daisy a perfection she neither deserved nor possessed."

"Exactly," agreed Thomas. "Because Gatsby had been hit in the gut. It's possible that Jem could have been just as nutty as Daisy. Now we'll never know."

"Is living with the illusion wrong?" asked John.

"How did it work out for Gatsby?"

"How did it work out for Thomas?"

Thomas slumped in his seat. "Easy as long as there's plenty of alcohol about," he replied, flippantly. "Fuck," he sighed, "I feel like I'm in a confessional."

"Sorry."

"No don't be, it's the first time I've told anyone, anyone who gave a toss that is. And since I'm in a confessional..." Thomas hesitated. "If I am really honest with myself, its guilt, plain old guilt. I felt at some level my feelings had somehow cursed him. It sounds stupid now. At the time I was reading Classics and had come across the story of Apollo – who, of course, happened to be a discus thrower – and his muse, the beautiful Spartan, Hyacinthos. For Thomas the teenager, the parallels were just too uncanny." He gave a huge sigh and forced a laugh. "It just felt like one big Greek tragedy."

John stood up and again touched his friend's shoulder.

Another deep breath. "Don't worry. I did the grief thing eight years ago. You can give me a hug though."

The two embraced.

They stared towards the quayside where some of the inhabitants were staring back. A boat seemed to be heading out in their direction.

"Oops! Seems like we have upset the locals."

"For God's sake, isn't this a private anchorage?" asked Thomas.

"Yes but it might be *straights* only."

"Quick, start talking about tits."

"Eh?"

"I'll tell you what!" exclaimed Thomas loudly in an Essex accent whist simultaneously expanding his chest. "Her tits were the size of…"

"It's okay they are going by."

Thomas gave a wave to the crew of the launch. "Do you think we got away with it?" he whispered through his teeth.

"Difficult to tell. Better be off with the tide."

"Did I look convincing as a *hetter*?" fished Thomas.

"Had I not known, I would have sworn I was sailing with James Bond."

Thomas's expression turned to one of smugness, "Absholutely."

Chapter 28 – Train North

The train slowed suddenly and Gretchen's head jerked forwards. She glanced at her watch and stared out of the window, unseeing, as the scenery of the west-coast mainline blurred by. Then she re-positioned her rolled up fleece against the window and once more closed her eyes.

There were already a couple of climbers on the crag. Gretchen guessed they were in their late teens or early twenties and, judging by the odd word that floated down, were Spanish. They climbed with very little equipment and wore only shorts and headbands to tie back their long hair. Gretchen's father nodded "Hi," to them and they responded in kind.

David surveyed the adjacent pitch. It looked straightforward but, as ever, he still referred to the guide book. While he was doing this, Gretchen watched the Spanish climbers.
"Dad, why do British people look so old fashioned when they climb?"
David laughed. "That's so funny – some of my friends would have a fit if they heard you say it. But I know what you mean. I started in the boy scouts and I've never got out of that 'be prepared' mindset. Look," he said, removing a small bag from which he removed a cagoule and a small bar.
"Kendal Mint Cake!" exclaimed Gretchen.
"Well you never know when you may get caught in a hurricane." He looked at the cloudless sky and they both laughed.
They spent the next few minutes stretching before putting on their climbing shoes and harnesses. Gretchen carefully fed the rope through her hands into a tangle free pile and tied the lower end to her harness with a figure of eight knot.
"How much do you weigh now?" asked David.
"Forty six kilos at my last judo match."
"Better find you an anchor then. I don't think you'll hold my seventy eight."
He ran a sling around the trunk of a small tree, gave it a tug and clipped it to the back of her harness. Gretchen ran a length of rope through her belay plate while her father tied himself to the end with a bowline. David rechecked the knots, the chin straps and harnesses and put his bag out of the way. "Okay, I'll go up to the second bolt, jump off and see if you can hold me. When I get to the top, I'll belay you up and we'll both abseil down. You all set to climb?"
"I am."
"Well in that case, 'climbing'," said David as he placed his foot on a fault in the rock at knee height, found a solid purchase and began.

Gretchen watched closely as he made the first few moves, stop, remove a quick-draw from his belt and clip the karabiner onto the first bolt. She then took in the slack, playing out as needed.

"Tight," he called after clipping on the second bolt now about six metres above.

Gretchen took in another tiny amount of slack.

David leant back off the wall and Gretchen giggled as she started to rise but was then held firm by the tree.

"Okay?" said David, looking back at his daughter.

"Nohey problema," she said, grinning from beneath her oversized helmet and nodding towards the climbers next door.

David grinned back. "Climbing now," he said, accentuating his northern twang.

Gretchen watched her father progress easily up the slab of limestone. This was her first expedition alone with him and she thrilled at been given the responsibility, mentally ticking off all the safety procedures while at the same time trying to take it all in.

Now at twenty-two metres David clipped onto the main hawser and shouted, "Off belay." He then pulled the rope through his plate until he heard Gretchen shout back, "That's me!"

Gretchen felt a thrill as she touched the hot rock. She had memorised her father's route but she could see now why he'd warned her not to try to follow in his footsteps. Her lack of height meant having to work the pitch her own way. Starting was harder than she had anticipated but she knew that her dad wouldn't be impressed by climbing without thinking, economy of effort was key. The texture of the rock-face resembled a beginner's attempt at cake icing and the shards bit into Gretchen's fingers.

Once under way, she was pleased to find that she made short work of the first three quarters and carefully collected the quick-draws as she went. Stopping on a narrow ledge, she shook her hands out and looked up to her dad. "This is great," she beamed.

"It certainly is," he replied returning her smile, taking obvious pleasure in her achievement.

The last few moves proved slightly harder. Her foothold had given way once or twice as she'd tried to gain purchase against limestone, overly polished by previous climbers. Her fingers had taken all the weight and rather than start again she had briefly hung by one hand as she unclipped the karabiner. Cursing herself for rushing, she made sure of her foothold, turned her legs outwards and crouched to regain her breath. "Slow," she told herself and, standing again, she mentally mapped the last few holds. Soon she was standing with her dad, clipped into the top bolt.

"*Do you want me to shout, 'off belay?'*" she asked standing eye to eye with him.

"*You, young lady, are a cheeky monkey,*" said David fumbling in his pocket and taking out his camera. He held it pointing back towards them, at arm's length, as they huddled together. "*There, that will be one for the album. What's the chance of getting Tom and your mum up here?*"

"*To Spain? Good,*" Gretchen thought. "*Up here? Not so good.*"

"*What do you think they would like to do?*"

"*Well Tom likes the town and music.*"

"*And your mum likes reading. It's been too long since we all went somewhere together.*"

"*What about Chamonix again?*" asked Gretchen.

From his pack David produced two small cartons and handed one to his daughter. "I don't think your brother was too impressed. Hmm, I'll give it some thought." Together they stood in the sun, leaning off a vertical face and drinking the juice.

"*It doesn't get much better than this,*" said David, squeezing his daughter's arm. "*Okay to abseil down?*"

"*Just another minute.*"

"*Sure.*"

"Tickets please!" a voice boomed down the carriage and Gretchen unrolled her fleece and pulled out the card. When the collector reached her, she asked their whereabouts.

"We'll be arriving in Preston shortly. Gateway to the North!" he added turning to the next passenger.

Gretchen yawned, sat up and got out her Ipaq. It turned on with a bleep and she selected File/Travels/Climbs/New. Like her dad, Gretchen had been keeping notes on the places she had visited. From her pocket she pulled out crumpled Post-It notes that she had scribbled on over the last few days and thought back as she re-read them.

After her visit to Anne Darwin's grave, Gretchen had wandered around Malvern. Unusually for her, she'd even sat in a little coffee shop enjoying a hot drink, still wondering about the revelation in the churchyard. Analytical as ever, she'd misunderstood her father's impulse and needed a complete stranger to show her what should have been obvious.

From there, she had driven onto Snowdonia to practise some more scrambling and increase her fitness. She had arrived at the campsite in the late afternoon and after going over her maps, had visited a couple of acquaintances down at Plas y Brenin to get the next day's weather forecast. It had been 'good with a rain band mid morning lasting up to an hour'. Gretchen had climbed over Tryfan and up Bristly Ridge by the time the rain had come through where she'd sat the squall out in her bothy bag. Her aim had been to get through seven peaks in seven hours which would give her time to get back to London and re-pack for the trip to John's boat on Thursday.

She tapped away at the Ipaq transferring routes, times and observations from her notes. Wednesday's notes were done as the train pulled into Preston. She poured out a cup of tea from her flask and watched passengers getting on and off struggling with cases, hugging and waving. She was reminded of her brother's game, *people watching* in which he tried to interpret the human dramas. An older man wearing glasses and a dark leather jacket sat outside the station café reading. She wondered if he looked lonely or content.

The train was soon speeding through farming landscape, the ground rising on the east up to The Dales, smaller than the Welsh Peaks but vaguely familiar from childhood holidays. Gretchen returned her thoughts to yesterday. Could her kayak trip with John and argument with Thomas really been just yesterday? The week had hurtled by in a grim echo of this train's progress north. She headed the file 'Backwaters (Walton) – 29/05/03', and read through her remaining paper notes. As usual, the entry began with the facts and figures she had gleaned, putting an asterisk next to those that needed checking, before listing observed species.

She then began a couple of sentences describing the exploration with John but stopped midway, her gaze drifting. Despite her brother's behaviour it had been an enjoyable day and she mulled it all over. Tom had found a good match in John. He shared her brother's interest in history, understood his job, and had a demeanour that would complement Tom's. As long as John was forgiving and Tom reasonably discreet, she reasoned, they could really make a go of things.

But then Gretchen had her own reasons to hope for a more permanent union; for the first time in ages, she felt that she would have a friend to talk openly with, someone who seemed worldly-wise and where sex would never intrude. She recalled ruefully her past friends or more pertinently, the lack of them. Her life seemed to follow a recurring pattern when it came to friendships. At junior school her sporting friends had been lost when she'd gone to the Grammar. There she had kept her head down and worked hard. In hindsight she could see that because of this, she had received a degree of unwanted bitchiness from a group of girls. Her indifference to their jibes only served to aggravate them further. The threat of actual bullying, however, receded after it became known that she had broken the shoulder of an older boy who'd attacked her brother. Her one remaining friend from junior school had eventually sided with the bitchy girls and, from the vantage of the library window, Gretchen would watch her smoking with them.

In her 'A' level year, Gretchen had joined the school debating society and initially had enjoyed the company but it hadn't worked out; as ever, there were games of group politics that she neither understood nor enjoyed. Choosing her own path was again interpreted as a criticism of theirs. An athletic boyfriend and a place at Cambridge seemed to increase her alienation and she cut a lone figure on the running track and studying in the library. She didn't know how the death of her boyfriend was reccived as she immediately left to pursue the adventures of her dad's journal.

At university she made some friends in the climbing club and, on her brother's advice, she had even dumbed down her ability. Unfortunately a boy had been persistent in his advances, which she could've handled, except his girlfriend was the president of the club. It was just simpler to leave.

Gretchen rubbed her temples and finished inputting the names of the Backwater wildlife. The train was passing Morecambe Bay now and heading up into The Lakes; a place she knew well having caught many deer in the area. The Deer Trust, she reflected, was a source of genuine friendship, somewhere she felt comfortable. She scrolled through her Ipaq and re-read the entry of the 23rd, 'Deer catch at Lulworth', wondering if those soldiers could possibly give a thought for conservation when they were about to fight a war. Then she began to chuckle, thinking of Sergeant Beckett sitting on Private Smith and of the Corporal being repeatedly kicked in the testicles. Her mirth subsided, replaced by a wave of tiredness. She rolled up her fleece and went back to sleep.

Chapter 29 – Port

"More provisions?" said John above the drone of *Bexsy*'s engines. "We've only been gone twenty four hours."

"Don't be difficult, you said we were going out passing the marina."

"Yes but 'passing' in a boat is not like 'passing' in a car. It will be an hour detour."

"So what's the hurry? We'll get to where we are going an hour later."

John continued to protest but Thomas cut him off.

"I'll make another pudding for you."

"I submit," said John.

"Ah, crumbled at the prospect of my crumble."

John knew when he was beaten and steered *Bexsy* towards the inland channel.

It was some time before Thomas returned with two more carrier bags.

"You're back, thank God. I was about to send up a distress flair, 'man lost in shops'."

"Sorry, intercourse with locals. Simply too much fun to hurry."

They left Hamford Marina, heading out into the bay and this time turned east.

"Goodness, that's a big lake," said Thomas, staring at the North Sea.

"Well, remember you said you wanted to take part in the next D-Day commemorations off the French coast."

"Would this be the commemoration where we drive to Calais and hire a Gin Palace in a sheltered harbour?"

"No – this would be the commemoration where you and I have to sail *Bexsy* to France irrespective of the weather."

"Ah."

"Well before we embark upon such a venture, I think we should test your sea legs."

Thomas looked down and watched his knees wobbling.

"Oh come on, it's a glorious day," said John, "you'll love it."

"Well I'm not wearing those waterproof trousers; they make my bum look big."

"You don't have to wear them, but I'd wear a spray jacket."

"And what colour is that?"

"Yellow."

"Do you have anything else?"

"No."

Thomas pulled a childish expression. "And no shouting at me."

John smiled. "Promise. Now hold the wheel and keep *Bexsy* pointing into the wind – that's away from the shore. I'll raise the sails."

In no time, they were sailing out against an onshore breeze, *Bexsy* needing much work from John to tack against the wind. The old lifeboat had been designed for stability, not speed, and the large brown main and foresails muscled the mast, which groaned under the stress of dragging the hull through the water. Thomas watched the bow wave as the rounded hull met the incoming tide. Occasionally, from the windward side, two white crests would meet and send spray from bow to stern. Thomas had put his hood up but having caught his reflection in the chrome plate decided wet hair was more swashbuckling. "Such was the wreck of the Hesperus," he sang, "being protected from the spray, Christ save us all from fashion like this, in Walton on the Naze."

There were numerous boats off the coast, their crews enjoying the sunshine and clean winds. Though John had struggled to maintain the formality of being the helmsman, Thomas had somewhat surprisingly proved a good deck hand as well as being great fun. Only once had it nearly ended in disaster. They'd been 'close hauled' on a port tack for ten minutes, the spray almost continuous as *Bexsy* lumbered through the swell. John had eventually backed off a little onto a reach, calming the situation.

"What are we doing now?" Thomas shouted above the wind.

"Close reach."

"Still on port?"

John nodded.

"Have an idea!" Thomas said aloud. "Just going below."

"Don't be long!" John shouted back.

Suddenly John heard a voice bellow "Starboard!" and, looking underneath the mainsail, could see another boat on a collision course.

"Where the hell did he come from? Tom!" John shouted, "Ready about!"

Thomas ambled out of the galley, two glasses in hand, surprised to find no one at the helm and John wrestling with a rope. The approaching boat had ultimately given way with a great deal of cursing from the helmsman.

"What was all that about?" inquired Thomas, sipping his port and watching the wheel, which was rolling aimlessly.

"Oh," replied John, looking flustered but trying to stay civil, "we just went the equivalent of the wrong way round a roundabout and the other people had to give way to us."

"Well no harm done," observed Tom, handing John a schooner of port, "it's a big road."

Despite the foresail flapping madly, John took the glass, first checking for nearby craft before taking a sip. "Tom," he said, "you don't have to tie the ropes when you go below, the cleats are… Christ what now?"

Bexsy was grinding noisily to a halt and John fell backwards spilling his drink.

Thomas, managing to stay upright and hang on to his drink, looked over the side and was surprised to see sand. Then he looked back to the coast nearly a mile away. "Whoever heard of a beach in the middle of an ocean?"

"Fuck!" cried John grabbing for the engine controls. "It's like sailing in an Ealing comedy. I thought you were watching the depth gauge?"

"Oops, I thought you said depth charge – I was watching for submarines."

Luckily the damage was limited to a bruised coccyx with the engines able to quickly reverse the situation.

They spent the next few hours going in large circles as John went through the basics.

Thomas was a fast learner if, by the end of the day, a rebellious one. "Prepare to jibe!" he shouted at the top of his voice.

"What?" asked John, looking at the wind direction.

"Rhyming slang", replied Thomas, peeing over the side.

It was early evening as they entered the mouth of the River Orwell and John allowed his friend to take the helm while he dropped the sails.

"I have the bridge, Number One," announced Thomas, taking the wheel in one hand and the throttle in the other. "Star date, two thousand and three. The Klingons are defeated and we have all retired for tea and scones. Mr Chekhov!"

There was no reply

"Mr Chekhov!!" Thomas repeated louder.

"Yes," said John in a weary tone.

"Stop writing those Russian plays and set the phasers to stun."

"Very drole. Do your Sean Connery."

"Gentlemen," said Thomas, standing proud and projecting his voice to a watching heron, "tonight we shail into hishtory."

"Very good," said John, swinging down from the deck. "If dinner is as good as your impressions, I'm in for another treat. Do you want to make a start while I sort out top side?"

"Take her in Number One," said Thomas, relinquishing the wheel, "I musht shay, I've had an exshellent day."

"Aye aye, captain," replied John smartly and then under his breath, "and I've had the best day of my life."

* * * * *

Later on that evening, Thomas sent Gretchen a text message.

> Hope all well with u.
> At a place called Pin Mill.
> Havng gr8 time discusng Dunkirk over apple and bramble crumble.
> Where r u?
> T XXX

A few minutes later, Thomas's phone buzzed. He picked it up and read:

In Fort William B & B.
Was asleep but now not.
Glad u r havng a gr8 time.
XXX 2 u both.
G

Chapter 30 – The Facts

At 07:15 John wandered up onto deck to find Thomas already there, in dressing gown and with empty mug. "My God," he said.

"Yes I know. *Me*, up before the larks."

"Do you want another cup?" He indicated the empty one on Tom's lap.

"Yes please, darling: coffee, two spoonfuls of cocoa, milk and a Sweetex."

John did as asked and returned with a drink that had the colour and texture of mud. His frown didn't go unnoticed.

"It's a Mocha, well a low fat version – got to look after one's figure."

John giggled.

"What?"

"I'm sure your sister would approve." John sat down with his plain tea. "I meant to ask, Fort William, what's it like?"

"Oh lord, only been there once. From the dimmest of memory, it's an outpost on the very fringe of civilisation – beyond that only fur trappers and Indians and beyond that, one simply drops off the edge of the world."

"No lemons then?"

"No – just the very wildest of haggis."

John looked across at Thomas whose pen hovered over a notepad. Thomas caught his friend's stare and winked.

"What made you beat the larks?" asked John.

"Well, as you can imagine, I have work of national importance but I have been constantly distracted by some of these other boaters. First there was a man in a barbaric cardigan and then a woman cleaned her teeth on deck while gargling. Sounded like the finale to Starlight Express. If this is a display of what happens when people leave the town, bring on Big Brother."

"So… grumpy because?"

"Grumpy?" said Thomas, casting his eyes around the boat and then the river. "Grumpy because I have nowt to be grumpy about."

"I see. What were you working on?"

"Oh," said Thomas, glancing at his notepad, "you've probably forgotten, but we are interviewing next week. We have whittled down – what a glorious expression – the list of applicants from any number of hopefuls and some scrummy possibles, down to five probables. Shaun asked me to do a morning's induction of some kind. So I thought I'd do a quiz."

"I can see you as a Quizmaster."

"Me too, a sort of Jeremy Paxman in classic attire."

"I was thinking more of a Richard Whitley but carry on."

Thomas clasped his chest and looked pained. "You know how to hurt a man. But as I was saying, a quiz to help stimulate creative discussion."

"Give me a 'for example'."

"Well I thought we'd start with the old chestnut about the Royal family's name change."

"Remind me," asked John directly.

"Not until you drop that 'Director of the Company' manner, Mr Freelance."

"Sorry, I keep forgetting my place. *Please* remind me."

"That's better," said Thomas, referring to his notes. "So, 1917, George the Fifth drops the *family* name 'Wettin' and the *'House of'* name 'Saxcoburg Von Gluckon', changing them both to what?"

"Windsor," replied John. "What would that be a discussion on?"

"Re-branding."

"Ah yes, I like it."

"Good," said Thomas, putting a tick on his notepad. "Next, why was Neil Armstrong the first man on the moon's surface?"

"Hmm," thought John, "I would say because he was the most competent but you're going to tell me that's wrong."

"That would be wrong. This iconic hero was chosen because he was the most expendable – the other two being vital for getting the rocket-ship home safely."

"Which they did."

"Which they did. The story put about after the fact was that big Neil was picked for having 'the right stuff', when really he was picked for not having the right stuff. I thought that was a good intro into 'spin'."

John nodded. "That could go in numerous directions, what else have you got?"

"I was going to use a prop. A couple of weeks ago I was drinking at *Tapps* and noticed, high on their shelves, a dusty old bottle of Vin Mariani."

"What's that?"

"Aha! That's just what the staff there said. It's a mix of wine and cocaine, banned in the 1920s. The interesting point for discussion though is that Vin Mariani was the first ad campaign to really harness celebrity endorsement: Jules Verne, Sarah Bernhardt, Alexandre Dumas… even a Pope."

"I'm amazed."

"The facts I know eh."

"What else?"

"I was thinking about something you told me from the flood story – about Noah getting drunk and naked – the discussion would centre on the use of judicious editing."

John rubbed his chin. "Now I know you don't take advice from me but if you don't know the candidates very well I would avoid any Abrahamic references; could be awkward. Be safer on… oh er… the occult."

"Okay," said Thomas, his pen poised.

"How about… The Fox sisters of New York," said John deliberating as he was speaking, "devised and carried out a hoax, which forty years later they owned up to. Despite the admission, which religion grew from it?"

"I've no idea," said Thomas.

"Spiritualism! And it continues to grow! That's like finding St Paul's diary with an entry saying 'I didn't actually see him'."

"That'll do," said Thomas scribbling furiously. He looked up. "And I thought I'd finish with Grae's calculation of doubling a millimetre forty seven times, taking you to the sun."

"Because?"

"Well – and I can't believe I'm stealing one of my little sister's toys – but she's hit on something that needs a leap of imagination."

"I haven's checked your sister's figures, you know."

"No need to. I have never known her wrong on figures, more's the pity."

"Well, my boy, that should keep you going for a couple of hours."

"Don't say 'my boy', makes it sound like we have an improper relationship. You're only seven years older than me and a lot fitter."

John hesitated, thinking Thomas's remark a little too defensive and wondering what had prompted it. Finding the answer, he judged, would have to wait.

"Sorry, *my man*," said John. "Do you want me to join you and the interviewees for lunch?"

"Why not, we'll go to Rory's and you can let slip my genius."

"And your modesty."

"I think it was you who once said that, in advertising, 'humility sucks'."

John shook his head and heaved a sigh. "Guilty as charged," he admitted, realising that he wasn't the only one who stored words.

Chapter 31 – Sandy

Sandy walked into the lobby of the Neist Inn and turned right. Though the room was narrow, it was bright and fresh sea air helped allay the usual scent of tobacco and food. Behind the bar, the shelves were neatly lined with bottles of whisky and, at the end of the bar, a large man with a greying beard was holding a glass up to the light.

"Morn'n Donald," he said, to the barman.

"Alright, Sandy."

"Aye, morn'n, gentlemen." Sandy addressed a group of men of various ages standing at the bar. They gave a collective cheer, a little louder than normal and accompanied by a few winks. Perplexed, Sandy scanned the room, seeing numerous people and turned back to the barman.

"Donald, I'm supposed to meet a women here, I'm guessing thirty-ish?"

"Ah, I knew what they said about you wasn't true."

Sandy looked back to the regulars and raised his eyes.

"She is waiting for ye in yon corner and," he leant forward lowering his voice, "she's a right cracker."

"Donald, you boys have been here so long, any woman is 'a right cracker'."

"Aye and not just the women!"

Sandy raised his hand to Donald as if to concede any further point and walked off up the room. As he approached the woman at the window table, he could see she was reading a climbing magazine.

"Hi, you must be Gretchen."

"And you must be Sandy," she replied shaking his hand.

"Glad you found us. I see you have a drink."

"Yes, thank you. You're rather hidden away here."

"Aye, for good and bad." Sandy sat down on the adjacent bench. "How did you get up here?" he asked.

"Oh the usual – boat, swam, taxi, five trains and a hire car."

"Well I did ask," said Sandy, not pursuing the answer. "Anyway, you'll be pleased to know that the weather for the next two days looks favourable."

"Yes I've been texting the local weather station. There's a couple of fronts coming through."

Sandy nodded. "They may clip us but us but it's definitely worth a go."

There was an outbreak of laughter from the bar and the two glanced over to see two smaller men trying to arm-wrestle the larger one.

"Is this your first crack at the Cuillin ridge?" asked Sandy, ignoring the disturbance.

Gretchen looked back to Sandy. "It is."

Sandy seemed hesitant. "And you're sure you want to attempt both the Black and Red Cuillin in one go."

"Yes, the *Greater Traverse*."

"Okay," said Sandy, "but before we go any further, can I ask about your fitness?"

"Sure," said Gretchen, pleased with his directness. Had he not asked the question she would have worried. And there was also a twinge of pride knowing that she could demonstrate her commitment. She described her regime.

"And your climbing experience?"

"Since I was a child – all over Britain, a little in Europe and further if I get the chance."

"There's nothing too technical on the ridge," said Sandy, "It's more the exposure. You okay with HVS and a lot of vertical exposure?"

Gretchen nodded.

"And okay to bivvy up there?"

"That would be no problem."

Sandy gauged her reaction carefully and smiled. "I get the impression, Gretchen, that you are way above the minimum standard. When was your last trip?"

"Wales last week," replied Gretchen, "Tryfan, to Snowden and around the horseshoe."

"Okay, that's plenty, much more than me, you'll probably be leading me."

"Really? I thought you'd be constantly at it."

"I do enough but I'm not in the best shape of my life. I'm going to grab a drink, can I get you another?" asked Sandy, getting up.

"Thank you, soda water and lime."

Sandy walked off leaving Gretchen wondering what he meant by "I do enough".

She hoped he was up to this and looked him over as he queued at the bar, trying to asses if he was 'in shape'. She could see that he had good posture as he stood at ease with the other drinkers. He was probably just under six foot with a wiry frame though his shoulders seemed noticeably broader than of those surrounding him. Through his light Gortex-top she noticed his left arm was permanently bent at the elbow around thirty degrees and also that a feint but wide scar rose from his neckline to behind his right ear.

"You," said Sandy, returning with the drinks, "are what we call 'a cheap date'."

"That's just what my brother says. What's that in your mug?"

"Mint tea."

"Oh, I wouldn't want to stereotype, but it's not the kind of drink I assumed a Scottish pub would carry."

Sandy grinned. "You wouldn't believe the grief I get from the locals."

Gretchen looked over at the men at the bar. "I'm sure I can."

"It's too early for alcohol and I have just drunk so much 'builder's tea' over the years."

"Addicted?" enquired Gretchen playfully.

"It was either this or rehab." replied Sandy in kind. "May I ask what motivated you to climb here, more specifically, to attempt the Greater Traverse?"

Gretchen hesitated. Sandy could see she was uncomfortable but given the danger that would bind them, felt that he was entitled to know a little more.

"Apart from it being the finest mountaineering in Britain?" she replied, hoping he would accept the question as an answer.

Sandy waited.

"I came here with my family when I was eight. My father climbed the ridge then... he died a few years later. Do you want more?"

Sandy regarded her a moment longer. "No, thank you. One last question, how did you get my name?"

"All the official guides had been booked."

"Oh, right," said Sandy, smiling to himself. "Well as I said on the phone, I've traversed the ridge many times with friends but I'm not an official guide. At the end I will be asking a contribution to charity of eight hundred pounds, which includes a couple of days board at my place, though if you want to stay here at the Neist that can be arranged."

"No, that's fine, thanks. How far are you away from here?"

"You passed it, back along the road about half a mile next to a phone box."

"Great, we have a deal," said Gretchen, raising her glass.

"We do," replied Sandy, raising his mug. "I suggest we take your stuff back to the croft and go through the operation. I assume you have many questions. Then you can get some rest and RV back here for some food, say 18:30?"

"Sounds good to me," said Gretchen, as she slipped the climbing magazine and her grey notebook back into her bag.

Chapter 32 – A Long Hot Bath

"Who are you texting?" asked John, looking up from his book.

"Grae," replied Thomas, pressing 'Send' again, "but not getting a reply. She has obviously left Fort William so is at this moment probably fighting savages."

"Or there's no signal?"

"Yes, all civilised messages sucked into oblivion. A tartan hole in the space-time continuum."

John looked at him.

"I've read science."

John raised an eyebrow.

"Though I might have seen it on Doctor Who. Anyway, you sceptic, what you don't know is I'm involved with this new range of hair colourings for mature people, the campaign being *science* based." Thomas's tone became deep and husky. "Welcome to Quantum World, where the laws of aging break down."

John nodded. "Sounds reasonable."

"I thank you," said Thomas, pressing 'Send' again.

"She could just have turned her phone off."

"True. She doesn't really need a social diary."

"Yes, you've alluded to this before. Having met her I'm astonished at her lack of friends. She has a lot of presence."

"Yes, alright, alright." Thomas took a deep breath. "She does have acquaintances but not the sort that gossip on the phone; they tend to be old or boffins. Having said that, she's very secretive – maybe she actually goes boozing with that evolutionary bloke Richard Dawkins and who could blame her – such a nice bottom."

"Dawkins or your sister?"

"Well you're just being mischievous now and that, as you well know, is my role."

"Sorry."

Thomas continued to consider the question. "I think if the option was either, her own company or those of us with feet of clay, it'll always be the former."

"She must have had friends at school," said John.

"Sort of. Grae used to meet with this real nerdy group that debated things but even then she would go her own way. I remember they entered a competition, the motion being something to do with fox hunting. The group decided to take an 'anti' position which Grae disagreed with."

"Why, did she hunt?"

"No not at all, but she'd done her own research and rather than go along with the few friends she had, she decided to enter the competition as an independent."

"At sixteen, what happened?"

"She won."

"No!"

"Yep, she had 'unearthed' – ha ha – this information that cats killed seventy odd million animals, or was it birds, a year next to – oh I can't recall how many foxes were killed by hunting, err a few thousand was it?" said Thomas, scratching his head. "Anyway her closing argument was something like 'every cat owner was far more cruel and injurious to nature than those who hunted and if you banned fox hunting, you would have to ban cat ownership'."

"Ouch!"

"Yes, it was a pyrrhic victory though. For she lost her only group of friends and after the newspaper account was printed, gained the scorn of every cat owner in the district."

"Don't tell me, 'Schoolgirl Calls for Cat Ownership Ban'."

"Something like that. Mum, after getting grief from the locals, told Sis to 'in future keep her opinions to herself'. I used to think Grae would be fine when she left our small town, but really London is not much different. I am assuming that her inability to tow the line is the reason she was sacked last week. By the way I have made subtle enquiries about all that but I've yet to hear back."

Thomas's phone buzzed.

"Ah, she lives," said Thomas, squinting at the screen. "On the Waternish Peninsula, Isle of Skye."

"And not a lemon in sight?" suggested John.

Thomas shivered.

"Anyway, Tom, I'm going for a long walk."

"Going to do your Jesus thing are you," said Thomas, looking at the surrounding water.

"Not feeling pious enough I'm afraid. I'd better take the kayak to shore. Do you want to join me?"

"No I exercised enough yesterday splicing the main brace. I'm going to take a long, hot bath. Oh no, wait I can't – we only have a bucket."

Chapter 33 – Lochbay

Gretchen followed Sandy's small blue van along the bay road, pulling off onto an unmade lay-by. She stepped out of her own hire car and looked down at a small tin-roofed byre.

"It's the croft you'll be staying in," Sandy called as he pulled a large orange Bergen from the van's rear doors.

"I was just thinking, the shed looked rather cosy, I've stayed in places far less welcoming."

The valley-slope stretched several hundred metres down to the shoreline and roughly the same distance above them to the hill crest. The road maintained this middle course all the way back down to the small harbour. The whitewashed dwellings were cut into the hillside at irregular intervals, their roofs a mix of tin, slate and thatch. The only unifying feature was that none were tall. The majority of the area was enclosed with barbed wire, though many of the posts were now rotten and the sheep wandered at will, blissfully unaware of title deeds. They grazed in between the tussock grasses, the carefully tendered pasture belonging to more profitable days. All the properties faced the bay which, as Gretchen took in the scenery, reflected the cloudless sky. Only a few trees had attempted to brave this Hebridean domain and had suffered the consequences. The stiff westerly winds had curtailed their growth, the tops bent over to leeward as if meeting some glass ceiling. "I see you get the odd gale," said Gretchen indicating the peculiar sight.

"Aye, it has a long run up across the Atlantic."

It was calm now as Gretchen scanned the rocky recess of the inlet and then the small group of islands that stood like sentinels at the mouth of the bay. "What a great view," she said.

"I think so. When I'm here, I try not to let a day go by without soaking it up. I even love it when it's lashing down with rain, especially when I'm in the conservatory with a brew. Actually rain is due in a couple of hours so you may see what I mean. Let's get the kettle on."

Sandy's croft was low-ceilinged, causing him to stoop in the doorways. It was whitewashed inside as well as out, though most of the walls were covered with photographs and pictures, creating a mosaic of gloss against the matt render. Even in the dim light, Gretchen could see that the furnishings were mainly leftovers from the 1960s.

"I'm afraid the slight odour is 'damp', but don't worry, the last person that died of pleurisy was months ago."

She smiled at Sandy's concern about how she might percieve his modest home. She hadn't noticed at all; what really attracted her attention were the photographs.

"Are these all of Skye?"

"Mostly."

"Wow, these are really good," said Gretchen. She looked systematically through the pictures. "Are these all your work?"

"Yes, they are," he said, taking obvious pleasure in her interest.

"I'm no expert but I can see these are not Happy Snaps."

"Thank you. Though it's difficult not to get good shots here," said Sandy modestly. "I must admit that I've occasionally camped out waiting for the right light. Are you a photographer?"

"Yes – well I have a good camera but I'm not sure that makes me a photographer. I've certainly not taken anything as good as these. And I've been to some pretty photogenic places. Oh," she said suddenly, pointing to one, "I've been here, when I was eight or nine. It's The Table."

"It is, up in the Quiraing. There's a better one here," he said pointing to a view of the unmistakeable green-baized feature.

Sandy talked about a few more of his favourite shots, explaining his efforts and admitting to the happy accidents that occasionally put him in the right place at the right time. "Anyway, it keeps me out of mischief," he said, seeing her glance at the clock. "Shall we look at the maps for tomorrow and talk through the plan."

For the next two hours they sat at the kitchen table, Sandy explaining the route as Gretchen took notes, constantly questioning, the pair deeply engrossed in their preparations.

"So you can see," said Sandy finally leaning back on his chair and stretching his arms above his head, "straightforward if all goes to plan but it rarely does; hence the contingencies."

Gretchen nodded in agreement looking up from the maps and papers. "No plan survives first contact with the enemy," she said, repeating an old mantra.

"And the enemy in the Cuillin is usually the weather." Sandy pointed to the child's picture of a barometer painted onto the wallpaper. On the wooden body was written 'Skye', with the hand pointing permanently at 'changeable'.

"There is a saying in the Hebrides," said Sandy. "'If you don't like the weather, there'll be some more along soon.' Most locals carry wet gear in their car as a matter of course."

Gretchen flicked through her notes underlining key words as Sandy cleared everything away. "So," she said, "just to recap, we aim to get away tomorrow at 03:30, drive to Glen Brittle, climb between fifteen and twenty peaks, bivvy on the ridge. On the second day we head across to climb the Red Cuillin and stay in the hut at Loch Coruisk. We walk out on Tuesday."

Sandy laughed, "But as you say, 'no plan survives first contact'. By the way, there are maybe fifty peaks if you count all the spurs but we'll be lucky to climb half of them in the time."

"Ah, is that why there are twenty peaks over three thousand feet but only twelve are 'Munroe's'."

"Probably, but I don't take too much heed of men squabbling over names," said Sandy rummaging around in his fridge. "Having said that, I am basing this climb around the Munroe's if nothing else. The good news is that I have several stashes of water and equipment which will cut down on our load. I will let some friends know our planned route, call times and our ETA home. I have to leave Tuesday night but may I suggest that you stay on here a day to recuperate."

"That's fine," said Gretchen, "for once I don't have a deadline."

Sandy made a thick sliced cheese sandwich and put it into his bag. "Right, I'm away for the afternoon so I'll see you at The Neist. Your bedroom is top of stairs turn right, help yourself to whatever there is in the fridge and the house. I recommend a brew and a rest in the conservatory but it's entirely up to you." He grabbed an apple and left.

Gretchen negotiated the tiny stairs with her rucksack, laying the contents out on the single bed before returning to the kitchen to make a sandwich and a cup of tea. She followed Sandy's advice and settled in the sunroom with her tea. The far side of the bay was, Gretchen estimated, a mile away and, from what she could make out, there were vertical cliffs covered in vegetation, the ground rising slowly behind. While she studied the terrain, clouds appeared on the horizon and the sky quickly darkened as spots of rain hit the glass. The squall arrived, just as Sandy had predicted, completely changing the scene from his croft. The effect was like being in a theatre box as nature played out a scene from the *Tempest*. Just as quickly, sunshine returned, the wind dropped and the small stream that ran from the gutter slowed to a trickle.

Gretchen lay out on the couch and closed her eyes.

From their perch, they watched the Spanish couple climb a third pitch out of the rock cave and disappear.

"We'll have a go at that next – you can handle the second pitch."

Gretchen was tying a loop onto the rope and didn't answer though her smile said it all.

David checked her knot. "Good to go," he said.

She lay back nearly horizontal to the wall, gave two small bounces, pushed hard with her third and, in a single move, gracefully dropped the sixty feet.

Her dad followed, slowly walking down the face step by step.

"Are you okay, Dad? You've gone a little pale."

David sat on a nearby rock. "I don't seem to have much energy today. I tell you what," he said taking his shirt off again, "I'll go and sit in the shade for a minute and you look at the guide book for the next pitch along – see what you think."

David rejoined Gretchen as she stared upwards, her hand shading her eyes as she tried to see past the overhang. "That's why we use commands like 'off belay'," he said, "for places where you can't be seen."

"How do you feel, daddy?"

"Better thank you. When I get home, I will see a doctor and take some time off work."

"That's great, we can go swimming in the river and you can help me with my maths."

"Sounds perfect but I have to ask you a question." He looked serious. "Do you think string vests will catch on in Spain?" Gretchen raised her eyebrows as David sniggered. He took out his flask. "It's so lovely being here with you. I wish Tom had come along. He doesn't realise these moments are so rare – he can sit and listen to music anytime." He fell silent and noticed that his daughter was looking at him. "I wonder how long climbing will be so peaceful here when the Brits realise they can get here for a tenner."

"Just think, hordes of men in string vests," added Gretchen wide-eyed at the thought.

David grinned again. "I know you are raring to go but do you mind if we just sit a while?"

"No that's fine. Do you have your camera?"

David gave her the small Olympus Trip and poured out the tea.

"Daddy, smile!" said Gretchen, and her dad raised his flask as she pressed the shutter. "I'm going to call it 'A Yorkshire Man Goes Sport Climbing'."

Gretchen could see the picture now, the components captured by silver halide as the camera-shutter fluttered open. Then she was in the frame, she could smell the heat and she could hear the cicada bleeping. Cicadae don't bleep. No they are definitely bleeping. Gretchen opened her eyes. "The phone," she thought, and gave a sigh. Moving only her arm, she picked up her mobile and read the screen. "If u r north of Fort William, please respond – if still alive."

Gretchen lay still for a second before stretching and yawning. She sat up and replied to her brother's text, "On the Waternish Peninsula, Isle of Skye."

She sat a little longer collecting her thoughts. "Okay, priorities," she said to herself. "One, kit and food for the climb – two, review the plan, any questions for tonight – three, have a shower – four, have a recce round the area getting to The Neist at six. Gretchen repeated them in her head before nodding, happy with the afternoon's tasks.

Chapter 34 – Pin Mill

Thomas sat at the only table in the pub that was still bathed in late-afternoon sun. He occasionally stopped writing to scratch his head, suck his pencil or pull a ridiculous face that suggested concentration but resembled indigestion. John had been observing this scene from the bar for several minutes when the barman eventually asked if he could help.

"Probably," replied John, "I'm just watching my friend in the corner there. He's either writing or trying to lay an egg. What do you think?"

"Ah," said the barman, "That would be Tom."

John gave a short laugh, "So, made himself known to you all already has he?"

"Yes indeed, he's been here most of the afternoon – a most amusing gentleman."

"Yes, he certainly can be. Tell me, what's he drinking?"

The barman hesitated as if considering the sacred bond between publican and drinker. He looked at Thomas and felt it reasonable to disclose the contents of his customer's current glass. "Pint of Abbot's by the looks of it."

"Great," said John, "I'll have the same."

"Hey, hey, the walker returns," Thomas said, as John approached.

"Yes, found the message tied to my kayak, though your kayak tied to it was a strong hint you were close by." John looked at him closely. "You seem very fresh."

"Do I?"

"Wait a minute – you've had a bath… How on earth? They don't do accommodation here."

"No but if you're charm itself, promise not to go through their bathroom cabinet and offer them twenty quid they are most accommodating – oils enough to satisfy Cleopatra… One can only wonder what forty quid would have bought."

"You can take the man out of Hampstead but… Cheers."

"Bottoms up."

They both took a long swig of the local ale.

"I wouldn't have you down as an ale man, Tom."

"When in Rome, darling, when in Rome," Thomas arched an eyebrow. "So, John Bentley, what did you discover on your walk?"

"Some beautiful churches and some nice country folk."

"You sure you just haven't been listening to *The Archers*."

John shrugged. He had also been giving much thought to his feelings for Thomas but, on balance, had decided to keep them to himself. "Play the long game," had come to mind but he had dismissed it, as it was no longer a game. He wanted permanence but was not going to make any of the running. It would be at Thomas's pace or not at all. "No," John replied, "there were no Eddie Grundies, though I did meet a postman and a vicar and I saw a fire engine; so more Trumpton than Archers. I walked miles and, I dare say, broke a few footpath by-laws."

"Are you mad? Farmer Palmer shoots for less. I know about these things. I've read Viz."

"So what have you been working on?" asked John.

"First of all, I have to tell you that sailing is a great creative force."

"Really?"

"Yep, it's so boring one can't help but face one's thoughts."

"Charming."

"No wait, it's true. Something Grae said about Mum. "'She only surrounds herself with so many pets to save herself from having to think', or something similar. I'd assumed it was just Grae having a go but this afternoon as I got cabin fever, I realised that I too have too many 'pets'– a hundred TV channels, games galore and far too many 'friends'; they all serve to distract me from myself."

"Well, this is all a bit 'on the nose'. Do I detect change on the horizon?" John took a drink of his beer.

"God no, but at least I realise, when I'm not being distracted by my *pets*, how productive I can be."

"So, what has this cabin fever produced?"

"A TV game show."

"Okay," said John slowly.

"Well it follows on from the talk we had on fox hunting, which I'm sure Blair and his babes will ban. But then – being British – there will be a backlash of guilt for doing away with a tradition because we do love our traditions. The other thing I feel sure about is that we are at the dawn of celebrity explosion, all looking for air time. And game shows are the ideal vehicle."

"Do you mean like Blankety Blank?"

Thomas nodded. "Except much higher production budgets and prime time instead of day time. So the game show to marry these unlikely bedfellows would be… Celebrity Drag Hunt." Thomas raised his hands in triumph, "Ta-dah!"

John laughed. "I'm assuming you mean drag as in 'chase' and not 'cross-dressing'?"

"Now you're just being silly. Hear me out. There is an endless supply of celebs who crave the exposure and it would be cheap because we'd use the countryside to 'lay our scene'. There would be 'pro's' and 'anti's' – the anti's trying to help the celebs through subterfuge and sabotage, and the pro's hunting down the celebs, who will naturally throw each other to the slaughter whenever and wherever possible."

"The unspeakable in full pursuit of the undefeatable," suggested John, carried along with Thomas's enthusiasm. "Though it's hard to imagine crusty road protestors wanting to protect Christopher Biggins."

"You have to admit that it promises spectacle."

"Practicalities?" wondered John.

"We'd start it as a one-off charity event to see if it flies, which is absolutely no risk." Thomas looked at his friend. "Thoughts?"

"Well, it is just barking enough to be taken up by the networks. Who will oppose it?"

"The extremes on both sides wouldn't thank us for trivialising their beliefs but the centre ground would go for it. We would play up the caricatures; the pros being tweedy and inbred, and the antis, balaclava'd and unhinged."

"Fitness?" said John. "Celebs are not generally known for their fitness."

"No, I'd thought of that, there'll be a number of different forms of transports for them to use. But there'd have to be obstacles as well; squeezing through 'earths' and perhaps eating rabbits – that sort of thing."

John wrinkled his nose. "I can't believe they'd be that desperate for exposure. Who'd be the sponsors?"

"Well dogs and horses would be co-stars of the show, again something else we Brits love, and so Spillers and the like would be the first prospects."

"Dogs and horses?" mused John. "In the Korean franchise they'd probably just make a huge casserole."

"Perhaps better not go there."

John nodded knowingly. "So how would you involve the public?"

"By telephone, betting on the celebrities – maybe even voting for their favourite obstacle."

"Call me a stick in the mud but where are we going to find people willing to submit to this?"

"Where were you when the Windsors went for *It's a Knockout*? If it's done with a good sense of fun..."

"Well what can I say, I think it's barmy and brilliant," said John raising his glass. "I would certainly pay a month's salary to see Jim Davidson 'chased to ground'."

Thomas got up. "Another tasty beverage?"

"Fabulous," replied John, "and a menu please."

"On the board," said Thomas pointing upward.

John watched Thomas chatting amiably to the people at the bar and knew that whatever kind of project Thomas was involved in would stand a fair chance, if only for a charity 'one off'. He couldn't believe Celebrity Drag Hunt would warrant a series but he'd been wrong about so many things of late.

Thomas returned with two more pints. "So," he said, "apart from 'honest country folk', what were you contemplating on your long walk?"

John took a deep breath. "Oh this and that, something I do need to talk to you about though is Andre – you really can't keep him."

"Spoken as if he were a poodle."

"I know he's dreamy but it's not professional. I genuinely don't think Rory Fox would have given you a chance had he walked in and been confronted by someone who said 'ciao baby'."

"Well, my sweet, you catch me in good mood and I will confess that I am trying to find a replacement."

"You are? But I thought..."

"Well you thought wrong. The thing I won't do is be pushed, as Rambo so eloquently stated."

"So why the volte-face?"

"Simply made the mistake of getting to know him. Under that facile exterior are just more hidden shallows. And also..." Thomas hesitated

"Tell me," said John, his expression becoming deadly serious, "That you didn't."

"Didn't what? Cross the Ruby Rubicon?" Thomas hung the moment out for effect. "No course I didn't – but Fraser from accounts did."

"Good Lord."

"In Shaun's office."

"Good Lord. He didn't catch them?"

"In *flagranti delicto*."

John roared with laughter. "He never said."

"Well you know what Shaun's like. 'Could you, um, gentlemen, ah, um, stop that and, ah, go some place else I, um, need to get on with some work, um, thank you'."

"When was this?" asked John.

"A couple of week's ago, just after you left for hols."

"Heavens, there must have been a furore."

"Well not really, Andre has acted like it never happened and Fraser has been off sick, having confessed to his wife, which then prompted a breakdown."

"Poor Fraser, I know what that is like. I'll drop him a line."

"Unfortunately our accounts are in crisis as Fraser knew and did everything."

"I leave the partnership and in two weeks all goes to pot. I don't mind coming in to check through the invoices."

"Thank you, lovely. I was going to ask you anyway, I was just picking my moment."

"You old fraud." John took a sip of his pint, relieved that the touchy subject had been resolved. "And thank you, Tom. I mean it. I know beauty is important to you… I salute a mature decision."

For once there was no smart backchat, no witty repost; Thomas just sipped his ale and studied the opaque liquid. "It would seem that chasing people for looks has been a bit of a losery," he said soberly. "I know all the clichés, I've even coined a few. When you and I met in that restaurant, I was on show. But too often, you know, I'd sit in cafés watching the young and beautiful and, as the saying goes, 'be consumed by the sadness of the unattainable'. Other times I'd just sit in *Tapps* being consumed. Not one of my liaisons has ever lived up to their turn 'on the pedestal'. The reality was always…" Thomas broke off.

They both sat in silence for some time, John not wanting to step in and Thomas not sure where his steps were leading. The meal arrived at a perfect juncture and broke the impasse.

"Hang on," said John, pointing a fork at his friend, "the clothes store, *the Boy from Ipanema*, the girls sitting in the café watching the young and beautiful… That's where you got the idea?"

Thomas took a sup of his beer. "Tall and tan and young and lovely," he sang.

John took over in his low flat voice. "The boy from Ipanema goes shopping."

They finished in a duet. "And when he passes, each one he passes goes – ah."

"So now you know," said Thomas.

John looked pleased with himself as he raised his glass. "Cheers," he said.

"Thank God we didn't use you for the singing. Cheers."

Chapter 35 – The Neist Inn

Rather than head straight down the steep grassy paddock to the shore, Gretchen walked onto the road and inland towards the back of the bay. It was about five o'clock and the sun was still high above the horizon casting a warm glow over the water. Despite the task that loomed ahead, she felt surprisingly tranquil. For some weeks now Gretchen had felt increasingly unsettled and had been at a loss to know what to do about it. Her early morning runs through London's streets helped shake the demons that crowded round each night and, during the day, it was work that provided a diversion. Away from work, a quest for knowledge had kept her distracted but distracted from what? Here however, in the clear air and light of a place that was just about as far as she could get from home without leaving her homeland, Gretchen wondered if she'd finally outrun her shadows. She tried to absorb as much of her surroundings as possible, walking slowly and stopping frequently. She gazed with curiosity at the plants and wildlife. Her frown, as she peered at a bird drifting on the thermals, dissolved into a grin. "Ha!" she laughed to herself, "another peregrine – same bird, different habitat, different habit."

Gretchen crossed a sheep grid and slowed as she noticed a group of newly emerging pale purple flowers. Realising they were orchids, she walked around them until her back was to the sun, crouched and took a photo.

As the road started to leave the bay, she turned right and wound down a small, partially made road that led to a few houses and eventually a short stretch of shingle where locals had beached their fishing boats. Ahead stretched half a mile or so of rocks and she hopped from surface to surface balancing, sometimes precariously, whilst investigating the rock pools. Sea creatures with legs scuttled away and sea anemone withdrew their tentacles as Gretchen overturned rocks and examined whatever she could catch.

"I have no idea what you are," she said to a large kind of sea woodlouse that flapped its long antennae at her camera.

Twenty metres from the shore, a common seal watched Gretchen and she nodded back. "Excuse me," she asked, "what do you eat?" It stared back. She cross-examined it some more. It flared its nostrils and sank below the waves. Gretchen waited for the seal to reappear but when it didn't, called, "Sorry I don't speak Gaelic!"

The rocks gave way to sand and Gretchen had to remove her shoes and socks to cross a stream which, as if suffering delusions of grandeur, had formed its own delta on the beach. The smaller rocks on this stretch were covered in mussels and whelks and Gretchen made a note that Wednesday's lunch could be found here. In clear sight now was a white building by the water and on its end was written in tall letters, 'INN'. Gretchen walked up the jetty, passed the nearby dwellings and into the bar.

The barman smiled. "Hello again, Miss, what can I get you?"

"An orange and lemonade please," replied Gretchen, "and can you open a tab, I'm waiting for Sandy Black from up the road."

"Oh right, our cider salesman."

"Oh, is that what he does?"

"Do you not know him?"

"I only know him as a climber."

There were three men standing at the bar, the tallest of which turned at the sound of this exchange.

"Sorry to butt in, Miss, I wouldn't let on you know he sells cider for a living. He's a bit touchy about the subject."

"Oh, thank you, I won't mention it," said Gretchen and then looking at his tee-shirt, read aloud, "'I love sheep'," adding, "Is there something I should know?"

His two friends burst into laughter, "She's sussed you out, Tiny," one teased. The other joined in, "Yep, she's outed you straightaway."

The barman put her drink down on the counter. "Thank you, Miss, we've known Tiny to be a closet sheep-fancier for some time but now, thank goodness, he has to hide it no longer."

Gretchen wondered at this local eccentricity as she took her drink. She looked at Tiny again studying his features briefly.

"Watch out, Tiny, I think she fancies you," said his friend.

"Well," said the other said, "she is only human."

"True," said the first, "but his girlfriends aren't," and promptly fell off his barstool.

Gretchen excused herself as their laughter became hysterics.

Sandy received a cheer as he walked in and, looking slightly puzzled, he collected his drink and joined Gretchen. "Locals in good spirits," he commented as he sat down, taking a long sup of his cider.

Gretchen smiled. "Yes, I had a chat with them."

"Oh that explains it. Ambrose farms over in Waternish, hasn't been a woman there since 1948, and Gavin and Tiny are fisherman. They'll be a little overcome by your presence."

"I'm surprised that Tiny is drinking in his condition."

"His condition?"

"I'm just guessing, hepatitis?"

"Tiny? No I think he's just had a flu bug."

"Well he's got jaundice and he looks tired. Is he a big drinker?"

"Not as big as some."

"Has he been away on holiday?"

Sandy looked across at Tiny and back to Gretchen. "You sure?"

"No, but if he is not being treated he needs a check up and, at the very least, a blood test."

"I thought you were an accountant."

"I did a year in medicine before switching."

Sandy looked at Tiny again and nodded. "Thank you, I'll have a word. Ah, that's good," he said, taking another sup of his pint. "So, medicine to accounting... may I ask?"

"Long story."

"How about the brief version."

Gretchen took a deep breath. "All going well until I made the mistake of working my first summer break in a GP practice."

"Oh?" inquired Sandy.

"It was the most depressing eight weeks of my life. So much seemed pointless. Only half the appointments really needed a doctor; of those, half were passed straight to a specialist."

"Were you expecting high drama and rare diseases?"

Gretchen sighed. "I suppose I was naïve but it wasn't just that. The surgery had its own dispensary so we medicated for *everything*. No patient left a consultation without a piece of paper. I helped out in the diet clinic. Guess what the failure rate was running at?"

"High I'm guessing."

"A hundred per cent. Not one patient had managed to keep any weight off for more than six months. Then a formal complaint was lodged about me. I told someone to 'lay off the cakes'."

"Seems a little harsh," observed Sandy.

"Well I may have said more than that. But then it transpired the clinic results were not important anyway; we just had to offer the service." She looked at Sandy. "How can you be motivated by jobs that only tick boxes?"

"I think you have just described the majority of working lives," replied Sandy.

"Maybe. Maybe that's why so many of the patients and staff, including the GPs were taking anti-depressants. Suddenly, a bright career seemed a gilded cage."

"Sounds like you weren't cut out for being a GP. It's a tough job."

"That's what the senior partner said to me."

"Forgive me, Gretchen, but accountancy is hardly known for its excitement."

She gave a laugh, "I know, I know. Talk about out of the frying pan. It was solving the puzzles that I loved. Had I stayed in medicine I guess I would have gone into research. I do occasionally wonder what interesting projects I've foregone but," she said, shrugging her shoulders, "too late now."

"So, did you get the interesting puzzles in accounting?"

"As a matter of fact, yes. I've been lucky to work on some good 'whodunits', which have taken me around the world. I have witnessed squander and greed at a fairly spectacular level."

"Are you working in the UK at the moment?"

"I was until last week... I was sacked."

"Ah, got too close to the truth did you?"

"Who knows?" said Gretchen studying the menu.

"So what now?" he asked.

"I'm climbing the Cuillin," Gretchen replied, "but before that I'll have the fish."

"This is really good food," said Gretchen, "how's your sea bass?"

Sandy gave the thumbs up. "I can't recall a bad meal here," he said, "though I've had some bad *nights,* but that's usually when there's a whisky tasting."

"I've read they've got a hundred types here."

"And I swear the boys at the bar can't even tell two apart so I bet them fifty pounds to a penny, each."

"What happened?"

"They won."

Gretchen laughed, "What all of them."

"Aye, I think it ended up costing me nearly five hundred pounds. I heard long ago not to bet against locals but I'm a slow learner."

"Have you travelled much?" asked Gretchen.

"Yes – a fair amount with work."

"Anywhere exciting?"

"No, briefings and the like, one hotel is much the same as another. What about you, anywhere exciting?"

Gretchen saw no reason not to talk about her travels to this stranger who seemed genuinely interested and she picked out a couple of interesting trips. Sandy seemed almost telepathic in that the questions got right to the nub of the matter and Gretchen found herself discussing all kinds of adventures.

"The thing about tracking by dung," she said enthusiastically, "is that when you have found a pile without dung beetles, you know you are getting close to the animal – the beetles arrive pretty quickly. I remember finding fresh, un-beetled dung and very slowly edging around a bush to see four adult White rhinos, not more than thirty metres away."

"Dangerous?"

"Not according to our guide though he was carrying a rifle." Gretchen went on to describe the difference between White and Black rhinos and the importance of not getting them mixed up. "I have seen a Black rhino accelerate," she said, "staggering!" As time flew by Gretchen found herself discussing her wider interests including the John Muir Society. Through all of this, Sandy never once interrupted her or ventured his opinions, merely asking short pertinent questions.

Sandy went to pay the bill and Gretchen looked out of the window to the crowd of drinkers, many still in their tee-shirts. She watched a teenage boy crawl under the seats and sneak several swigs of a man's beer. She caught herself smiling at the man's reaction when he next picked up his diminished pint. In London, from the eerie of her flat, Gretchen had only ever looked down on such scenes and often wondered at her brother's phrase, 'rhythm of the night'. Was that it? Was she feeling the rhythm?

"You have a lovely place here," said Gretchen, as Sandy returned.

"Aye, The Neist covers a multitude of purposes," he said, looking over at the bar. "Sustenance for the body and *spirit* for the soul."

"I'd read that religion is fairly austere here."

"Austere," repeated Sandy, "perhaps – more a bit dour. But folks are always falling out so there are many splinter groups."

"Can they do that?"

"Oh aye, there's plenty of precedent. Presbyterian split into COS and Free COS, then the Free COS had a split to form the Free Presbyterian COS, which then split to form... oh it's gone."

"Sorry, COS?"

"Church of Scotland."

"Ah, so they are still all Christian?" asked Gretchen.

Sandy choked on his drink. "Well you wonder. What does Forrest Gump say – 'stupid is as stupid does'. I would say 'Christian is as Christian does' but there's not a lot of 'turning of the other cheek' anymore. I'm guessing by the question, you didn't have any religious instruction."

"Hardly any. In fact I had more two days ago than I've had in my entire life. I've been so busy learning about the natural world, I've had little time for much else."

Sandy laughed. "Oh dear, you're no good for gossip then."

"Well I'm interested in man to a point but the history of tribes is far too complicated."

"Interesting view."

Gretchen picked up her glass. "There are more atoms in this glass of water than there are glasses of water in all the oceans but we can still calculate it. I couldn't calculate how the drinkers in this pub would react if you switched the beer from Guinness to... to..."

Sandy smiled. "You don't know any other brand of beer do you?"

"I don't."

"So you like to quantify?"

"My brother says even my posture upsets people. Apparently I do this..." Gretchen furrowed her brow and leant forward.

"Oo," said Sandy, the smile becoming a grin. "I feel like I've just been peered at through a microscope."

"It's not that bad is it?"

"No, not at all, and you don't have to worry about offending me, though a word of caution, I wouldn't talk to anyone about religion."

"I'll bear that in mind."

There were still people arriving at the inn but despite the busy throng, Sandy couldn't escape without a cheer as he and Gretchen left.

They picked their way along the shoreline; the gentle ripples at the water's edge and clear reflections from the expanse of the bay giving an impression of eternal calm. Only the boulders thrown high beyond the tide line hinted at another story.

The sunshine was still bright and Gretchen asked about sunset time.

"About ten," Sandy replied, "so we should have good day length on the ridge. So, are you feeling fully fit, no colds et cetera?"

"I feel okay. What about you, are you up to the challenge of dragging a heathen Sassenach around your magnificent mountain?"

"I think it may be you dragging me."

* * * * *

"Where are you going?" asked John as they started paddling back from the pub to *Bexsy*.

"Oh, bollocks," replied Thomas, somewhere from the darkness.

They'd taken ten minutes to launch their kayaks on account of Thomas refusing to muddy his freshly bathed feet. John, therefore, had had to drag his friend and canoe from dry land out into the estuary. By the time he had returned, the lack of moonlight meant the only trace of Thomas was the odd profanity floating out across the water.

"Shush," said John, in an urgent whisper, "there are people trying to sleep in these boats."

The black hull of *Bexsy* came into view and John grabbed the ladder, pulling himself tight alongside. He looked around. "Tom," he hissed, "where are you?"

Somewhere from the darkness there was an unmistakable splash of a paddle then a silence and then a voice. "Bollocks," it said.

Chapter 36 – Coire Ghrunnda

"Did the last Ice Age reach Spain?" asked Gretchen looking along the valley.

"I don't think so. Maybe some small pockets on higher ground." Her father placed his hands together in a prayer position and pushed to stretch his forearms before giving them a shake. "What are you thinking?"

"Just wondered what formed this landscape."

David started putting unwanted equipment back in his rucksack. "Another question for when we get home," he said, adding, "perhaps the question is. What IS forming this landscape?"

He looked at Gretchen. "Right, I'll get as high as that arête," he said pointing, "and put a sling across those two nuts – looks like there is a convenient ledge to belay from. I'll bring you up, then, my BIG daughter; it's your lead into the cave. Okay with that?"

"Perfect," she replied.

It took several minutes to find a suitable anchor point, to sort the ropes and do the checks but eventually they were all set.

"Climb when ready, Dad," said Gretchen.

"Climbing," said David, as he stood up on a low rock and reached for a handhold.

Gretchen watched again. He climbed so accurately and smoothly, expending no more energy than needed. Sometimes his body bent sideways, sometimes convex, always balanced. He stopped once, hands by his thighs in an underhand grip, and leant back to check the next set of holds. Gretchen slowly paid out the rope in small amounts.

"Off belay!" David shouted, as he began pulling up the rope.

Gretchen disconnected herself from the anchor and waited for the tug. "That's me," she said and immediately began climbing. The previous climb had taken a layer of skin off her fingers and they now started to smart on the sharp limestone. To relieve her fingers she looked for footholds, which she knew, in any case, to be the preferred purchase. However there was no avoiding some holds that relied on upper-body strength, and the tiny ridges bit into her flesh.

David clipped her onto the sling as she pulled herself up to his ledge.

"Blimey the rock is sharp," Gretchen said.

"Really, my fingers are so calloused, I didn't notice. You still okay to lead?"

"No hey problema."

"That's my Grae. Damn! I didn't bring my camera to capture this auspicious event."

"It's okay, Dad, there'll be plenty more."

"Come on then, birthday girl – let's see what you can make of this slab."

"Ready?" he said, pulling in the slack.

"Yep," she said, unclipping from the sling, "climbing."

Gretchen had to concentrate. This level of climb would have been un-challenging indoors but leading on rock was another world. She tried to keep her breathing even but the thought of a slip preyed on her mind. She found the process of placing the quick-draws and guiding the rope through the spring gate so much more tiring. Gretchen stopped at a ledge where she rested, changing hands several times as she shook out the lactic acid from one then the other. Looking up, she could see the overhang was not as insurmountable as it appeared from the ground. Any overhang needed strength but the holds looked big and plentiful. She smiled down at her dad and gave the 'okay' sign. He smiled back. Gretchen climbed quickly over the final eight metres of overhang, placing three quick-draws efficiently, her mind absolutely focused. The final move was fairly strenuous but Gretchen could feel that her hold over the ledge was secure. Pivoting on this, she used her flexibility to kick her foot up and levered her way sideways over and into the cave.

At 3 a.m. Sandy got up to find Gretchen gone from her room. The door was open, bed made and rucksack gone. He checked in all the other rooms and began to wonder. Finally he put his head into the conservatory and was relieved to find her fully clothed and ready but asleep in the wicker chair. Her arm twitched and she uttered a few words before lying still again. Sandy smiled. "Good morning," he said, loudly from the kitchen.

Gretchen woke with a start. "Morning," she said, a little too brightly.

"Want to share?"

"Sorry?"

"Your dream, where were you?"

"Oh I was standing," she yawned, "astride the San Andreas Fault."

"Really?" asked Sandy.

"Yep, turn right at the old gas station, down Soda Lake Road."

"The next question would be, 'was there an earthquake'?"

"Who can tell?" Gretchen said evasively.

Sandy's eye caught the bright wrapping paper and elegant bow.

"Somebody's birthday?" He asked.

Gretchen nodded. "Yes, thirty three today!" she replied. There was something though about the words 'thirty three' which resonated lightly within. She couldn't decide whether this was innocuous, as in the draft from a butterfly wing, or ominous, as in the tremor on a spider's thread.

"You should have said. We'd have celebrated last night."

"It's not important."

"Well happy birthday, Gretchen, I'm afraid I can only offer a cup of tea. No Bucks Fizz in this house I'm afraid. You'll have to wait until London."

Gretchen was staring at Sandy.

"What?" he said, trying to read her expression. "Gretchen?"

Her eyes relaxed. "Sorry, didn't sleep much, thank you, don't worry... I'll be fine once I'm moving... I'll be partying when I get back to London."

Sandy smiled reassuringly. "What's the present?" he asked, handing Gretchen the tea and giving her a chance to change the subject.

"A new altimeter watch, my old faithful died last week."

"What brand did you go for?"

"It's a GARMIN, do you know anything about them?" asked Gretchen.

"No, but a few of my friends have them and they wouldn't carry rubbish."

"It's showing us currently at sixty five metres, is that right?

"Sounds right, we'll check it against my map to see if it stays accurate. By the way, we're not planning to eat for about four hours, so I'm having some toast now, can I get you anything?"

"Yes, I'll have the same. I've still a little room in my bag if you need me to carry anything."

"Thanks but I've been packing my Bergen for so long, I know where everything is. If you are up to it, we can swap occasionally, as mine has more kit."

As they loaded up the car, Gretchen took a moment to look at the stars. The combination of clear sky, new moon and the lack of street lighting seemed a fitting reception for starlight that had travelled so far. As Gretchen waited for Sandy, she checked her watch-compass against the stars. At the sound of the car engine, Gretchen gave one last look and got in.

"Looking for UFOs?" asked Sandy.

Gretchen laughed. "Don't tell me people here see UFOs."

"Oh aye, all the time. Some think them a divine warning – others think it's a warning to lay off the Macallan."

"Macallan being a whisky?"

"It is. A very good one," said Sandy. Some moments later he added, "Whisky is almost a religion in the Hebrides so you need to treat that subject with tact as well."

"Life is complicated here," observed Gretchen.

The journey took them along a twisty road down the west coast. Gretchen tried to relax and focus on the next few days. She had felt so at ease yesterday. But now she felt as if storm clouds were once again gathering. She convinced herself that it was just pre-climb nerves and that inner calm would only be restored once the exertion began.

"I was checking the compass on my watch against the Pole star," she said remembering the earlier question.

"That would be Polaris?"

"Yes," yawned Gretchen, "well, for the moment."

"The moment," said Sandy, "why? Does it change?"

"Every few thousand years. Next one will be Vega."

"Mine of information, aren't you?"

"Hmm."

"You don't think so."

"Einstein's view was that imagination is more important than knowledge."

Sandy looked across and nodded but did not reply, sensing that 03:45 was probably not the time to pursue such a discussion.

The sharp contrast of stars on black canvas was gradually replaced by the gloom of predawn and a light mist settled on the south of the island. The mist became fog as they drove through the valley past Glen Brittle but cleared again as they reached the shore. Neither spoke while they checked their kit out of the car going through long-practiced mental lists. Sandy surveyed the loch and then the peaks where the corona of sunrise was just visible.

"Everything look okay?" Gretchen asked.

"Yes, the weather forecast would appear accurate so far. Are you ready?"

Gretchen tapped her Leatherman and nodded.

The path meandered eastward, rising slowly at the base of the corrie. The vegetation was still thick and they stopped briefly at a stream.

"That's Corrie Lagan," said Sandy, pointing upwards to his left. "We'll see it from above – it gets a lot of visitors because it's the most accessible part of the Cuillin."

Gretchen looked up the long steep-walled, glacial valley. Her father had mentioned it in his journal, though she couldn't remember the context.

"Onward and upward," said Sandy.

The track began to rise more steeply now as they circumvented the buttress of the Cuillin. Gretchen saw up-close for the first time, the gabbro rock that she had read about as it lay dark and indifferent.

"This leads eventually to Skorr Alastair, it's called Strawn na Keecha," said Sandy.

"Okay, and in English?"

"That was the Anglicised version but it translates as 'Promontory of the Nipple'."

"Oh, glad I asked."

Gretchen looked south to where two globular islands appeared in clear relief against the sun's first rays. "And they are the breasts?"

"No that's the Isle of Soay though I admit the Isle of Paps is more memorable." He stepped up onto a large rock. "The going will get tricky now as we lose the path. It's essentially a kilometre of boulders but the rocks have plenty of friction. We may walk-out this way on the Tuesday and if for some reason we're separated, follow the cairns, not the stream."

"Why's that?"

"You'll die."

"Fair enough."

They scrambled upward over boulders large and small; the mountain tops now clear as the warming air lifted the tardy haze.

Half an hour later they arrived in the natural amphitheatre of Coirre Ghrunnda, a small still loch, surrounded by rock seats and a backdrop of high imposing walls.

"Wow!" said Gretchen, "This is something out of Lord of the Rings."

"Aye, some people come, only to get this far but still leave fully satisfied." Sandy dropped his rucksack and started removing the water bottles. "Gets a bit heavier now I'm afraid," he said, dipping the bottles into the water. He looked at his watch. "We'll eat here before we start climbing." He handed Gretchen two bottles of water and sat back on a stone seat to eat a sandwich.

"Oh, what height does your watch say?" he asked.

Gretchen glanced down. "Seven hundred and two metres."

"Spot on," said Sandy, scanning his notes.

"Do you ever get tired of walking these hills?" asked Gretchen.

"No," replied Sandy. "There's always some kind of fulfilment. If I'm here with guests its through their enjoyment, but when I'm alone, well, I get a fair amount of something else. He dropped a pebble into the water and watched the ripple move unchecked across the surface.

"Where now?" asked Gretchen.

"Straight up," Sandy replied pointing to the ridge. "Are you interested in rocks?"

"Yes, why?"

Sandy picked up a large rock, dark green as to be almost black. He dropped it down on a larger rock of similar type. The rock rebounded with a definite metallic clang.

"Eh!" she said and repeated the experiment. "Must be a really high metal content, What is it?"

"Peridotite."

"Hmm, don't think I've climbed on it before." Gretchen picked up a shard of the rock and examined it. "Good friction. Hmm Peridotite," she repeated, "I'll look it up."

"More facts?"

"Indeed. Do you know much about the geology here?"

Sandy unwrapped a chocolate bar. "Some, you?"

"A little, I know that in the beginning the Hebrides split from the American plate and crashed into the European, and that Skye, seventy million years ago, was very much like Iceland today."

"Really?" Sandy chuckled to himself. "Actually what I know could be summed up in 'the Red Cuillin are made from granite and the Black from gabbro and basalt'."

Gretchen nodded enthusiastically. "Do you know the difference between gabbro and basalt?"

"No," mumbled Sandy through a mouthful of toffee crisp.

"Cooling rates, that's all. They look completely different but gabbro cooled slowly underground and basalt quickly above. Chemically they are identical."

Sandy smiled.

Gretchen checked herself. "Too nerdy?"

"Don't worry I'll let you know."

As they chatted however Gretchen realised that Sandy knew a lot more than he'd initially implied. He began tying up his Bergen. "Onward and upward," he said

Gretchen was already mirroring him and heaved her rucksack vertically, dropping her shoulder to catch the weight.

Chapter 37 – Doubting Thomas

Sunday mornings for Thomas were sacrosanct and he took every opportunity to luxuriate in the absolute unhurriedness of the day. His ritual began by measuring coffee beans into a small stylish machine of copper and chrome. He would then remove two oranges from the fridge and extract the juice into a tall glass, which was returned to the fridge. Pressing the coffee maker's *Start* button, Thomas would make his way downstairs and outside, usually wearing casual house clothes although on occasion, a smoking jacket. He first crossed the street to Ali's shop for the Sunday papers, and then back to the patisserie below his flat. He took time choosing the correct pastry which meant involving the opinion of the baker and sometimes everyone else in the queue. Back at his dining table, Thomas would slowly enjoy his purchase along with a perfect coffee and the newspaper headlines. A cigarette would accompany a more in-depth reading and a second cigarette would accompany the entertainment section. Breakfast followed which invariably meant two eggs. Though the method of preparation and cooking varied, the sound of the Dualit toaster kept proceedings ordered; clicking away with the regularity of a Swiss clock. Only when eggs and toast were deemed perfect would the chilled orange juice be taken from the fridge.

On this particular Sunday, Thomas woke to a throbbing of engines that echoed the ache at his temples. He peered up at the alarmingly low ceiling. For a few moments he wondered what had happened to his flat. And why were those workmen digging up the road today – didn't they realise he was trying to sleep? He woke again a few moments later, his bed refusing to stay still, and made his way above to find they were already at sea.

"Tell me," he asked, steadying himself against the rail, "were we going forward and twisting back at the same time back there?"

"Good morning, Tom, and yes we were."

"Thank God for that, I thought it was something I ate."

"It's called a yawing. We hit the swell from a large ferry."

"What are we doing now?" said Thomas, still looking nauseous.

"Pitching and rolling – keep your eyes on the horizon and take shallow breaths, you'll soon feel better."

Thomas did as instructed, taking in his situation. Having been unable to find his dressing gown, he stood in his blue striped pyjamas and Barbour jacket staring inland at a large brick tower as the boat moved beneath him. Soon the colour returned to his face and he was able to take deep breaths. "Good morning," he said, "shall we start again?"

"Feel okay?"

"Not quite the spring chicken yet, but give me some time, coffee and a fag and I'll be a-cheep, cheepin' soon enough."

"Don't go below again until we get out of this swell. You take the wheel, and I'll make you a drink." John pointed to a digital gauge, "What's that?"

"That would be the depth gauge."

"And what will you do?"

"Keep my eye on it. Anything below five metres and I'll shout."

"You've got it," said John going below.

"Anything above ten and I'll sing... Anything below three and I'll get naked and call Baywatch."

John stuck his head through the hatch. "Did you shout?"

Thomas glanced around for someone else before shrugging innocently.

John appeared with coffee and, after handing a mug to Thomas, took over. Thomas took careful sips trying to avoid spills. "So, I imagine we're headed for church and I'm guessing that the good Lord must be moving in both mysterious and early ways." There was a hint of complaint in his voice. "Or are you planning missionary work in Walton first?"

John genuflected slightly and made the sign of the cross. They turned into the channel leading into Hamford Water and the swell subsided, the breeze dropped and Thomas took off his coat.

"I was simply up early, so I thought we'd get under way."

"Where is brainwashing today, then?"

"Tom, please..."

"Sorry."

"If you must know I'm not playing at home today – there's a rather pleasant C of E down the road. I did try the local Rome-ish once but found *Father Michael*, far too... objectionable."

"Coming from the most tolerant man produced by a school full of tolerant men, Father Michael *must* have been objectionable."

John smiled. "Well maybe I caught him on a bad day. Had I not had a wealth of life experience I would have felt like some... lowly insect. He was just so unbelievably angry."

The warmth from the engines filled the wheel house and Thomas stood up on the deck. "What have priests got to be angry about?" asked Thomas.

"Sorry, what?"

Thomas raised his voice. "What have priests got to be angry about?"

"Well, as he wagged his finger at us, I did go through the usual suspects. Scared? – Unlikely. Hurt?"

"Do you think he was stood up by The Virgin Mary?"

John gave a wry smile. "Again, unlikely. Which just leaves… frustrated."

"Hello," said Thomas flashing his eyes.

John removed his fleece. "I don't often agree with your smutty mind but…" Thomas inclined his ear trying to hear. John raised his voice. "I concluded the same, the sermon contained the word 'sin' so many times, one could only speculate as to whose sin he was referring."

"Ah, methinks the priest doth protest too much."

"That was my thoughts." John slowed the engines as they approached an oncoming boat.

Thomas grinned.

"What?"

Thomas rubbed his chin. "The *repressed priest*, hmm, could be quite a useful character for a campaign."

"What? 'Who would rid me of this turbulent pries…'"

"No, I've got it, I've got it," interrupted Thomas. He stood up. "Irish beer, brewed in a little Irish community, a really chilled and at ease with itself little community." Thomas began to gesture wildly. "A chilled beer that's it. Call it… Bally… Cock. A new priest in town, annoyed at been given 'small parish' in Nowhere-ville. He starts his *fire and brimstone*, the congregation look at one another and… what's a village spokesman called?"

An elder?" suggested John, slowing the engines further, the oncoming boat doing the same.

"That's is, the elder stands up…"

A lightly framed brunette wearing a Tommy Hilfiger shirt – turned up at the collar – peered daintily across at the passing boat upon whose deck stood a man wearing striped pyjamas. He appeared animated and raised his open palms, exclaiming in an Irish accent "FATHER, I THINK YOU'RE IN NEED OF A BEER AND A BLOW JOB."

John closed his eyes and acknowledged the passing yacht by holding up his hand.

Thomas also gave a wave but continued in full flight, his Irish accent even stronger. "'But I'm sorry Father, we can only offer you the first.' Then the next shot would be of the young preacher sinking a pint of the cool beverage. Tagline – 'Chilled... for when others aren't', as we see a young maiden give the priest a wink."

John dropped his head to his chest shaking it slowly. "I don't know where to begin," he sighed. "Where do you get your sense of mischief from?"

Thomas, looking mightily pleased with himself and began rooting through the newspapers and magazines lying on the bulkhead. "Don't know," he said, "certainly not my mother." He eventually found a cigarette packet in which was one last Marlboro. He lit up and took a luxurious drag. "Oh," he breathed out, "another immaculate conception. Really takes it out of one."

John pointed to the depth gauge.

Thomas jumped up. "Sorry, erm, four point five metres. Why are priests celibate anyway?"

"Property."

"Eh?"

"Too expensive to keep wives and children."

"You're joking."

"No, celibacy only came in around the 12th century. Cash was getting tight. Religious justification came later."

"Ouch. That must have been tough for those already married." Thomas flicked his ash overboard and then scratched his head. "Knowing all this stuff, would you want your sons to get married in a church?"

"I would want them to be married, or not, wherever they truly felt was right for them."

"Okay, if you were to get married again... well a blessing, would you want to get that at a church?"

"Yes. I can't help it. I…"

It was Thomas's turn to shake his head.

"Tom, in my darkest hours, the church sustained me. The traditions, as incongruous as they may seem to you, connect me. They ground me. I don't want to become *dis*connected."

Thomas still looked bemused.

John slowed *Bexsy* right down as the jetties came into view. "Your scepticism is why I have to leave advertising. I'm tired and I need to believe again."

In Thomas's mind flashed an image of Christ – jeans, tee-shirt, leather jacket, sitting astride a large motorbike. He decided not to mention it.

Chapter 38 – The Cider Salesman

Sandy scrambled steadily up the rock face, occasionally looking back.

"This rock is fantastic," shouted Gretchen. "So many good holds."

"Aye. I can't think I've scrambled anywhere in the world as pleasurable as this."

Gretchen was slightly puzzled. He'd said 'anywhere in world', yet last night he'd given the impression that his travels had been boring; 'briefings and hotels'.

Sandy stopped. "Right you go first from here," he said, "the next pleasure is all yours."

Gretchen scaled the last few metres of dark rock to arrive at the ridge. "Oh my God! THAT is really stunning," she said.

"Over there," said Sandy pointing east, "that's Loch Coruisk, and there," he said pointing north, "are the peaks of the Black Cuillin and further still are all the Red Cuillin. Are you sure you still want to do the lot?"

"Even more so! That's…"

"As good as the Ngorongoron crater," teased Sandy.

"Close."

"Praise indeed, though you will have to choose your superlatives carefully, there's a lot more to see."

Gretchen laughed. "I'll be frugal."

"Right we need to drop our bags here and jog that way to Nan Ache to make up some time – summit then run back. There's some exposure but it's a fairly tame introduction. Then we'll summit Darven before moving on to…"

"The TD Gap," Gretchen interjected.

"Aye, and I suppose you'll be wanting to lead."

"If it's dry, I'd like to have a go."

"We'll see."

Sandy led at a walking speed to start, letting Gretchen acclimatise to the exposure. However he soon quickened the pace when it became obvious that she was in her element. They covered the distance to the peak of Nan Ache in no time.

"Your first summit, congratulations," said Sandy.

"This is great. Are we going any further this way?"

"No, there's a lower peak called Garven, which we may climb on the way back."

They jogged back to their bags and, after collecting them, continued at a similar speed. Despite his carrying the larger Bergen, Sandy's pace and confidence surprised Gretchen. She began to feel, possibly for the first time since childhood, that keeping up may be a problem. This was such a foreign feeling that she put it down to his local knowledge and reassured herself that she would adapt quickly.

"This is a nice little scramble," said Sandy, looking up at a thirty metre turret.

"Is this THE castle?"

"No no, this is a smaller version but worth a look." Sandy tilted his head surveying the sky.

"I can't get over the friction on the rock," said Gretchen, pulling herself over a boulder. "I'd have thought there'd be some weathering after seventy million years."

"Age shall not weary them," whispered Sandy to himself.

"Sorry?"

"Nothing. Aye, the gabbro's so hard that there's been no soil formation, hence no vegetation."

"Just this lichen," said Gretchen pointing to the mottled patches of stained rock. She looked around. "It's uncannily wild. It's... I'm lost for the word."

Sandy smiled. "Don't worry, everyone finds a word to describe it eventually. I'll expect yours by the end."

From the top, Sandy pointed out the next three peaks.

"We'll go over to Doo Mor as well. It's a different view point. We'll take a break on Skoor Alastair."

Even with their rucksacks the pair moved easily over the rough terrain, occasionally having to down climb; the re-climbs only once needing rope.

Arriving at the TD Gap, Sandy immediately set up the abseil while Gretchen appraised the route opposite.

"Why is it so feared?" asked Gretchen. "Its not graded too high."

"It's got a difficult crux which is okay for most in the dry but I've seen E2 climbers come off in the wet. Given that the weather changes quickly, it's easy to underestimate. And looking at the clouds I would say we best get a move on."

They dropped quickly into the ravine and looked up the chimney-shaped single pitch, both feeling the rock.

"Okay with this?" asked Sandy.

"Yep, looks good."

As Gretchen clipped the wire nuts and cams onto her harness, Sandy couldn't help being impressed by her confidence and ... there was something else about her. It wasn't her looks. Sandy had met too many beautiful people devoid of personality to be impressed by the outwardly pretty. He frowned and started to look away as Gretchen met his eye.

"You are okay with me leading?" she asked.

"I have faith."

"Thanks. Slack."

Sandy paid out some rope. "Climb when you're ready."

"Climbing."

Within half an hour, they were on Skoor Alastair.

"You are now officially the highest person on Skye."

"My God!" exclaimed Gretchen, turning three hundred and sixty degrees. "My God, this is something else."

"For an atheist, you use his name a lot."

She laughed, "Yes – lost for words, again." She gazed around. "Awesome in today's usage just doesn't quite capture it."

The rising air from the warming rock danced around the two climbers who stood quietly lost in their own thoughts. The cry from a hooded crow broke the spell.

Gretchen looked at her altimeter, "Nine ninety?" she asked.

"That's it," Sandy replied, removing his water. He checked the levels before drinking half a litre and returning it to the bag. Gretchen did the same, still taking in the view.

"Do you have your camera?" asked Sandy.

Gretchen pulled it from her pocket, handed it across and removed her helmet.

"Don't move," he said, "light's great." In the viewfinder Gretchen looked out towards the sea; behind her, stretching into the distance, were the peaks still to be faced.

They sat down and he offered Gretchen an energy bar.

"Thanks," she said, taking it. "I allowed for three thousand calories a day, mainly dried – is that what you work on?"

"I work on about five a day when I'm on exercise, though I have burnt over ten thousand in a day."

Gretchen frowned; this was more calories than needed for two marathons. "I'm sorry to ask," she said, "and you needn't answer, but you do seem unusually... well, 'in shape' for a cider salesman."

"Cider salesman?" Sandy looked puzzled and then smiled. "Ah. You've been talking to the boys at The Neist."

"Have I been conned?"

"I'm afraid you have. They do it all the time, I should have warned you," said Sandy, shaking his head again. "I'm stationed in Herefordshire near a big cider maker. When I first came here, I brought dozens of bottles with me, not knowing if I could get any in the Hebrides. They put two and two together and concluded I was in the cider business."

"What do you do?"

"Army. The Neist boys know. They have just made up this character for me – international cider sales rep – which is, frankly, much more interesting than the real one."

Gretchen laughed. "That explains it – the fitness, the scrambling round the world, ten thousand calories... the addiction to tea. Well, well."

"I'm pleased your mind is at rest," said Sandy.

"Can I ask what you do for the army?"

"No, but I do get involved in counselling work for those on active duty."

"There's nothing in your house that indicates the army," observed Gretchen.

Sandy thought for a while. "Let's just say a few years ago I had *issues*. I bought the house as a way of escaping. After a year climbing the Cuillin, I was ready to go back. Now I'm lucky, my commanding officer gives me time off when I ask."

A dark band of cloud moved around to the north. "We'd better keep moving; there's not much shelter here."

Chapter 39 – Pallbearers

"Ahoy there!" said John, as he stepped back aboard *Bexsy*, a spring in his step. "Good Lord, I think the expression 'ship-shape' is in order."

"Yes," admitted Thomas, "while you've been away, I've been busy as a newly-married bee – shopped, cleaned and polished."

John went below and started laughing. "I bet this is the first time flowers have ever been arranged on *Bexsy* – or any other sailing craft."

"Well sailing folk are missing out. How was the service?"

"Lovely. Sun streamed in through stained glass and all that – I communed both literally and metaphorically."

"Lucky you."

"I do feel lucky, Tom. As you like to quote at me, 'the Jesuits got me early with an unseen hook on an invisible line'. But why does that matter if it makes me feel good."

Thomas poured out coffee and sat down, moving the flowers to make room for warm croissants and preserves. "It *doesn't* matter if it makes you feel good. If I have an issue, it's because I'm envious that one can sleep well just by mumbling a few *Hail Mary's*." He heaved a sigh. "Though I suppose it's cheaper than my therapist."

A mobile phone rang and Thomas picked it up. "Thomas Thorpe," he answered. "Max, thanks for ringing back."

The phone call lasted about ten minutes, in which time John prepared *Bexsy* for casting off.

"Are we going somewhere?" asked Thomas, pouring his cold coffee overboard.

"I thought we'd go back to Hensie Creek for the day, I like the quiet. Do you need any other essentials from the store – lemons et cetera?"

Thomas rummaged through one of his cool boxes. "Oh no! I'm down to the last two," he said in his best Noel Coward, "I can't live like this, it's really too much."

Bexsy chugged slowly back towards the main channel.

"That was Max Pickering by the way – the guy I asked about Grae."

"I gathered, and?"

Thomas lit up a cigarette. "He had gleaned, very off the record, that her cards were marked early on because she failed to do the political thing."

"Ah."

"I can just hear her, responding to an invite to some Michelin Star nosh-up, 'Thanks but I'm going to wrestle a deer'."

"Yes it does seem unfair," said John running the scenario through his mind. "Staying true to oneself, does she ever go out?"

"Oh, all the time if you count lectures. And who counts lectures?"

John started the engines, walked forward, pushed off the bow and walked back to the wheel house.

Thomas was still deep in thought as John returned. "Sorry I could have helped there."

John smiled. "No problem."

"As good as she is at her job," Thomas continued, "she will, I fear, always struggle in 'the smoke'. It's either get pissed or piss off – which is lucky for me since I struggle to remember a time when I was sober."

"Sad but true." John reflected.

"You were supposed to contradict me there, lover boy."

"What do you think she'll do?"

Thomas exhaled a stream of cigarette smoke which lingered only briefly in the warm summer air. "I'm sure there is plenty of work for what she does," he said. "She's sort of a corporate Poirot. Perhaps she should go freelance."

"Sounds like that might suit everyone," said John. "You said she was thinking about a PhD."

"Ah," said Thomas, "another peak for her to conquer – constantly striving. You've no idea how wearing she is to be around."

They entered the main body of water and *Bexsy* slowly turned inland following the occasional signposts that indicated the channels.

"I found your sister very easy to be around," said John.

"Ah, that's because you're a gay man, you don't count."

"Thanks."

"Mum thinks she's not been at ease with herself since Dad died. I just think she sees taking anything easy as a kind of weakness. She took it on herself to look after the family, learning about tax forms and the like, saving me from a beating at school. In fact I've rarely seen her flustered and never seen her cry. Not even at Dad's funeral. Mum and I were so worried about her." Thomas gave a short laugh. "I remember Grae fighting Mum over the funeral arrangements – she wanted to somehow carry the coffin herself." Thomas paused, shaking his head in recollection. "She called the pallbearers – who were Mum's family – 'a bunch of fucking losers'. It's the only time I've ever heard her swear."

"I'm guessing they were close," said John, "Gretchen and your dad."

"In-bloody-separable, especially when he was home, I never got a look in... Anyway, during the funeral service she wore this long white dress and stood completely impassive throughout as everybody else fell apart. Then we noticed blood stains spreading down the sides of her dress. Mum shrieked thinking it was some kind of stigmata but she'd been squeezing some shards of stone into her palms so deeply that they bled profusely."

"Hell, that must have been a sight!"

"Oh God, the whole thing was horrible. Years later I asked Peter about it, you know Pete-the-shrink?"

John nodded. "What did he say?"

"Something like… err," Thomas affected a doddery Viennese voice, "'Using physical pain to displace emotional trauma is not uncommon and acceptable in the short term'."

"Short term?"

"Yes, not a substitute. 'Bereavement', he told me is err…'a necessary process'."

Chapter 40 – INTJ

"Are you okay to up-the-pace a little?" said Sandy again, glancing up.

"Sure," replied Gretchen willingly.

There's some shelter beyond Skoor Cheerlach that I've used. Is your wet gear near the top of your bag?"

"Of course."

"Sorry but you'd be amazed how many people I bring up here who have to empty the contents of their Bergen in the middle of a squall."

They crossed over the Great Stone Chute, a moraine of thousands of tonnes of rock debris, and climbed up a short but vertical face back onto the ridge. After summating Skoor Cheerlach they walked along a narrow promontory, their confident steps belying the shear drops on either side, until confronted by a ravine.

"There are several ways down," said Sandy, "but we'll belay and take shelter. I think we have a front moving in behind us."

"Sideways rain! I've heard about this," said Gretchen, as she ate another sandwich and watched the rain fly over the top of them.

"As long as the wind stays behind us, we should stay dry but I'd put a fleece on, the temperature will drop as we sit here."

"This is just perfect," said Gretchen.

"I was up here with a management team last month, they weren't quite so enamoured."

Gretchen visibly shivered. "Why would you want to bring people like that?"

"I fundraise for a charity; corporates pay big bucks." Sandy took a bite of a pastry. "I'm sensing you have something against management." He looked at her slyly, "Or is it teams?"

"Well I can't remember when I was last impressed by a manager but no, I was once sent on a team building course… wasn't the highlight of my career."

"Oh?"

Gretchen took a deep breath. "It was an 'outward bounds' type thing and I'd made some effort to get in-shape. When I turned up, however, it transpired that the other eight blokes had done none at all. On the first morning the instructors assessed our fitness as a team – it was pathetic. I was annoyed because the instructors downgraded the physical side to suit the group. I thought the point was we adapted to the environment, not the other way round. Anyway, the tasks were relatively straightforward but three guys from a government agency just argued over every point, twice putting us out of time." She put her water down and sat up. "And, while I was acutely aware of the fact that we were failing, they didn't seem to care. Then, after a night outdoors, they moaned because there'd been no breakfast even though it was their tardiness that had lost us the meal. By the time we came to the final exercise – to cross a lake and get our lunch – their whining was driving me to distraction."

She could sense that same irritation spreading through her just recalling the memory. She felt, from any objective standpoint, her subsequent actions could be justified but glancing across to Sandy's impassive features she began to have doubts.

"We were shown a collection of oil drums, ropes and boards," she continued, "so it was obvious some sort of raft was needed. I asked if anyone had done this before and one said he had so I asked him to sketch on the sand how it worked. As soon as he started to explain, the three started arguing, on and on. I re-read the task and thought it was fairly ambiguous, so I… swam across and left them to it." Immediately she began to feel uncomfortable.

"They didn't make the time limit did they," said Sandy.

"No, they hadn't even begun the build."

"What happened?"

"The instructors took a boat across to pick them up."

"No, what happened to you?"

"Apparently I failed the course but I'd already left by then. I guess if you were my instructor you would have also failed me?"

"Without hesitation," replied Sandy directly. "Can't leave a team. However I would have already dealt with the individuals."

"What? Shot them?"

"As tempting as it would appear, everyone has a part to play," said Sandy seriously. "I'm assuming you didn't attend the debrief?"

"I'd long gone."

"That was your biggest mistake and had you been in the forces, you'd have been given your discharge papers."

Gretchen was really stung by this remark but didn't respond.

"Okay," said Sandy, his head slightly inclined, mouth on the verge of a smile, "first thing, I have found that sometimes the unlikeliest person can radically increase mission success. I guess you'll have had to do some sort of psychological assessment in your career?"

"Yes, a few years back."

"Which one?"

"Myers-Briggs."

"Great – there are four elements, yes? I'm guessing two of which scored 'Thinker, Judger'?"

Gretchen nodded. "That's right."

"And the others?"

"Err, Introversion and... Intuition."

"Okay, so that would give... an INTJ." Sandy thought for a moment. "So let's take an opposite, say someone who's a 'Sensing, Feeler'. In my experience they would be good at organising and respecting others. They can also be very efficient as long as they understand their own task. They don't have to know the overall goal; in fact knowing might freak them out. Looking back, did you recognise this in any of your team?"

Gretchen thought back. "Mm, I think I did."

"Did you recognise yourself as the leader?"

"I didn't want to lead them. If I'm honest, after the physical," she grimaced, "I'd already written them off. I guess I thought I could just get the job done quicker myself."

"Hmm, independent. Gretchen, I have worked with many like you and, if you'll allow me, I'll tell you what I've experienced in the field – an effective team cannot be outperformed by an individual." Sandy looked straight at her without blinking. "I suspect, with some justification after seeing you out here, that you could have led that whole team successfully AND learnt much in the process."

Gretchen had not thought about it in this way.

Sandy laughed, easing the moment. "I can just see you swimming across the lake while all the others looked on."

"I feel guilty about it now," said Gretchen.

"How did you feel before?"

Gretchen looked sheepish. "Proud?" she offered.

"Ha," said Sandy, "we've all been there – *pride* the deadliest of sins." He got to his feet, gingerly stretching out his hip.

"Muscle soreness?" Gretchen asked, relieved to change the subject.

"I don't have any muscle left – I'm just skin over scar tissue." He winked.

The rain had stopped and from where they sat, they could see the sunlight spreading across the rest of the peaks, hastily moving out to sea.

Chapter 41 – Mollie's Ribbons

Bexsy chugged up the narrowing creek, the tide already lower than Thursday's visit and John had to drop anchor several hundred metres further away from the quay. He was watching the waterfowl amass on the emerging feast as Thomas joined him. "It's been a fabulous weekend John, thank you."

"My pleasure, pity Gretchen had to leave so early. I really like her."

Thomas stiffened slightly but then caught himself. "Sorry," he said, "having a sister like Grae has made me quite sensitive. She is a remarkable person."

"You're a remarkable person too."

"It's kind of you to say so. Obviously Mum says it all the time but then that's what mums do."

"Does your mum ever say that to Grae?"

"I think she tries but Grae doesn't seem to accept praise and also what can one say if there's no frame of reference. Mum's a normal mum and Grae, well, is on another planet."

"You said she'd not forgiven your Mum?"

"Not true, that would mean bearing a grudge which is a human trait. Grae doesn't have them... Did I tell you that Grae didn't attend her own graduation?"

"What!" said John.

"Mother was so upset. She'd sacrificed so much to get her to Cambridge."

"Gretchen told me she started work the day after her exams but I assumed she'd gone back to graduate."

"Mum and I went instead, making some excuse about Grae being stuck on the other side of the world." Thomas smiled at the memory. "Mum went on stage and got Grae's 'first' while I scoffed the strawberries and cream and shouted 'bravo'."

"That does seem unusual behaviour."

"What scoffing strawberries and cream or shouting 'bravo'?"

John gave his friend a wearisome look.

"Oh Grae has had a long history of this. When Dad was alive she used to put her certificates and ribbons she received on his pillow for when he returned from work, which he really loved. It encouraged her to try all the more, she was always winning stuff. After he died she continued winning but never collected another prize. All too often, there'd be an empty place on the medal rostrum. It was so embarrassing. Prizes sent to her went straight in the bin. She called them Mollie's Ribbons."

"Where do I know that from?" asked John, making his way back to the stern.

"Mollie is the silly filly in *Animal Farm*. She wanted to wear the ribbons given to her by the humans."

"And you're saying Grae saw herself above this?"

"No she was never arrogant, just genuinely indifferent. She'd say 'I can't take any credit because coming first just depends on who else turned up'."

"She has a point," said John.

"Fourteen year olds shouldn't have a point. She was an insufferable cow."

John giggled.

"Contrast all this with my sports days," Thomas continued, "I was so inadequate I was desperate for any recognition. I was in the rugby team..."

"I didn't know you played rugby," interrupted John.

"I was big for my age – too many pies. I can see the sports master picking me.

"'Thorpe!' says he."

"'Sir?' I reply.

"Position?

"Wing, sir.

"Sprinter, eh?

"No, sir – coward, sir.

"Ah – Joker, eh?

"No, sir – coward, sir."

John laughed.

"Well as you can imagine," Thomas continued, "he didn't accept this answer and put me in the pack. Any feelings I may have had for my comely props waned as we linked arms and mauled the opposing team. Such brutality I can't tell you. Every scrum was like a car accident – I just shut my eyes and waited for the crash. After only one game I was transferred out of the pack and onto the wing, and then out of the team altogether."

"How did you end up in track and field?"

"Oh, our school was a *healthy* school – one had to have *a* sport. Obviously track was out of the question: javelin needed too much technique, shot-put was punishment for the fat kids so I ended up with discus. I didn't mind, the training was brief and left me with plenty of time to lie on the grass and write poetry. It was an ideal vantage point from which to watch my sister compete."

Much to the chagrin,
The ice queen raced,
Angle unknown,
The rostrum un-graced.

"Clunky I'll admit but I was in the maelstrom of youth. So… where was I?"

"Graduation."

"I was, oh yes – so you see, Grae not attending graduation was no big surprise and nothing malicious – if she could walk away from one of the world's most prestigious institutions without a second glance... well I dunno. Perhaps she really did feel it was worthless but she should have given a second thought to others."

John retrieved the flowers from the sink and placed them back on the table. Thomas reached forward and removed a drooping petal.

"So you think this all started after your dad died?" asked John.

Thomas hesitated. "I had read in Dad's grey notebook – before Grae snatched it away from me – something about 'not sitting on one's laurels' and that 'every new dawn wiped the slate clean'. I'm not sure whether Grae has just lived this as a code or if the whole thing is a sort of bravado."

"She hardly mentioned your Dad when we were out canoeing."

"No, hides it well. But have you wondered why a girl, who wrestles deer, hangs off mountains and is the epitome of action, still has long hair?"

"Go on," said John quizzically.

"Because Dad adored her long hair. In fact he adored everything about her. In the same way he loathed everything about me."

"I really can't believe that," said John.

"It's true. You used the term connected. Well, we were well and truly disconnected."

"Really, that's not what Grae told me. Her very words were 'Dad thought Tom's stories were excellent'. Apparently he kept copies in his briefcase."

Thomas felt like he'd been hit in the gut. "Dad kept copies of my stories?"

"That's what your sister said two days ago," said John hesitantly, only realising now that he should have thought before blundering in.

Thomas looked stunned. He walked back to the rail and grabbed hold of the shroud.

"Tom?"

Eventually Thomas replied. "I didn't know this. Why didn't I know this? Mum would always be praising my stories but as I said, that's what mums do. Dad, well, Dad was never there. Why didn't Mum tell me he liked them?"

"Maybe she did and perhaps you just heard what you wanted."

"I can't have filtered out something so important."

"I wouldn't be so sure," said John gently. "I know I did. I was packed off to boarding school at six and resented my father hugely for years. I definitely highlighted the bad and omitted the good."

"Don't you any more?"

"No."

"What changed?"

"I read. I used to think my hurt was unique, that I was being victimised by my parents but then I discovered these feelings are universal; grist for the mill. You know what Philip Larkin says?"

"What, 'They fuck you up, your mum and dad?'"

"Yes, the second verse says – 'But they were fucked up in their turn by fools in old-style hats and coats'."

"I remember."

"Well that was just the start. Everyone, it seemed, had something to say on the subject. Eventually I came across Oscar Wilde's quote on parenting. Do you know it?"

Thomas shook his head.

"'Children begin by loving their parents – as they grow older they judge them – sometimes they forgive them'. By the time I'd read that, I realised that my resentment was my problem."

Thomas stared down at the muddied water, the ripples preventing a clear reflection. "Do you think I'm stuck somewhere?"

John shrugged. "If it's any consolation I think your stories are wonderful. The one on Vimy Ridge moved me to tears."

"Thanks, but… well you know, its not proper writing. I compose ads for vacuum cleaners."

"Don't knock it, I bet Evelyn Waugh couldn't shift ten thousand vacuums."

Thomas started patting his pockets, searching for a cigarette. "I worry that if I did write from my heart," he said, "those close to me would be in constant fear of drowning… Are you sure that's what Grae said?"

"Scout's honour and she seems the least likely person I've ever met to exaggerate."

"Well roger me with a pair of old loafers, I don't know what to say."

"I think 'rogered with old loafers' is fairly expressive," John reflected.

Thomas continued to stare down at the water, the weight of *Bexsy* squeezing air from the mud, the bubbles drifting imperceptibly seaward.

"I'm going to explore, do you want to join me or do you 'vant tobee alone'?" asked John

"Was that your Garbo impression?"

"I'm afraid so."

"In that case, think I better come along, I can't let you wander around these parts with an accent like that – they'll call immigration."

Chapter 42 – Inn Pin

Sandy led Gretchen up an easy scramble along a narrow crest. They emerged at the base of an enormous razorback of rock. Sandy caught the expression on Gretchen's face. "The Inaccessible Pinnacle," she said quietly.

Sandy patted the base. "Isn't she beautiful?"

He watched her take in the sight, her brown eyes following the contours of the climb, flicking this way and that until they lost focus and she looked downwards. She knelt and touched the rock. "My Dad talks about the Inn Pin in his journal. He calls it the 'last Munro'. What does that mean?"

"Aye, *Munro baggers* find it so daunting they tend to do all the other two hundred and eighty two first."

"Is that's why it's so well known?"

"Aye, that and its unusual shape, it's the Sydney Opera House of the Cuillin."

Sandy removed the rope from the Bergen and dropped it to the floor. "Right, I'm going to take the rucksacks around to the bottom of the west face which is where we'll end up after we abseil back down. You can rest here."

Sandy saw Gretchen about to protest. "I'll only take ten minutes and besides, I want to relieve myself. If you wish to do the same, now's your chance."

Gretchen held up a hand of resignation, removed a small carton of juice from a side pocket and handed him her bag. "Okay, but I carry your Bergen the rest of the day."

"Deal."

High pressure increased over the Mediterranean spilling air onto the Costa Blanca. Forty miles inland down a remote feral valley, sporadic gusts of wind picked up fine particles of limestone. One such gust initiated a small whirlwind which, as it grew, began to scatter debris., Before it could truly gain momentum however, it collided into a large tree; its energy lost to the branches, the leaves shaking with impact; the whole tree coated with a film of chalk. Above them all the olive groves looked on from their terraces. Higher still, a climber struggled to her feet, unable to suppress a look of glee. She breathed heavily, partly from the exertion of the overhang but also from the exhilaration of her first lead climb.

"Slack!" she called down and walked to the back of the cave clipping onto a bolt. She then took a couple of paces forward until she felt the reassuring tug on her sling. "Safe!"

Gretchen was laid against a smooth rock slab when Sandy returned. She got to her feet and yawned. "Are you *relieved?*" she asked.

"Much, thank you." Sandy picked up the rope and began uncoiling it. "I'm sure you can solo this," he said, "but let's short rope it as there are a couple of polished bits."

"No problem, I know it's made from basalt, so I guessed it could be slippery." Gretchen took half of the rope, looped it and put a hitch into her belay plate.

For the next ten minutes, Sandy climbed cautiously, checking for loose and slippery patches, stopping on Gretchen's shout and waiting for her to catch up before moving on again. Only once, about three quarters of the way up, did Gretchen find herself holding her breath as her foot slipped out of the seemingly sure hold. Adrenaline surged through her body as she briefly stared down the sheer face. She glanced ahead and was reassured to see that Sandy had instantly taken evasive action by moving to the opposite side.

"Well done," he said as she emerged over the top ledge. "Keep tight to the boulders and I'll just tie us off."

"Ha! The *not so* Inaccessible Pinnacle!" she said taking off her helmet and shaking her hair down. "I'm impressed that Munro walkers do it at all. It's not for the feint hearted."

"You're not there yet," said Sandy pointing to the Bolster stone.

Gretchen looked up at the stunted obelisk balanced on the tip of the mount. "Does everyone climb up there?"

"No one."

"In that case..." Gretchen replaced her helmet and climbed onto the lower of the boulders then across the tallest. Despite intermittent gusts of wind, she slowly stood upright and held out her arms wide. "How do I look?"

"Like a person balancing on a thin column of rock that's balanced on a thin slice of a peak three thousand feet above the sea. But don't look down."

Gretchen slowly clambered down. Her companion was seated at the base of the stone. His eyes were closed and facing up the sun. He handed her a small dented flask. "Cider?"

Gretchen was momentarily confused, then caught on. "Very funny," she said, "what is it?"

"It's a lemon mineral drink, still cool."

"Thanks." Gretchen drank from the flask while Sandy pointed out the various peaks and the path they had followed.

"The Ridge, with all its spurs, is packed with this kind of stuff," he said. "It has taken me years to find them and I know there's so much more – it's what keeps me coming back."

"Surely though the 'Inn Pin' is a high point?" reasoned Gretchen.

"You'd think so but in reality it's just one of many. Let's see how it goes but if we get to The Tooth in reasonable time, we can have a look at the Naismith Route, which is as breathtaking."

"I've heard of Naismith," said Gretchen.

"I should think so. There are Naismith routes all over the world."

"Is that where the Naismith Rule comes from?"

"It is – twenty minutes per mile plus thirty minutes for every thousand feet ascent."

"We used it for planning university trips."

"Did it work?"

"No never."

"Not surprised," laughed Sandy, "They were much tougher in the old days."

"Who was he?"

"Ah," murmured Sandy warmly, "William Naismith is one of the reasons I'm proud to call myself Scottish. He was a true adventurer; founded the Scottish Mountaineering Club. He said it was a 'disgrace' for any Scotsman with sound lungs *not* to be a mountaineer. There's a picture of him down in the bar at Sligachan."

"He sounds like a real hero."

Sandy sighed. "Well, heroes rarely live up to their myth so I'd rather not dig too deep."

Gretchen didn't reply and Sandy looked across at her.

"Everything alright?"

She remained silent.

"Gretchen?"

"Yes, fine." She seemed a little startled but quickly regained her composure. "Is the Scottish thing important to you?"

Sandy thought for a moment. "It's hard to be Scottish and not be touched by it. My C.O. told me that nationalism and insecurity are two sides of the same coin and he was fervently Welsh – knew what he was talking about."

Gretchen gave him a puzzled look, making Sandy laugh out loud.

"Sorry – bad joke – we could never be sure if he was being serious or just Welsh. We all play with stereotypes. How do you feel about being English?" he asked.

"Well, my parents spent a lot of time in Europe so I could just as easily have been French or German. It says British in my passport – like yours I suppose which makes us the same on paper." She shrugged her shoulders. "I'm not certain I've ever thought about it."

"That's part of my point," continued Sandy, staring back towards Skorr Alistair. "An unspoken cornerstone of Scottish identity is a mistrust of the English; which is pointless if the English don't care about being English." He glanced across at her, "How much do you know about the Jacobite Rebellion?"

"I'm sorry, history wasn't my subject."

"But you have heard of the event?"

"I'm afraid not. You're going to tell me it was important?"

Sandy gave a chuckle. "Well it is to some," he said standing up. "Entire identities are built on a two hundred and fifty year old event."

"Why would people base their identities on a historical event?"

"People go to war over much less." Sandy removed two leashes from his harness, secured Gretchen and himself before untying the rope. "It gets stranger than that," he continued. "Some of my friends are nostalgic for a past that was not even theirs – their ancestors being recent immigrants to Scotland."

"I'm sure it's the same in England," said Gretchen getting to her feet.

Sandy began preparing for the abseil by feeding the rope through the hawser as he searched for the central mark.

Gretchen undid her loops of rope and handed them to Sandy.

Sandy, satisfied with the equipment, shouted "Below!" He listened for a second then threw the doubled rope over the edge. "To answer your question," said Sandy, "I guess my Scottish-ness is rooted in this landscape…" He remembered the previous night's conversation in The Neist. "More John Muir than John Swinney."

"Who is John Swinney?" asked Gretchen, running the rope through her belay plate.

"You may well ask," replied Sandy. "He is our First Minister – I rest my case."

Gretchen checked her harness and then walked backwards over the edge.

The clouds obscured the sun, allowing Sandy to lift his sunglasses.

She began edging backwards to find the fall point and stopped; holding herself at forty five degrees, she looked up at Sandy who was framed by the Bolster stone. "Speaking personally," she said, "the Scots that I've climbed with are far tougher than the English."

Sandy smiled.

Gretchen disappeared from his view to the sound of running rope. Thirty seconds later the call 'clear!' drifted back up to Sandy.

They pressed on over six more peaks. Some of the precipices they crossed would have paralyzed all but the hardiest of souls. Only once, her boot hovering over a particularly cavernous space, did Gretchen raise the issue. "Three hundred metres?" she asked.

Sandy looked down, his expression unconcerned. "Err, three or four."

Gretchen stopped often to examine a rock formation, take a photograph, or follow birds with her compact binoculars. In the distance she had seen the unmistakable shape of an eagle. It had wheeled closer and closer before finally dropping out of sight into one of the many corries. She began to scribble in her notebook until she heard Sandy whisper urgently. The Golden Eagle was parallel with them, not thirty metres away, held on the updraft. It seemed to appraise them before making the tiniest adjustment to its wings and continue its climb.

On more than one occasion Gretchen had noticed that Sandy had ducked out of the photograph causing her to ask if it was some kind of breach to official secrets. "No just shy," Sandy had replied adding, "but I would have to kill you."

Sandy was pleased that Gretchen was interested in all aspects of the Cuillin but this had put them way behind. Also her insistence on carrying the much heavier Bergen was taking its toll. At the first hint of dusk they were still an hour from their preferred camp. Sandy made a decision; they would stop at Drim nan Rarve. He told her the plan.

"I'm okay to carry on."

"No, I've had it for the day," he lied.

Chapter 43 – Hot Pig

For their last afternoon on the East Coast, John had decided to opt for fun over effort and explore the nearby creeks. "Are you sure you want to join me, I'm happy either way," John asked as he began preparing his kayak.

"Not going too far?"

"Not too far."

"Can I take some nibbles?"

"You can take some nibbles."

"Can I take some drinks?"

"You can take a drink."

Thomas stroked his chin as if giving the matter some great thought. "Can I take…?"

"I might as well say no now," interrupted John, "since we'll explore the limits of my patience to failure anyway."

"Sun-cream, I was going to ask if I could take sun-cream."

John rolled his eyes. "Yes, if you like."

"Then I'd love to accept your warm and courteous invitation, thank you."

The two of them paddled slowly side by side in the tranquil waters. They said little as their strokes gradually fell in sync. Without any conscious effort, they found themselves some distance from *Bexsy* and heading for a series of objects protruding from the mud. As they drew close they could see the exposed timbers of a long deceased coastal barge. The curved oak beams – some broken, some missing – resembled the ribs of a long slim torso and the old wreck took on a persona.

"If I were wearing a cap, I'd doff it," said Thomas.

"I know what you mean," replied John. "I wonder what life she had."

"Oh she was a rare beauty, trawled up and down these waters looking for a good time."

John inclined his head. "Really," he said as if accepting this as incontrovertible.

"In fact," continued Thomas, "she was known as the 'trawling trollop'. In the late eighteenth century, Caroline of Brunswick was highly influenced by her fashionable lines."

"I assume you have this on good authority."

"The highest," replied Thomas, "I know a thing or two about these parts."

John suppressed a smile and the game was on; Thomas's role to stretch the bounds of credibility, John's not to react, the scoring system hidden in the subtleties of friendship.

"Tell me about the church," asked John, pointing to distant spire.

"Yes that is the church of…" Thomas paused and looked around as if taking his bearings.

"Kirby?" offered John.

"Correct, well done. Yes the church of Kirby has an unusual tale."

As they drifted with the tide Thomas told the story of the dyslexic vicar of Kirby who had prayed for the soul of an ailing member of his flock. Unfortunately the cleric had misread the names and his parishioner had passed-on but another recently departed had returned."

"Never heard of that," said John.

"Oh, happens a lot," replied Thomas learnedly, "when praying, one needs to be clear."

"I'll bear that in mind. What happened?"

"Oh the usual – apparitions at the altar, manifestations in the… crypt. Had to call the exorcist. Whole lot covered up of course."

"Of course."

"Which is why you haven't heard of it."

John sucked in his cheeks to avoid a smile but he knew it would ultimately be in vain. And indeed it proved to be so for Thomas was unceasing with his onslaught. John questioned skilfully but Thomas always countered with a tit bit of fact to keep his friend wrong-footed. It was the story of Nazi gold in Frinton that finally saw victory. "Did you not know that Albert Spear designed the original pier… Weren't you aware that the Mitford Sisters were frequent visitors… That Hermann Goering had a beach hut."

"Enough, enough you win," laughed John, "I admit I'm canoeing with Hans Christian Anderson."

In that curious way of lazy days spent in the fresh air, they had returned to the boat, exhausted. Having ministered to *Bexsy*'s needs, John sipped at his wine and marvelled at his companion's ability to conjure another sumptuous meal from their stores. He also noted with some amusement that the day's story-spinning seemed to have taken its toll on Thomas and, as a consequence, the food had been eaten largely in a contented silence.

In the western sky, thin wisps of cloud trailed into the distance, distorting the colours of approaching sunset. Thomas leant against the rails assessing the changing light. After John had finished clearing away, he joined him.

"I'm pitching to God who is badly in need of an agent to sell his sky," said Thomas.

"Who's the competition?"

"Saatchi."

"Why is God selling?"

"Gambling debts."

"Okay," said John slowly, wondering where this was going.

"So what three words would describe those colours?" said Thomas pointing westwards.

"Hmm," considered John, looking up. "Vermillion?"

"Too bold."

"Yes, you're right, okay… Bittersweet? Is that a colour?"

"No – but I'll accept that."

"Russet?"

"Okay."

"Sanguine?"

"So," said Thomas, "so to reiterate, that's bittersweet, russet and sanguine."

"What were you thinking of?"

"Mivvy, abashed and… hot pig."

"Hot pig?" giggled John. He checked the sky again. "Do you know I think you may have just described a new red? Okay, my turn," he said. "Three emotions you see in the sky. Wait, let's write them down and compare."

John picked up a copy of *Vogue* and scribbled across a picture of a white Gucci deck-shoe. Having turned the page to hide his thoughts, he proffered Thomas an ad for faun Versace chinos.

Thomas poured a second port and paused before scribbling his three words and handing back the magazine.

"Right, I've put humorous, sublime and boundless and you," said John, turning the page, "have written... oh! Anxious, melancholy and sunken. Are we looking at the same sky?"

Thomas swirled his port in the tumbler.

"So," continued John, trying to remain upbeat, "so in God's business our description of his efforts would be 'russet sublime' and 'melancholy hot pig'. Even given your winning personality, I can't see our presentation beating the Saatchi's."

"I just realised," said Thomas, "it's not only Gretchen's thirty third birthday but it's also the twentieth anniversary of Dad's death. I hope she's alright."

"Ah," said John, relieved to have got to the heart of the matter. Is she not good on anniversaries?"

"It's hard to tell, she has always contrived to be away somewhere on her birthday. She's very secretive but I do know she takes Dad's journal and visits the places he'd been to. About nine years ago by complete coincidence I met a guy who had travelled with her. Did you ever meet Sam?"

John shook his head.

"He was still in the closet when Grae met him but by the time I bumped into him at Peters's Place, he was out, happy, and monogamous more's the pity. Anyway, we realised our connection while he was telling me about a holiday in Tanzania the year before. He told me an anecdote about this pretty girl who had leapt off their truck to chase after a snake, trying to photograph it."

"Not your sister."

"Who else would chase a black mamba – which is a deadly serpent not a condom."

"Thank you."

"Caused all sorts of a stink apparently. There were several more anecdotes, off which I could have dined for months, but Gretchen being

Gretchen, I'd never heard them. Anyway, I digress. What Sam also told me was that her mood completely changed on what he subsequently realised was her birthday, and which would have been the tenth anniversary of Dad's death. They had camped on the rim of some famous crater – how can a crater be famous? – and spirits were high. The first rays of morn did indeed present a most magnificent spectacle, though Grae would not come out of her tent. She was, in Sam's words, 'the saddest person I have ever seen'. So withdrawn was she, they thought she might be ill. Luckily Sam cared for her and as the day progressed, she came out of herself. By the time they had reached an old museum, she was much improved but still obviously struggling." Thomas swallowed and took a deep breath. "Breaks my heart when I think of her like that, just hanging onto Dad's journal."

"So when you're not being angry with her, she is on the same planet."

Thomas didn't answer.

"Was Gretchen with your Dad when he died?"

Thomas nodded. "They were away together climbing." Thomas suddenly let out a laugh, "You invite the Thorpes out for a weekend of fun and all you get is a family row, an early departure and tales of woe."

"What can I say?" said John. "You are two of the loveliest people I know."

Thomas took his friend's hand and kissed it. "And you are so kind," he said, a tear running down his cheek.

"Steady," John said, looking ashore. "They'll be watching us and if this goes any further, the locals may come out shooting." He handed his friend a tissue. "Another port?" he asked, "We've about an hour before the tide will let us head back to the marina."

"Actually, I'll have a cup of tea but I'll make it."

Chapter 44 – State

"We'll short-rope this last section," said Sandy, "it can get a little tricky."

Indeed, Drim nan Rarve wasn't straightforward and always required care but Sandy had also noticed that, in the last section, Gretchen had noticeably slowed. Her usual alert posture had gone. No longer was she scanning the surroundings for sights and sounds. Her head had dropped and Sandy wondered if it was fatigue or introspection. Short-roping would not only be safer but equally allow him to take the heavy rope out of the Bergen, which he knew she would not otherwise relinquish. She completed the knots for the technique proficiently but he could tell she was not fully with it. It wasn't just the obvious symptoms of fatigue; her eyes, formally attentive, appeared distant. They were only a few minutes from the top but still a good twenty or so from their destination, so Sandy initiated a conversation, intent on keeping her 'in the moment'.

"I know a bit about *you*, Gretchen," he said, "but I've been fairly scant with info on me. Would you like to ask me any questions?"

"Oh," replied Gretchen, immediately picking up, "I'd not asked as I didn't want to pry but yes, what's your background?"

Sandy chuckled. "That's quite broad but I'll have a go. Well," he said, starting the lead, "I'm thirty eight, from a small village near Cupar, which is in Fife. That's in Scotland by the way," he smirked.

Gretchen returned a smile and waited for him to turn and give the okay. He found a suitable position and nodded to her.

She climbed to him. "Anything else?" she asked.

"Okay, my father was the local doctor, mother a Methodist teacher. I have two brothers and was a mischief-maker as a child." Sandy set off again.

She caught him up.

"Well... at school I was more interested in sport than lessons, though did enough to scrape into Edinburgh. At Uni I continued to be interested in anything other than studies, but it was climbing, in particular, that really caught my imagination."

They did another short pitch.

"I'm still listening," said Gretchen.

"Afterwards," Sandy thought for a second, "I worked for an outdoor pursuits company, all in operations, which, to cut a long story short, led to the army." He stopped talking as they neared the summit. The last few metres involved a steep scramble up a narrow outcrop. There were parlous drops both sides and Sandy continually glanced back, monitoring his companion's progress.

Having made the top, they both spent a minute admiring the view in the changing light.

"As you warned me," said Gretchen, "I'm all out of superlatives."

The wind was fairly constant along the ridge now and they sat on a couple of rocks sheltered by the broken crest of the peak in the shape of a half dome.

"Down the valley there," said Sandy, pointing south-east, "is the site of a famous battle between the MacLeods and MacDonalds. There's a large boulder, called the Bloody Stone, that marks the spot where all the bodies were piled."

Gretchen looked and nodded. Then, out of the blue, she asked, "How did you end up being a counsellor?"

"Ah," said Sandy, slightly taken aback, "Well I can tell you that that's not what I'm paid for. Umm…, as I said, I had a few 'issues' and was lucky to find a therapist who was… well, very effective. His technique seemed so simple yet worked and I thought it could benefit others. Unfortunately he had no more spare time so I studied under him and learnt it."

"How does it work?"

"No idea. At its very core is just the repetition of a couple of simple questions, six or seven times."

"Sounds too easy."

"I know."

"What are the questions?" asked Gretchen looking intrigued.

Sandy looked at his watch. "Alright, I'll ask them a couple of times to give you an idea but then we'd better push on. Let me think. Okay."

Sandy turned towards her and dropped off the rucksack as she had done, surreptitiously mimicking her posture. "Over the last couple of days," he began, "you have mentioned the phrase 'in shape' a few times. He moderated his tone. What is 'in shape'?"

Gretchen wasn't sure if that was the question but, as no further clarification was forthcoming, considered it. What is 'in shape?' She started immediately. "Well, 'in shape' would be defined as… the preparedness to meet a task… I guess *I* use it to mean in 'physical shape'… so the body can perform when needed." Gretchen's eyes were in constant motion as she searched for answers. She didn't just want to give *a* response; she wanted to give the *definitive* response. But the more she hunted one down, exploring the recesses of her mind, the more dead ends she met. Gretchen started involuntarily rubbing her thumb over the calluses on the palm of her hand as if reassured by their presence. Sandy said nothing. Eventually Gretchen looked up and regained eye contact with him.

He spoke again in a cadence that matched hers. "And in-shape can 'meet a task'... and in-shape means 'in physical shape'... and 'the body can perform when needed'. And what kind of body is a body that can perform when needed?" he said, imperceptibly rubbing the palm of his hand.

Gretchen concentrated, not sure if she could remember what he'd asked let alone respond to it. "What was it? What body was a body...?" She closed her eyes and screwed up her face as she tried to see what he meant. "It's a body," she said, carefully, "it's a body that's in control... that's self reliant that can cope no matter what happens it can cope by itself because you need to do that, you need to able to do that... in case... you're ever left alone."

There was a long pause.

"And we'll leave it there," said Sandy, his passive eyes giving way to a slight frown. "Time to go and set up camp. Gretchen!"

She blinked and stared at him.

"Let's go."

Gretchen sat immobilised for a couple of seconds until the command registered. She got to her feet and, in a well-practised move, heaved her rucksack vertically dropping her shoulder to catch the weight. However, it was not her rucksack; it was Sandy's Bergen weighing considerably more. She stood looking into the ravine, her balance approaching the point of no return. Instinct and her good reflexes made her pivot swiftly throwing the Bergen into space. But it was not enough and silently, she fell.

Chapter 45 – In Deed

Thomas emerged with tea and cake.

"Ah – another foodstuff squirreled away. What is it this time?"

"An ancient Yorkshire recipe from Grandmother," said Thomas, adopting the accent, "cut and cum-agen cake."

"Cut and come again cake?"

"No, 'cum agen'."

"Cum."

"You've got it."

John took a bite. "Delicious," he said, "perfect with tea."

A fox barked somewhere onshore followed by the sound of pheasants taking to the wing, raising their alarm as they did so.

Thomas tapped a Marlboro onto the cigarette box and reached for his lighter.

"Gretchen and Dad were in Spain," he said. "when Dad had time off, he often took her climbing or exploring. She idolised him. As it was her thirteenth birthday, he had organised a special treat, climbing somewhere on the Costa Blanca."

The cloudy sky, while retaining the heat of the day, excluded the light of the stars. The small cabin light provided enough fluorescence to prevent night-vision but insufficient to illuminate anything. The two men therefore sat in near darkness.

Thomas continued. "I know from a chap called Mark – one of the climbers who was there – that they both had breakfast in buoyant moods, Grae wearing a shirt that I'd bought for her birthday. If there was any luck about the day, it would have been the fact that Mark and his group had arranged to meet them at a certain place for lunch."

John put his plate down, the tiny clink breaking Thomas's flow and he stared into the darkness.

"While Mark was climbing," Thomas continued, "he thought he heard a girl shouting. He listened keenly for some time but, on hearing nothing further, assumed it was just the wind, which had started to gust. Something about the shout though had unsettled him and he went to check it out. As he approached, he could see a climber suspended twenty or so metres up the rock face. Nearer still it was apparent that the climber wasn't moving. Above the figure the rope ran up and over an overhang into a recess. He shouted but there was no reaction. He continued shouting as he got closer. Then he saw the face of a girl appear and recognised Gretchen. He could see that she was distraught. He called her name and shouted reassurance but she disappeared again."

Thomas thought about Mark, a man to which they owed much yet whom he'd never met. His sister had always declined contact; the reason given that she'd 'moved on' and yet, twenty years later, the Christmas cards still came. Thomas recalled Mark's avuncular voice on the telephone and the kindly written words. For once Thomas didn't want to exaggerate. "Mark," he continued, "could do nothing by himself so he shouted over and over that he'd be straight back with more people and ran off to get his friends. He sent one for help and the other three ran back to the crag. There was still no sign of Grae so, while his friends got ready to get Dad, Mark climbed up to the cave. As he cleared the overhang, he saw the huddled mass of my sister. 'Daddy!' she had shouted."

John heard his friend heave a huge sigh.

"Mark replied but apparently Grae just stared at him, wide-eyed and imploring him not to tell her anything bad."

Thomas flicked his lighter open, the flame illuminating his face. John, respecting his friend's privacy, looked away.

Chapter 46 – Crux

As she began to fall Sandy had dived around the rock bracing for the impact, which was almost immediate as the short rope was only hitched to eight metres. There was a 'crack' and then nothing. He had been able to tie-off quickly and get back to the edge. Gretchen was hanging by her harness, moving though not speaking. "Gretchen, can you hear me?"

"I'm alright," she called back. "I think I banged my head... there's blood but I can move my arms and legs. I'm sorry... I lost your Bergen."

"Don't worry – I'll get that later. How *alright* are you? Can you climb back?"

"I may need some help," she smiled weakly.

There were several good holds and Gretchen, with the help of Sandy's strength, was able slowly to get back onto the ledge. However, as soon as she was back to safety, her skin colour turned a pale grey and she feinted. Sandy had seen it many times and worked quickly, getting her inside her sleeping bag and raising her legs. More worrying though was the dent in her helmet, under which a bruise was already evident, and the blood that seemed to be coming from her ear. He needed to call for help. His phone had been in his Bergen but hers was in the top pocket of her rucksack. As he felt the empty pouch, he remembered her using it and putting it back in her fleece. Sandy looked around and then let out a yell at the dawning realisation; the fleece was tied to his Bergen. Chiding himself for his elementary error, he looked down the steep ravine. He couldn't see the bag but some of the spilled contents were just visible. He sifted through his options. He looked at her, then across to the setting sun, checked his watch and began anchoring the rope.

"Gretchen, if you can hear me, I have to go for my bag and get a phone. We need to get the rescue team. I am sure you're okay but I want to get you off the mountain."

She was well sheltered but still only a few metres from the edge so he cut a hole through her sleeping bag and ran a sling through it from an anchor point to her harness.

Gretchen was coming round so he repeated his intentions. "I'm alright," she replied, trying to get up but fainting again.

Sandy had just about finished memorising his route as she came around again. "I'll be back soon," he said and dropped away.

"Don't leave me," she whispered to an open sky.

In the distance, she could see the two Spanish climbers getting into their car. There was another car which probably belonged to the British climbers they'd met for breakfast. From her position she could see a large section of the valley; the landscape a contrast of the craggy and the ordered, the wild and the repressed.

"Safe!" *she shouted again, listening while she pulled the rope through. There was no reply though the wind was blustery. The rope came to a stop.* "Is that you, Dad?" *She waited for a reply. She gave a couple of tugs. Waiting a few minutes, she shouted again. As she listened, Gretchen tried to recall word for word what was said before the climb to see if any instruction had been misunderstood.*

After ten minutes, Gretchen began to panic and started shouting, at the same time tugging the rope. She continued pulling, her shouts now tinged with hysteria. Eventually she sat and leant against the wall, trembling but at the same time trying to calm herself with slow breathing just as her father had taught her. "That's right," *she consoled herself,* "I am my father's daughter and I can get through this."

She heard something or was it the wind? No there it was again. She scrambled forward to look down. She could see the Englishman from the hotel running forward. He looked up at her. In that instant, Gretchen knew something was terribly wrong. She shrank to the back of the cave, still hearing his shouts. Then there were more voices caught on the wind as it whipped around her sanctuary; as long as no news reached her, there could be no bad news.

"I am my father's daughter and I can get through this." She heard it again – a young girl's voice getting fainter. Gretchen began to whimper as an ocean of heartbreak pushed against a dam of reserve. Wave after wave struck the wall. There was no gradual yield to the pounding. The collapse was instantaneous and big tears fell and fell. "I waited!" she shouted into the wind. "I waited, I fucking waited, and you…" she cried again. "And you never came, you never fucking…" The cry gave way to a shriek and then to wail of anguish. "You… you, you," she wept, "never came," she repeated, over and over, the softening voice giving way to uncontrollable sobbing.

A thought started to grow in her. "Maybe you never came," she said to herself, "because you are still there?" The realisation that all of this had been a test of her vigil, swept everything else aside. "I am my father's daughter and I can get through this." She looked at the belay rope. All she would have to do is climb down and he would still be there. "Dad!" she called suddenly, "I'm coming." She tried to stand but was pinned by the harness. She turned to free herself. "Dad," she shouted, "wait, I'm coming. I am coming for you!"

There was a noise from the rock face.

"Sandy!" she thought, "Sandy could help me."

A hand emerged over the lip of the rock. "Sandy," she shouted urgently, "I need your hel…"

The figure that emerged however was not Sandy. The figure stood up, his red jacket catching the last rays of the sun. Gretchen stopped struggling, paralyzed by the sight. The figure looked back at her in the way he'd always done.

"Grae," he said, "I made it."

"DADDY!" cried Gretchen, "I knew you'd come."

He moved to her side and knelt down to hold her. She buried her head in his chest, comforted by the coarse fabric.

She pulled away to study his face, those familiar eyes looked back. She wiped her tears away and sniffed.

"Daddy, I've been searching everywhere," she said. "I dived off the rocks at Crystal Cascades and felt you, I went to the Olduvai Gorge and met Buck, and he remembered you."

She hugged him tightly.

"I felt the Sequoias," she began again, "and they were just as you said and I visited Annie's grave and got your message. Dad, why have you taken so long? I got to the top, I tied off and waited and waited but you never came."

"I'm here now," he said, "I'm here now."

Chapter 47 – Time

Bexsy rocked gently, letting out a series of groans as she started to float. This had hardly registered with her crew as Thomas continued to retell the story of the same day, twenty years past.

"By the time Mark was able to communicate with Grae, the medics had arrived and she was lowered down. At least by then Dad was in a stretcher though he never regained consciousness and died in the ambulance."

John eventually spoke, "Do you think that time does heal all wounds?"

"God knows and you're the one with the direct line."

"Ah," laughed John ironically, "God has never answered my prayers and I have made not a few requests I can tell you... Are you okay?"

"Yeah, it's been so good this weekend, you know?"

"I know."

"Just to talk," said Thomas, breathing in deeply and looking up to the stars as he exhaled. "Just so good to be open... without having to be pissed."

John raised his eyebrows at his friend.

"I haven't drunk that much."

"Just teasing, you have been a model of temperance and great company to boot."

"And you have been a great listener, thanks."

"We have enough tide to cast off," said John standing up and addressing his mate. "Are you ready to Rock and Roll, as we used to say in the seventies?"

"Sixties wasn't it?"

"Just weigh the bloody anchor."

"Aye aye, Captain."

Thomas went forward as John turned on the deck lights and started the engines.

"Warp factor three!" shouted Thomas.

"All ahead slow," replied John, swinging the boat around.

Bexsy's main beam lights came on and the vessel slowly chugged east.

Chapter 48 – Ambulance

Gretchen nearly fell asleep in his arms.

"Daddy," she said quietly, "I'm really making a hash of life."

"How's that?"

"I've travelled, I've seen and done but I'm no further forward and... I'm tired, so tired."

He held her close but didn't reply.

"In your journal you wrote about 'not dwelling on missteps or doting on laurels', well I've tried to live by both and..." Her voice trailed off.

"Grae," he said quietly, "those words may have been true for me when I wrote them but I was just a man trying to make sense of the world."

"I'm tired," Gretchen said again. "Remember," she said sleepily, "you told you me that 'people are not their behaviour'? What did that mean? Did it mean that everything I've done up until now..."

"Doesn't dictate the future," he finished. "Yes, you are only what you are now, this instant."

Gretchen fell silent.

"And you've achieved exactly what you set out to achieve," he added.

"But I don't think that I'll ever be what you want me to be."

"What *I* want you to be?" he laughed. "You know you have always gone further than me. Think about it. If I have been your benchmark, then you have beaten it consistently."

"How can I have?"

"How about, I get a third class degree, you get a first, I do the three peaks in a car, you do it on a bike, I attempt to traverse the Black Cuillin, and you the Black and Red. The list is endless."

"I haven't done the last though," she noted.

"You know you will."

Gretchen thought for a while. "So why have you come back?"

"To help you remember."

"Remember?"

"The last part of the story," he said, "that you have been trying to forget. You know what I'm talking about, don't you?" He looked into her eyes intently. "DON"T YOU!"

Gretchen took Mark's hand, not knowing him, just recognising a shape.

"We have to get down," the shape was saying.

Her mind seemed to separate as she knew that the shape must be followed. Suddenly she had clarity as emotions abated and the world became one of function. "Mark, do we have enough rope for an abseil?" she asked.

"Yes if we single the rope. Listen, you've had a shock, are you up to this?"

Gretchen nodded and pulled out her small elastic tie and began looping it around the rope. "Check me," she said.

Mark looked at the harness and the knot. "That's all good, look at me again." Gretchen looked at him. "It's about a hundred and seventy feet – just take it slowly."

Gretchen nodded again. She walked backwards slowly over the lip, took several steps to cover the overhang, looked down once, gave a single bounce and was gone.

At the bottom, the ambulance crew had placed her father on a stretcher and an oxygen mask over his face. Gretchen rushed to his side but stayed calm. "Dad, Dad," she said urgently, holding his hand, "can you hear me?"

"El es la respiración, pero no es consciente," said the paramedic.

Phil translated, "He is breathing but not conscious."

All the way down the slope where the track would allow, she held his hand and repeated her call.

As they reached the ambulance, Gretchen lifted the blanket and felt in her father's pocket. She gave the car keys to Mark. "Can you…"

"I'll do everything Gretchen, don't worry, we're already trying to get hold of your ...ily."

The paramedics had transferred him to the ambulance bed and were attaching monitors as Gretchen got in.

"We will follow you to the hospital," shouted Mark as they closed the doors.

Gretchen held her dad's hand alternating between squeezing and stroking. She talked constantly to him about climbing and sport, her school work; anything to maintain that glimmer of light. The ride seemed endless and she laid her head on his pillow. There was a twitch from his hand and she stiffened. There it was again; a short squeeze.

"Dad! Dad, can you hear me?" Gretchen urged as she stroked his hand furiously.

David opened his eyes and tried to speak through the mask.

Gretchen looked at the medic, who nodded.

Gretchen slowly lifted his mask away.

"Daddy, I'd thought you'd gone."

"I'm sorry, I'm so so sorry. I have let you all down."

"No, no you haven't, you're back, and everything's going to be alright."

"I love you and Tom so very deeply."

"You don't have to say that, we know. We love you very much."

"Listen, there's no time." David smiled. "I need to talk. You... you have my nature and Tom has my humour but you both have so much more. I love Tom's stories. Can you give him my journal – he might be able to make something out of it. Please be good to your mother, she has raised you, I have been away too..." David gasped and the medic restored the mask.

David's breathing stabilised and he motioned to the mask. Gretchen looked around at the medic who shook his head. Gretchen implored the medic who, after checking the monitor, changed the mask for a nasal cannula.

David's mouth cracked into a tiny smile. "Well done," he said, his voice losing its strength. "I know you will both go on to have great lives... You'll go much further than me. You think I'm a hero but I can't begin to tell you the mistakes I've made."

Gretchen couldn't hold back the tears any longer.

"I'm just sorry," he whispered, "I won't be there... for you're highs or your lows."

David's eyes began to close, "I can see laughter... and discovery and children and..."

He suddenly grew pale.

"Daddy?"

"Calm Grae, calm," he whispered, *"I am calm. I will always be with you..."*

"Daddy!"

The medic saw a change on the monitor and moved quickly. Gretchen sat aside, numbness spreading outwards from her chest, consuming her body. By the time the medic looked at her, his expression and words heavy with sorrow, Gretchen was able to reach out and touch his arm and nod her understanding.

"You had to remember," he said, searching her face, "I told you I was far from perfect."

She closed her eyes.

"You have chosen to remember me like an album of hand picked photos, all smiley and bright. Grae, in reality you know that album also has..."

"Don't," Gretchen cut across him. "What do you want from me?"

"To let me go," he said with quiet certainty.

"I can't."

"To let you go."

She buried her head in his jacket. "I'm scared," she sniffed. "I will never see you again, will I?"

"No, you won't," he said softly but then chuckled. "Although if this was one of Tom's stories... I'd have to return because I'd forgotten my hat or something." Gretchen choked through the tears at the thought of her brother's surreal tales. There was a sound behind them and they both turned to look.

"It's time," he said.

Gretchen held him tight as Sandy's hand appeared over the ledge.

Chapter 49 – Magical Artefacts

Gretchen had slept for nearly two days. She awoke, late Tuesday afternoon, to a young doctor feeling around her wrist. He was staring at her as her eyes opened.

"Forty two," she said.

"What?"

"My resting pulse rate."

The doctor pushed his fingers against her skin, waited and then frowned.

"Have you found a pulse or have I died?"

"It's…" He moved his fingers around her wrist, "a little feint. I'll just go and get the nurse."

Gretchen took her own pulse. It was forty two give or take a couple of palpitations.

A ward sister approached, small in stature though covering the ground at great speed. "Good morning, Miss Thorpe and how are we feeling?" she asked in a flat Irish accent.

Gretchen inhaled deeply and exhaled slowly, "Fine, thank you."

"May I just take your pulse?" she said, feeling for the radial artery.

"I just made it forty two. If you don't count the ectopic beats."

The nurse was quiet looking at her watch. "Ah," said the nurse, "our apprentice obviously mistook them for…"

"Arrhythmia?" suggested Gretchen.

"I see you're on top of it. Honestly, some of our housemen are shite, as if I'm not busy enough." The ward sister filled in the chart quickly and fixed Gretchen with a smile. "Welcome to the Calcutt Memorial Hospital, Miss Thorpe. Another man in a white coat will be along to bother you shortly," she winked. "Good to have you with us. Oh and by the way there is a man waiting to see you who we had to expel for smoking."

"Grae, for fucks sake, you're all right," Thomas said, walking up the ward, relieved to see her.

"Hey Tom,"

"You *are* all right aren't you? I mean there's no broken pancreas or splintered kidneys?"

"Just a bang on the head – concussion."

"Concussion! Excellent, any sort of 'cushion' can't be too serious."

"No, just need a bit of rest."

"That is a comforting," said Thomas, furtively texting John.

"I'm assuming Sandy rang you."

"He did indeed," replied Thomas, "masculine voice – clipped – rather thrilling – I'm guessing military?"

"He is actually, though it took me a couple of days to realise. Did he tell you what happened?"

"Yes, hurricane, frost bite, living off witchetty grubs, the whole thing."

Gretchen smiled. "It's good to see you, Tom."

"And I'm glad to see you looking so well."

"I confess, Tom – I can't remember feeling so at peace, must be the sedatives. Had I known that drugs could make me feel this good, I'd have got your friend to *score* me some."

"You'd have to join the queue, darling. Listen, would you mind if I buggered off for half an hour to find a place where one can iron a shirt. It's been a long journey. I made a mistake and got a bus from Glasgow."

"A bus! You?"

"Well it was more of a luxury coach. Thought if I took a car I might get crushed by a stray... tossed caber."

"Go and find a hotel. I'll see you later oh and..." Thomas was looking at the young doctors. "Tom!"

"What?"

"Can I borrow your mobile phone?"

"Better not let nurse see it," Thomas replied.

"It's okay I'll go outside to use it."

"It's not that, up here phones without wires are treated as..." he looked both ways and then leaned forward whilst modifying his voice allowing everyone to hear, 'magical artefacts'."

Gretchen couldn't help herself smiling. "See you soon," she said.

Thomas gave her his 'winning smile'.

She watched as her brother negotiated, in an exaggerated fashion, the two housemen bent over the same patient. She sat listening to the fading sound of his brogue shoes squeaking against the polished floor. Her rucksack caught her eye – half concealed by the bedside cabinet. She closed her eyes and tried to think; working backwards placing her memories in order. Instead, her mind was filled with various disparate images. She wondered if making a list would help and looked around for a pen and paper. Seeing none Gretchen thought of ringing for assistance but checked herself. She relaxed back into the pillow and rested.

* * * * *

"Hi, I'm here to a visit Gretchen Thorpe, she was admitted in the early hours of Monday."

"Yes, she's through those doors, bay on the left."

Sandy walked along the corridor and saw Gretchen in the far bed.

She looked up. "Hi Sandy, I thought you might have already left."

"I'm on my way now. Just thought I'd call in on the way past."

"Thanks, that's kind of you. What am I saying? It's kind of you to save my life. I really messed things up, I'm afraid."

"The mistakes were mostly mine but let's not debrief. How's the head?"

"It's fine. Thanks for ringing my brother and... well everything else."

A man wearing a suit approached them.

"Ah," said Sandy, shaking the man's hand. "Gretchen this is Nadir. He's been looking after you."

"Actually Sister Beck has been doing everything," said the man, "I have just had to field the calls from Sandy."

Gretchen glanced up at Sandy who had coloured a little. "Well thank you anyway, Nadir," she said warmly.

Nadir raised his hand in a wave, "Good to meet you, Gretchen, and I'll see you shortly, Sandy."

"I'm taking him across to Inverness," Sandy said in response to Gretchen's quizzical look. "Oh, I found your fleece – though I think your phone has had it."

"That's okay, it's only my social phone – did you manage to find all of your gear?"

They both took a cup of tea from the drinks trolley as Sandy explained how and where he'd found the contents of his Bergen. He also explained the course of decisions taken after the incident.

"How did you get a helicopter?"

"I called in a couple of favours."

"Now I'm really embarrassed," she winced, "for concussion!"

"It's okay; they needed a training exercise."

There was a silence.

"Emotional," she said.

"Sorry?"

"That adjective you wanted to describe the Cuillin."

"I'll add it to the list. Oh by the way, Tiny from the pub does have jaundice and is having tests. I'd like to say he thanks you but..." Sandy saw her expression change. "What?" he asked.

"I saw my father," she said calmly.

Sandy, realising the earnestness in her voice, pulled the curtain around.

"You went off," she continued, slightly frowning, her words slowing at the recollection. "He came back for me. I don't understand. It was him as clear as I'm talking to you now. We talked... well, about stuff. He…" She broke off and looked up at him. "Do you believe me? Am I going mad?"

"Do you really want an explanation?" Sandy said slowly and deliberately.

Gretchen scratched underneath her identification bracelet, her eyes fixing on a print of an autumn landscape. "No," she said eventually, "No I don't."

"Gretchen. You are certainly not mad."

"How do you know?"

"I have seen too many corpses to know what madness is."

"Sorry," she said, suddenly feeling grounded.

"Believe me," said Sandy matching her emphasis, "you are as sane as I am."

"But you were in therapy," said Gretchen, a small grin evident.

Sandy grinned back and suddenly they were no longer smiling, just gazing at each other.

"The little place," asked Gretchen, clearing her throat, "near Hereford, that makes cider. That would be Credenhill?"

Sandy continued to gaze at her. "Goodbye, Miss Thorpe," he said, extending his hand.

"Goodbye, Major Black," said Gretchen, saluting.

Sandy turned his handshake into a salute and left.

No sooner had Sandy slipped out of the curtain than the disembodied head of Thomas appeared.

Gretchen gave a tired laugh. "It's like a Morecambe and Wise show," she joked.

"Wow," Thomas said. "Was that *the* Sandy?"

Gretchen nodded.

"All muscle," Thomas observed.

"Scar tissue apparently, did you find a hotel?"

"An *otel* – I certainly did."

The ward sister put her head round the curtain. "All alright in here?"

"Yes thank you, Sister Beck," said Gretchen.

She smiled. "Can you open the curtain when your visitor leaves and don't let him fire up a Marlboro."

"What?" cried Thomas in mock indignation. "No smoking in hospitals? It'll be the restaurants next, you mark my words." He took a deep breath. "Now, don't be mad at me," he winced.

"Tell me," said Gretchen.

"Mum wants to pick you up."

"Okay."

"What do you mean 'Okay'? I've wasted five ciggies building up to telling you that and you're 'okay!' How did this miracle come about? Was it your strong-yet-vulnerable guide?"

"I'm not sure."

"Not sure? You're sure about everything."

"Well, if you tried to ply me with crystals I would be sure... Tom, I need to tell you something."

"Oh God, it's not serious is it? I need more sleep if it's serious."

"It's about Dad."

Thomas was still.

"I told you he didn't regain consciousness. Well he did, in the ambulance. I don't know why I didn't tell anyone. It wasn't very long and sometimes I wish he hadn't woken at all. He wanted me to give you this." She handed him the grey journal.

"Me?"

"He thought you may be able to use it for your brilliant stories."

Thomas took the book reverently. "I'm, I'm..." his voice dried up.

"He wasn't conscious for long... he said he was sorry for not being there for us... and that I should look after Mum. So essentially I failed in the two tasks."

Tom crumpled in his chair. Gretchen passed a tissue.

"Did he say anything else?"

"That he loved us very much and that he'd always be with us."

Tears formed in Thomas's eyes and Gretchen slowly heaved herself out of bed and put her arm around him.

"You mustn't get out of bed," he choked.

"Its okay, the catheter's out."

"Too…" he breathed in, "much information."

They sat for a while, both looking at the cover of the notebook, lost in their own thoughts.

Gretchen broke the silence first. "I'm afraid the drink-trolley has already gone or I'd console you with tea."

"It's alright for you," Thomas said, wiping eyes again, "you're on sedatives."

That reminded Gretchen and she pulled the chart from the bed frame. She quickly scanned the key words until she came to 'Meds'. Scrawled beside it was written, 'None'.

Chapter 50 – Jock

Air rich with the aroma of freshly brewed coffee met Gretchen as she opened the door to her apartment. Thomas looked up from where he was arranging sprays of yellow roses and freesias. "Bugger!" he protested. "You're early."

"My goodness, Tom, have I walked into the right flat?"

Thomas hurried over to kiss his sister. "Just thought I'd brighten up the place for your arrival. How's the week with mother been?"

"Fine, thanks, I slept a lot. I told her about Dad, but she wasn't really too bothered."

"Oh she was. She rang me to talk it through. She was deeply upset to think of you coping with the whole thing. On the phone for hours."

"She was? I didn't pick that up. I think I need some kind of machine to interpret what people say."

"Ah, a subtext machine. Put me out of a job though."

"Subtext, that right. I just assume if someone is saying something, that's actually what they're talking about."

"What people say is usually the last thing they mean, my lovely. But let's not dwell on all that."

Thomas finished the flowers, stood back and inhaled through his nose. "In a couple of days, the fragrance will coincide with the bloom."

"Thanks, Tom, I do appreciate your pains."

"Pains?" said Thomas frowning. "I enjoy these things. I've got rid of your junk post, the rest is there," he said, pointing to the kitchen top. "Your work mobile has buzzed several times this morning. If it's been doing the same for the last two weeks, it must be overflowing."

Gretchen picked it up. "One hundred and fifteen missed calls and my text box is full. I'll get to it later." She dropped her rucksack and picked up the mail, scanning for any that she didn't recognise.

"I assume you'd like a brew? Sis?"

"Sorry?"

"Tea?"

"Oh, can I have a hot chocolate," she said, pulling out a handwritten white envelope and opening it. The letter inside was from Jock and typed on an old fashioned typewriter.

12 Buchanan Place
London SW7
27th May 2003

Dear Gretchen,

I have been unable to get hold of you by phone so thought I'd better drop you a line. I have made some enquiries regarding our conversation and while it's down to the ballot box, your candidacy would be welcomed. All I can hope for is that you gain from your community work the same sense of fulfilment that I have had.

On a more sombre note it would seem that our friends at animal rights may get their wish after all since an old complaint has reoccurred and I may have run out of remission. Should this come to pass, I am writing to let you know that I have left you my entire book collection. This may sound more like a punishment than a gift, so please don't feel obliged to take them.

I wish you all the very best.
Jock

Gretchen read it again, lost in thought.

"Problem?" Thomas asked.

"That old friend of Dad's I had lunch with – Jock McBain – sounds like he is very poorly."

"I'm sorry to hear that. Is the letter from him?"

"Yes, he wants to leave me his library."

"Is that a good thing?"

Gretchen sighed. "Well the irony isn't lost on Jock."

"Nice guy?"

"I've only met him once but he seemed so."

Thomas left a respectful pause. "Here's your chocolate, good to have you home."

"Thanks."

Thomas sipped his cappuccino and then looked enquiringly at his sister. "John doubted you'd be home long, he thought you'd be training straight away to have another crack at the Ridge."

"Now forgive me if I'm wrong," said Gretchen, "but based on your comment ten minutes ago 'people not saying what they mean', is that really John or are you asking me if I'm going back?"

Thomas started to laugh. "Hallelujah – at last, you are catching on."

"I'm not as thick as I look," Gretchen replied, saluting with her cup, "and no I won't be going back to Skye; the chapter is finished, the Grey Book has been relinquished."

"So what next?" asked Thomas.

"Apparently that's the exciting bit, I have no idea."

* * * * *

The small church, it transpired, was no longer a church, having been deconsecrated. There was still the sense of grandeur though; the vaulted ceilings, stained glass and reassuring stonework but this was matched by various forms of art and a floor covered with warm, burgundy coloured, carpet. The choir had also been redesigned. Pulpit, stalls and altar had been replaced with carvings of universal symbols of charity. Mother Theresa and St Francis were joined by Mandela, Ghandi and other Nobel Prize winners. Gretchen read the lists of names and then read the history of Humanism. Other mourners started to arrive although Gretchen assumed the correct term would be 'celebrants', this being a celebration of Jock's life.

"Are you Gretchen?" asked a woman.

"Yes, I am," replied Gretchen.

"Hi, I'm Jane, Jock's daughter. I understand you're having the library."

"Hello, yes, but I'm more than happy for anyone else..."

"No no, the family are pleased there is someone interested. Dad's wishes were for them to go into storage, to be paid for from his estate until you could take them."

"Oh, that's a relief, I only have a flat."

Jane's voice became low and urgent. "This may seem an odd request... I understand you lost your father?"

"Yes, though many years ago."

"It's a big ask," said Jane, "especially as we've never met but I wonder if we could have a chat some time. Dad seemed to think very highly of you and well..." She took a deep breath. "I know you've got another engagement afterwards, do you mind if I ring you."

"No fine, anything I can do."

The service had not been what Gretchen had expected. As she had only ever been to one funeral before, her reference was limited but she'd seen enough in films to have a general idea of the stock hymns and readings. However, the songs played were Jock's favourites; the eulogies were as funny as they were loving. Gretchen felt that she had a good sense of the warm, generous and humorous person that they were celebrating. The venue had a screen in place of the apse and, in the closing section of the service, pictures of Jock slowly emerged accompanied by the music of Louis Armstrong;

childhood to old age; sitting exams to protesting in front of a bulldozer; and finally from cuddling his children as babies to proudly shaking their hands on graduation. While much of the proceedings were uplifting, the last pictures had too strong a resonance for Gretchen and she wept openly.

She walked slowly across London's parks, threading her way through green spaces large and small on her way to Notting Hill. She had for some weeks felt a growing sense of composure, her mind and conscience were not clear but they felt free. The apparitions that had haunted her still came but Gretchen no longer took flight. She just let them stay until, as if becoming bored, they evaporated without trace.

She paused to run her hands over the smooth bark of a beech tree. The branches appeared sturdy yet Gretchen knew the faintest crack of a beech could cause a shear, often with dire consequences for those below. She looked up at its full summer canopy and smiled. "Don't give me all that bravado," she said, "I know your secret."

Chapter 51 – 4Cs

The sign for the 4Cs Restaurant was simple black writing on grey with a green border. Through the window Gretchen could see her brother on a mobile phone, simultaneously giving instructions to the waiters. She walked in.

Thomas put his hand up to greet her. "Fabulous, fabulous," he said into the phone. "See you then in..." he looked at his watch, "two hours, okay, bye."

"Grae, darling!" he said with a big grin and then remembered. "Oh, how was the funeral?"

"A fitting send off I think you'd call it."

"Good, good, you okay?"

"I'm fine but I seem to be a bit early. Can I do anything?" asked Gretchen.

"Yes, I wanted your opinion on this before it goes." Thomas handed her a small laptop computer and a headset. "Go into 'My Documents/Green Spirit'."

"Green Spirit? Ah, you followed up my lead?"

"And nicked some ideas from a certain grey notebook." It's just a pitch, but see what you think."

Gretchen opened up the laptop and turned it on. She looked around at people arriving in ones and twos. Some of the faces she recognised. There was Tom's doctor, Bunty, and Tom's co director, Shaun Hacket. The others, she assumed, must be John's friends and the two strapping young men at the bar could only be John's sons.

Gretchen clicked on the file and inserted the ear piece. The screen opened up into a note which read 'Green Spirit proposal – Bentley Hacket 2003 – 90 seconds'.

The opening scene showed a Roman soldier covered in grime and sweat, building a wall. Next to the soldier's foot, a seed dropped, bounced in slow motion and fell into a small crack. As the seed grew into a small sapling, the picture split into two screens and Gretchen watched, trying to place the haunting music. In one screen were animated clips, in the other the growth of the tree. The clips were roughly five seconds in length depicting the rise and fall of various civilisations while, in the other screen, images appeared of insects, birds and mammals interacting with the growing tree.

Gretchen recognised the theme tune from the *Last of the Mohicans* and the crescendo coincided with rich pictures that had quite an overwhelming effect. Suddenly the music stopped and an overweight, bored looking man filled the screen. He started a chainsaw and swung it at the tree. The strap line emerged, 'Hardwood – where did yours come from?' Finally, the split screen faded back in, a lifeless stump on one half and patio furniture with drunken revellers on the other.

Gretchen handed the laptop back to her brother.

He raised his eyebrows.

"Well the chronology is inaccurate," she began, "and you are preaching to the converted."

"Sis! If you knew what this has taken..."

"It's really moving, Tom. I love it."

"Excellent," said Thomas, beaming, "I'll get it in the post. Oh, Rory," he said to a man in chef-whites, "I'd like to introduce my sister."

"Rory Fox," he said, shaking her hand, "By 'eck, you're nothing like your brother."

Thomas turned to address his sister. "By which he means, if I can translate, that I am t'creative genius and you are obviously t'bookkeeper."

"No," said Rory, his Lancashire twang as strong as Thomas's imitation, "I mean she's gorgeous and you're a puff."

"Well that's me back to therapy," said Thomas. "How's it all backstage?"

"We're ready when you are," replied Rory, "John's just putting the icing on the cake, literally I might add. That's not one of your euphemisms." Rory gave Gretchen a wink and left for the kitchen.

"Isn't he fabulous?" said Thomas.

"Just as you described."

"We try and get him to say words like euphemism just so we can hear the sound *yoo*."

Gretchen was introduced to several of her brother's friends and made small talk following Thomas's guidelines: 'Ask them what they do, don't get technical and *only* if they get fresh, may you intimidate them with some tale of daring do.' To her surprise and relief she found that a careful use of the former meant that she didn't have to deploy the latter. And to Tom's equal surprise and relief, she found herself laughing out loud, mainly at his expense.

"Your sister looks well," said John, "in fact she's positively glowing."

"Yes, clearly falling off Scotland agrees with her. Had I known that, I'd have pushed her years ago. Shall I gong to order?"

John nodded.

The ting-ing of a wine glass hushed the crowd.

"Welcome everyone," said Thomas, "to John's coming out..." Thomas affected a light clearing of the throat, "of impoverishment party." A low chuckle rippled through the gathering. "I'm pleased to say that the two reasons for his destitution, George and Edward, are dining with us today, so please feel free to treat them badly."

George and Edward grinned and raised a glass of wine to their 'Uncle Tom'.

"Right, the seating," Thomas continued. "There are place names, anyone out of place will have to answer to Rory."

"Hello, Gretchen," said John giving her a warm hug.

Gretchen reciprocated. "How's everything at the office?"

"Oh, the usual, never a dull moment with your brother. I'm playing bookkeeper as we're a man down. What about you?"

"Oh the usual to: catching up, bridge building, meeting with old acquaintances, lots of apologies. Did Tom tell you about a guy named Mark who rescued me when Dad died?"

"Yes, Tom told me he'd been trying to get in touch."

"I went to stay with him and his family in Colchester. I didn't appreciate anyone else was affected by the incident. I've just been so self-absorbed. I also spent some time with Mum though I think we both know that we are so very different. We rescheduled her birthday by the way."

"How did you get on with her husband?"

"Fine, he treats her well, which is all I guess I can expect. It's possible that she may not have found life easy with Dad and maybe, if he were still alive… well who knows." Gretchen became quiet. "Has Tom forgiven me?" she asked.

"Well," said John, "I can't deny there was some anger when he got back, but it was never directed at you. It was mostly at himself. He called it self-imposed melancholy."

"You know, my brother is more like Dad was than he realises; Tom likes his facts and Dad, now I remember, liked his mischief."

John smiled at the irony. "So how are *you* doing?" he asked.

Gretchen took in a long breath and picked at the calluses on her palms. "I have no idea. Dad used to say that regret is a wasted emotion… I hope I've been doing the right thing for others but I'm not sure where that leaves me." She glanced around the room. "Changing the subject, your boys are a handsome pair."

"Thank you, the eldest is doing some work for Tom."

"Really?"

"Yes, the four of us spent a week on the Backwaters, the boys call it 'Uncle Tom's therapy' – the grumpier he became, the more they took the piss until finally he said to George, "Clearly you think you know best so you better come and work for me."

The first course was served and a couple of late arrivals were pelted with bread rolls. Rory looked out of the kitchen and everyone stopped misbehaving. The chair next to Gretchen remained empty which was fortuitous as she and John were able to spend the whole lunch chatting and laughing with Tom, who sat opposite.

As coffee was served, Thomas checked his watch and tapped his wine glass once more. "Ladies and Gentlemen, there's no such thing as a free lunch... but today's an exception so let's get a speech out of the man paying the bill."

The restaurant erupted as John stood up. Thomas had once described him to Gretchen as 'modestly public-school English', and as he stood looking uncomfortable and trying to calm everyone down, she saw what he meant.

"Thank you," John said, "thank you all for coming. Firstly I should say that Rory is doing an amazing deal for me yet the food has been nothing less than superb." Everyone clapped Rory who was sat at a side table and gave the tinniest of nods.

John continued. "Um... at school, we were discouraged from quoting Americans so forgive me when I say..." He took in a deep breath and spoke evenly but with an evident sense of relief, "Free at last, free at last."

The speech went on to thank those who'd helped him out over the years and then John told two anecdotes, he being the butt of each, which brought the house down.

"However," John said, "there is another reason why I have asked you all here. Rory?" he asked, "do you have the cake?"

"Yes, John, I do indeed," said Rory bringing it towards the table.

"As you know, Thomas and I have been seeing each for four months but laughing with each other for the previous eight years. We have decided to make it a permanent arrangement and so are to have a civil partnership."

Once more there was cheers and claps from all except Rory who shook his head as he handed over the cake knife.

"And what's more," said John, "we're going to ask Rory to be our 'matron of honour'."

"Oh bloody hell!" said Rory, though his words were drowned by laughter.

Gretchen caught her brother's eye. She raised her glass to him. He winked back and checked his watch.

Gretchen froze. The noise of the restaurant receded as she was transfixed by a figure talking to a waiter at the door; the broad back, the familiar tension in the walk. She looked back at her brother, her mouth open but otherwise speechless. He glanced over his shoulder, a grin spreading across his face. He cupped his hands over his mouth, effecting what he took to be an impersonation of Joe Cocker and sang over the din. *"Love lifts us up where we belong, where the Eagles fly, over mount…"*

Gretchen blushed uncontrollably like a little girl.

The figure at the bar turned around slowly and Gretchen saw Sandy's profile just as she had back in May when he walked into the Neist Inn, when she had pretended not to notice. Thomas was on his feet shaking Sandy by the hand and pointing to Gretchen and the empty seat next to her.

Chapter 52 – The Misty Isle

Leaning forward and taking small steps against the increasing gradient, Gretchen carefully skirted the loose scree that peppered the Quiraing. Despite the heavy load, her breathing remained even as she controlled her ascent. There was something though, high in the stomach. The first time her feet had trodden this path was as a child. Then, she had tried to match her father's stride but had steadily fallen behind until every five minutes or so he would stop, turn and wait; there only ever being an exchange of smiles, never a hint of complaint.

The angle now had become very steep and Gretchen slowed, focusing on the footholds until steadily she stood upright and looked across 'The Table'. It was an outcrop of rock topped by fine spring green resembling a billiard table thirty metres square. It looked a lot smaller than before when she had thrown a Frisbee to her brother who, still wheezing from the climb, had missed the catch. The plastic disc had hovered over the precipice, about to disappear, when a gust of wind had dropped it back at his feet.

A haze appeared in the distance blending sea and sky. Gretchen knew their height above sea level. She also knew the curvature of the earth. In former times she would have calculated the true distance to the horizon but now, as she looked out over Staffin Bay, she felt no need to think beyond the mirage. Tilting her head back, she took a deep breath and slowly exhaled.

"Are you having a moment?" a low voice from behind said.

Breathing in again, Gretchen nodded.

"Lucky you."

Sandy looked at his wife of three years; her hair now short and flecked with grey but her eyes more vital than ever. She had taken to the croft with relish. The byre was now a state-of-the-art study but other than that, the steady life of Lochbay had not fazed her. Even Thomas who made much of his 'missionary work in the Hebrides' enjoyed the odd weekend, always bringing lemons and always declaring that 'the wallpaper was killing him'.

There were voices now; Gretchen glanced across at Sandy and their eyes locked as she unclipped the Bergen and swung it from her shoulders.

"Shall I?" she said, walking to the edge.

"Aye," replied Sandy, "I'll sort out Fred."

Gretchen looked down at ten assorted Australians and Americans; the first guests of the newly formed 'Skye Trek'.

"How you all doing," she half shouted into the wind.

A mix of "Struth!", "Gorden Bennett!" and "Bloody Hell," drifted back.

Gretchen anchored her feet, softened her knees and pulled each walker up onto the top.

There were more exclamations, this time at the geological oddity.

"Do you like our Table?" said Sandy, undoing the papoose and gently lifting their baby out. Fred moved his head around to follow the voice and gurgled.

"It's great mate. Is this... Meall na... Suir...amach?" said an Australian, reading his notes.

"No," smiled Sandy, "we have a way to go yet but you're all doing well."

Gretchen peeled some oranges and took out some warm milk for Fred. She sat feeding him as her husband pointed out the unusual rock features in the distance and took photos of the group. Sandy then went over to a cairn, returning with a small football.

"Okay two minutes a side, anyone kicks it over the edge has to go and get it and believe me, you don't want to be doing that."

Holding Fred over her shoulder and lightly patting his back, Gretchen watched him refereeing the most pedestrian game of football she had ever seen, laughing as the Australians – ever-competitive – won one-nil; the Americans complaining to the ref. Her father once advised her to 'never marry for money' and she knew he would approve of Sandy because she did; it was as simple as that.

Sandy crouched down by her side. "How's the wee one?"

"Fred is fine, but we are both heading back now. You'll need to crack on as well."

"How are your Cambridge friends?"

"Pru's very fit but Clive will need your help."

Sandy nodded. He stroked his boy's cheek and, squeezing Gretchen's arm, stood up.

"Okay!" he said in clear voice, "time to move out."

It was a mark of Sandy's natural authority that everyone had put away their gear and within a minute they were all standing with him.

"We are saying goodbye to my wife and child." He stopped, a grin spreading mischievously across his face. "Actually, we're saying goodbye to my wife and children as I am informed as of this morning that she is with another."

"Another what?" said an American as cheers and laughter spilled forth.

Gretchen watched them go, a bright orange Bergen followed by an array of colours. She transferred the papoose from rear to front-facing and snuggled Fred into the canopy. Surveying the small lochs in the distance she could see a haze moving inland. "Looks like they'll be experiencing the real 'Misty Isle', Fred." Fred gurgled as if in agreement. Gretchen could just make the tiny dot of her Land Rover away in the distance and looked down at her son. "Right," she said, "race you back to the car."

Chapter 53 – SW1 2006

Except for Thomas, the lounge was empty and he sat at the bar writing in his small notebook. He paused occasionally, drumming his fingers on the counter as his eyes cast around without focus. Something distracted him, perhaps a sound or a smell and he tilted his head sideways in an effort to chase down the source.

Breathing hard, David stopped on the steep slope of the Quiraing. He glanced back to check his daughter's progress; her face as stoic as ever as she tried to match his pace. Continuing, he scrambled up the last few steps and climbed onto the cropped grass of The Table.

Thomas was already there, stooped forward, hands on knees trying to get his breath.

"Outstanding Thomas," said his father, inhaling deeply, "I couldn't keep up."

Thomas emitted a short rasping bray.

David patted his son on the shoulder and took out the map.

Gretchen appeared, clasped her hands behind her head and kept moving.

"Where next?" asked David.

"Accident… and Emergency," gulped Thomas and promptly keeled over.

David laughed.

"What?" said Gretchen as she walked to them.

"Oh just your brother," he said, winking to the prostrate form.

From the door at the back of the bar a man dressed in white shirt and black waistcoat appeared.

"Roddy," cried Thomas, "You're back from the north."

"Good evening Mr Thorpe, what can I get you?"

"How did your trip go?"

"Good, thank you. Your usual?"

"On speakers with your father again?"

"I am thank you." The barman held up a cocktail glass, raising his eyebrows to his customer.

Thomas nodded. "I'm relieved to hear that Roddy," he said with a sigh, "though I'm even more relieved that you're back. Your stand-in thought a Tall Black Russian was a spy novel."

"As you mentioned novels Mr Thorpe, may I say I enjoyed yours very much."

"Glad to hear it," said Thomas. He put away the notebook and watched the barman mix his cocktail.

The barman placed a coaster on the mahogany and centred the drink with care.

"Excellent Roddy; retail is detail." Thomas took a sip. "Fabulous," he exclaimed. "By the way, has John been in looking for me?"

"I believe Mr Bentley was here asking after you."

"Oh. Am I in trouble?"

"I couldn't say."

"No, no of course not."

Thomas took another sip. "Relationships. Not easy are they?"

The barman pondered the question a while. "My wife didn't hang around long enough for me to find out."

"Ah. Three in the relationship were there?"

"Four I believe."

Thomas grimaced but decided against a reply. He finished his drink.

"Well, I suppose I'd better face my misdeeds. No point delaying."

The barman took a fresh glass from the shelf. "Your usual again then?"

Thomas replied without hesitation. "Why not?"